Dear Strangers

Dear Strangers

MEG MULLINS

VIKING

VIKING
Published by the Penguin Group
Penguin Group (USA) Inc., 375 Hudson Street, New York, New York 10014, U.S.A.
Penguin Group (Canada), 90 Eglinton Avenue East, Suite 700, Toronto, Ontario,
Canada M4P 2Y3 (a division of Pearson Penguin Canada Inc.)
Penguin Books Ltd, 80 Strand, London WC2R 0RL, England
Penguin Ireland, 25 St Stephen's Green, Dublin 2, Ireland
(a division of Penguin Books Ltd)
Penguin Books Australia Ltd, 250 Camberwell Road, Camberwell,
Victoria 3124, Australia (a division of Pearson Australia Group Pty Ltd)
Penguin Books India Pvt Ltd, 11 Community Centre,
Panchsheel Park, New Delhi—110 017, India
Penguin Group (NZ), 67 Apollo Drive, Rosedale, North Shore 0632,
New Zealand (a division of Pearson New Zealand Ltd)
Penguin Books (South Africa) (Pty) Ltd, 24 Sturdee Avenue,
Rosebank, Johannesburg 2196, South Africa

Penguin Books Ltd, Registered Offices: 80 Strand, London WC2R 0RL, England

First published in 2010 by Viking Penguin, a member of Penguin Group (USA) Inc.

1   3   5   7   9   10   8   6   4   2

Copyright © Meg Mullins, 2010
All rights reserved

Publisher's Note
This is a work of fiction. Names, characters, places, and incidents either are the product of the author's
imagination or are used fictitiously, and any resemblance to actual persons, living or dead, business
establishments, events, or locales is entirely coincidental.

LIBRARY OF CONGRESS CATALOGING IN PUBLICATION DATA
Mullins, Meg.
Dear strangers / Meg Mullins.
p. cm.
ISBN 978-0-670-02143-7
1. Strangers—Fiction.   2. Life change events—Fiction.   I. Title.

PS3613.U454D43 2010
813'.6—dc22   2009031483

Printed in the United States of America
Set in Fairfield
Designed by Alissa Amell

For my mother and my sister
In memory of my father and my brother

Dear Strangers

Miranda likes the dark. She always has. Even when she was a child and most kids she knew loathed it, Miranda revered the way the night changed and quieted the world. Overlooked corners of the house turned into cozy hideouts, lit by diminutive porcelain lamps; her parents' voices became soft and serious as they spoke of small triumphs and troubles, while outside the darkness of night unveiled a vast and glowing universe that seemed much more interesting than the day's lone sun against an empty blue sky.

When adolescence struck, Miranda's affinity for the dark expanded. As Eli Banks put his hands on her shoulders and nudged his face in close to hers, opening his mouth before they'd even touched lips, she had closed her eyes and silently thanked the night for her very first kiss.

Even now, Miranda pays it homage. She credits it with allowing people anonymity and privacy and, conversely, the confidence to reveal a deeper part of themselves. Which is why, this very instant, she's standing in the darkness of a stranger's front yard with a lens cap clenched between her teeth. Most of the house is dark, but she can see through one lit window into what looks like a small study. There is a desk against one wall and a brown leather couch on another. After she secures the camera to the tripod, Miranda slides the lens cap into the back pocket of her jeans and looks through the viewfinder. She adjusts the lens so that the room fills the frame.

Miranda checks her watch. Her subject, if he's going to abide by the request in the anonymous letter she sent, should appear any second. She considers just taking a photograph of the empty room. Like the set of a play in a dimly lit theater before the actors appear, its dreary tidiness is evocative of some imminent arrival.

She doesn't take that photo, though, because a tall figure has invaded the viewfinder. He carries a briefcase in one hand and walks with the swift assurance of a businessman entering a boardroom. But he is not dressed for business. Aside from his reading glasses, all he appears to be wearing are trouser socks, a white broadcloth shirt, which is wrinkled along its hem from being tucked into pants all day, and pale blue boxer shorts.

With his free hand, he begins to work the shirt buttons from the top. The first one gives him trouble, nestled as it is beneath his sagging chin. His fingers twist and turn, fumbling blindly. Finally, he succeeds. With less effort he undoes another few until his shirt bulges open at his chest.

The skin below his neck is paler than his face, making his head look artificial, like a loaner. It's sitting atop this foreign stretch of white skin while its native self is still reviewing *flowcharts back at the boardroom. Or cutting someone's sal-ary. A grim smile suggests he is replaying a conversation in his mind.*

Miranda is feeling impatient and anxious, as she always does on these evenings when she's uncertain, still, of what she will find. Not every subject reveals an authentic private moment; some are clearly staged and do not deliver what Miranda wants.

He sets the briefcase down on the desktop and unlatches it. When he pulls a newspaper from its contents, Miranda understands this is his real life—one sock fallen to his ankle, a rubber band around his wrist—and it is exactly what she'd hoped to see.

She takes the photograph.

With his newspaper in one hand, he settles into the couch and gazes at the window as though looking for something. Or someone. In the dark.

Like so many others, his look startles her by its famil-iarity.

Then he opens the pages and reads the day's headlines.

Miranda imagines the news. War, fraud, betrayal. Corrup-tion, burglary, layoffs.

Are these the words he wants close to him now? When he's undressed and alone? Are these the words that console him at the end of the day? With his reading glasses still propped on the end of his nose, he gazes again at Miranda. Or at the place in the dark where he supposes she is. Like any of the pieces of news he's just acquired, she is also simply words on paper, words on a letter he received in the mail. Her presence exists for him only because he believes in what he reads.

Her fingertip responds to his good faith. She moves it across the release button, then previews the photograph.

The black thatch of hair on his chest is like a crater cast in shadow. His face is red, his eyes guarded. Even halfway undressed in his own house, in the middle of the night, he could be a loan officer sitting across from her at the bank.

Miranda quickly packs up her gear. With the tripod cradled beneath her arm and the small pack slung across the opposite shoulder, she bows her head as she walks across the green grass of this stranger's yard.

Navigating the darkened sidewalks of her route home, Miranda wonders who claims that man. Anybody? Does anybody love him the way she hopes to someday love someone? This man, who takes comfort in headlines—is he anyone's favorite? Does anybody see him this way and love him for it, or despite it? Or is his life lived just so, his habits carved into a solitary tread?

Why is the dark, with all its metaphorical implications, the place of secrets? Why, when it is precisely in the dark that everything is seen? During the day, the masks are on; at night, they come off. Miranda loves her own mask—rhinestoned cat glasses when she wants to look studious, a pair of knee socks to make her feel distinctive, pigtails as evidence of belonging to a certain tribe—but it is her place in the dark, this part of her, that she treasures. Here she doesn't have to imagine the private pieces of people's lives. Instead, she witnesses them. She's not waiting for them to smile, as she must with the schoolkids whose blouses are all wrong or whose shoes are too tight. She's not trying to be a photographer; she just is a photographer.

In the sky, Saturn and Jupiter are adjacent to the moon, all of them illuminated like small, bright reminders of the day's existence, even within the night, and of the sun's inevitable return. A metaphor, she thinks, for everyone: discreet parts within us always, just on the other side, waiting to appear.

1

Oliver looks down at his hands on the steering wheel as he brakes for the stop sign on Hillcrest Drive. They are the hands he was born with, he thinks, surprised by this small revelation—the same hands that grasped unknowingly the fingers of strangers, the same hands his mother kissed when she tucked him in at night and the same hands that held tightly to his father's. Shaped by molecules deep within him that he cannot see or feel, his hands are also surrounded by countless molecules in the air, pressing against his skin, adhering to his form. These minuscule, invisible particles are the unseen forces that hover about us all the time, making our own identities manifest.

This is how Oliver thinks of that summer twenty-one years ago: a set of invisible forces that were pushing against them all of the time, silently shifting them into who they are and are not.

At first glance of the street of his childhood, nothing has changed. All of these houses were here twenty years ago; most of the pine trees and aspens were also. The banana-seat bikes that used to litter the lawns have been replaced by Razor scooters and electric toddler cars, but everything else is familiar—especially the silhouettes of mailboxes on their posts stretching out into the street, making a ladder of shade on the warm asphalt. Just being on this block can make Oliver feel like he is still seven years old and certain that, even though death is rumored to be permanent, there must be exceptions. Loopholes, he's heard his parents call them. Surely, his father would not have let this happen. His father, whose body was solid and strong, whose voice held no hesitation, who nearly always had the answer to his mother's hardest crossword clue, would not die on a warm summer night when there were so many lives depending on his. Certainly, he would change the rules or go to court or pay a fine or persuade God, or whoever was in charge, to turn permanent into impermanent. Nonfiction into fiction. Today into yesterday.

But Oliver is not seven anymore. And everything has changed.

Reluctantly, he heads downtown, to the address his mother left on the answering machine. Oliver parks the car, unloads his equipment and begins his work.

He wishes he could stay out here all night. The afternoon's blue sky has quickly turned to violet and the sparrows and thrushes that fly overhead have become sharp silhouettes of black that look as though they've been cut, meticulously, from craft paper. He pops the camera from its tripod and holds it to his eye as he looks skyward, recording this onset of dusk. With this color change, the temperature has also changed. Though the asphalt beneath his sneakers still radiates the heat of the day, the air above Oliver's head feels thin now, and cool, and he envies the birds that his camera records mingling with the dark tree branches, becoming hidden in the canopy of sycamores that line both sides of this block. Either of these changes, the sunset or the cooler air that accompanies it, would be enough to compel Oliver to linger here, even if he weren't dreading what comes next.

It's almost as bad as the constant requests he fields as a truck owner: to make a trip to the dump for his landlord or pick up his sister's new refrigerator from the big-box store or move a friend's futon and accessories from one low-rent apartment to another. Being a self-professed video guy, Oliver is also asked to record weddings and school plays and now his parents' dance recital. Or, to be more precise, his mother and his stepfather's Swing Night.

He would have liked to say no. In fact, if he'd been in his right mind, he would have. He is not shy about disappointing his mother or Mr. Nice Guy, as Oliver still refers to him in his mind. For nineteen years his mother has lived next door to his childhood home. With the neighbor as her husband: Mr. Nice Guy.

Christened so by Oliver's father. Because each time they left a car door open after unloading packages, each time there was a piece of mail misdelivered, each time he found one of their balls in his yard, Mr. Nice Guy would come to the door with his bright toothy grin and correct these mistakes. As if he were life's hall monitor, reminding people and things where they belonged. Oliver remembers well the doorbell ringing during dinner and his father, after leaning from his place at the table to look through the front window, shifting his gaze back to his mother, saying "It's Mr. Nice Guy, honey."

With a slight furrow in her brow, Oliver's mother would silently, gently reprimand his father for this recurring joke. Then she would open the door, thankfully accept whatever it was that had been returned or corrected and invite the neighbor in for a plate of meatloaf. Without fail, Mr. Nice Guy would accept, pulling up a chair between Oliver and Mary, like an overgrown third child.

The night that Oliver found his father, it was Mr. Nice Guy whom Mary ran and fetched. Mr. Nice Guy who leaned over their father, his hands trembling, and failed to revive him. Mr. Nice Guy sat with them on the porch while the ambulance light glowed miserably in their driveway, and when their mother scrambled out of her car, her sewing bag falling out with her, he dropped to his knees and collected all of the fabric scraps, scissors and spools. Then he searched for each and every straight pin that was scattered on the concrete.

Oliver doesn't remember him ever finishing. He never stood and walked back across their yard to his own. In fact, after the ambulance took their father away to his colleagues at the hospital, Mr. Nice Guy was still on all fours. Their mother led Oliver and Mary into the house, leaving him there, on his hands and knees, his head bowed, the night dark and quiet.

Oliver would certainly have denied his mother's request that he record Swing Night if she hadn't just bought his lunch—their biannual attempt at a grown-up relationship belied by Oliver's meager wallet, which sported only a five. The food was mountain-gourmet: elk steaks, venison ravioli, fried artichokes and raspberry pie. Certainly the most nutrients Oliver had been exposed to in months and the tastiest food he'd ever had. His initial discomfort as they sat among men in business suits, some of them his own age, had melted away as soon as the warm nut bread and garlic-rosemary butter were placed on their table.

He was still giddy from the food when his mother looked up at him in the parking lot and said, squinting into the midday sun, "I need a favor, Oliver."

He stepped into the sun's path, blocking it for her, and said, "Sure, no problem."

She smiled at him, her short hair framing her petite square face and its amusement. "Before you even know what it is?"

Oliver shrugged. "I can't swallow cocaine in a balloon. And syringes still freak me out. So, unless you've started running drugs or injecting steroids, I think we'll be okay."

"Good. It's our Swing Night. Next week. Martin and I would love to have it on video. Wednesday at eight P.M."

Oliver grimaced. "Wednesday? Night?"

His evenings, Wednesdays included, were reserved for sitting in front of the grocery store, watching. But he did not want to explain this to her and he could not quickly conjure a reasonable excuse.

"Thanks, Oliver," she said, filling the small pause in his reply. "We appreciate it." She then reached up and kissed his cheek, then got into her car.

Oliver recognized her methodology. She often walked away from him when she was satisfied that they'd said all that was required, aloof to the deep and wide conversations he imagined they might have, the endless trenches of things he'd like to say.

As he unloads his equipment this evening, with the sun still throwing long shadows across the sidewalk, he tries to remember some of the sweetness of last week's raspberry pie. It is useless. The only taste in his mouth is the bitter one of obligation.

He grabs a bunch of exterior shots. The storefront of the single-story brick dance studio. The neon sign that hovers above it. The students arriving in their sequined and bejeweled costumes, their shoes a study in patent leather. And now he captures the beauty of the day's end, the way this piece of earth darkens and cools as it turns away from its closest star—perfect for the bin of footage he collects for his bread-and-butter work.

With a heavy sigh, he eases the camera into its case and slings it across his body. Then he folds the tripod and props it on his shoulder. He crosses the street toward the lit-up building, his own silhouette a lopsided, wingless creature in the night.

Inside, Oliver blinks through the bright lights of the mirrored studio. His sneakers squeak loudly against the waxed floor. In his dark corduroys and wide-collared black shirt, he is Lucifer to the troupe of pastel, aging angels gathered here. He finds his mother across the room, in the front corner, her aqua chiffon skirt becoming a cloud of sea foam around her waist that matches the green of her husband's shirt. Together they jitterbug or Lindy or jive. Oliver cannot tell one dance from another. It is possible that if Mary were here with him, she would whisper the names in his ear, but it is more likely she would stare, slack jawed, as he is, while their mother and their father's replacement twist and shimmy across the wood floor.

It is not the dancing that surprises him. Oliver has encountered it frequently in the kitchen after dinner, the two of them bound in a kind of Lawrence Welk waltz. The sink abandoned midstream, a stack of dirty dishes their only other audience, they like to indulge in a loose, undirected down-up-up jig. But now the sheer pace of this practiced choreography is stunning. The world is falling apart all around them and, night after night, they practice their dance steps. People are lost, abandoned, forgotten and dying. But here is something that can be rehearsed. Sequins glitter, skirts twirl and success is apparent and possible. Is this why his mother's generation seems to float above the angst of his own? When she advises him to "lighten up," perhaps what she means is that he should learn to dance.

He makes his way through the other midlife dancers to a high black stool near the windows. Somehow, Oliver finds room for both his feet and those of the tripod on top of the stool, and he sets up the camera for a wide shot of the entire dance floor.

There is a nice-looking instructor who assigns the floor to the first three couples. Everyone in the room applauds this action. And then the music begins.

Looking through the viewfinder, he watches his mother's and Mr. Nice Guy's feet work in unison, like four feet controlled by one brain. A perfect match, he thinks, watching the sweat begin to soak through in long, unforgiving streaks from beneath Mr. Nice Guy's shirt.

Oliver can't help wondering if his father danced.

There are too few memories. And dancing is not among them. Often what he can't remember feels like a betrayal, a failing on his part. He should know more. It was seven whole years. Countless meals, baths, hugs, and probably dances. Oliver yearns to have the empty places in his mind filled.

He himself likes to dance, though in uncoordinated, undefined shuffles and gyrations. He likes to play music loud and let his own voice drift into the decibels.

What they are doing now is performance.

"Holy cow," he says aloud as his mother is hurtled over Mr. Nice Guy's shoulder. He had no idea the guy could lift her, let alone do it quickly and on the beat. They finish with a spin and a dip and Oliver can see both of their chests heaving with exhaustion, their hearts tested and proven.

Later, as they stand outside in the middle of the parking lot, Oliver says, "Man, you guys should go on the road."

Mr. Nice Guy reaches for Oliver's hand. "Thanks, buddy. Thanks for coming out tonight."

The two men shake and then his mother pats him on the shoulder. "It's just fun, you know," she says. "It keeps us young. And when our knees and our hips go out, we can sit around and remember."

"Not really your specialty—remembering," Oliver says, putting his tripod into the back of the Ranchero.

She laughs, lightheartedly, uninterested in and unmoved by her son's criticism. "But now we've got video," she says, "to help us remember it all."

"Indeed," Oliver says. "Indeed you do. Hey, do you remember Dad dancing? I mean, did you guys dance together, ever?"

Mr. Nice Guy stands there with his arm around Oliver's mother and smiles blankly at the asphalt beneath his feet. Oliver watches his mother's face as she searches for an answer.

"No," she says, finally. "He didn't. We didn't." She pauses, then puts her hand on her hip. "But I do remember that you were quite a little square dancer. Remember, Martin, when he was in fifth grade?" She gazes up at her husband.

Mr. Nice Guy nods agreeably. "Sure," he says, as they drift across the parking lot toward their car. "I remember that."

Oliver's mother turns her head back and says, over her shoulder, "You wore the little red kerchief around your neck? All the girls wanted you as their partner because you actually knew how to do-si-do."

Oliver watches them buckle up and back out of the parking space. His mother looks diminutive in the big sedan. As they pass beneath a street light, it throws its strong beam onto the passenger's side of the front seat. His mother's face becomes, briefly, a bright, pale circle, like a stone lit up in the night. Then she slips back into darkness and the sedan disappears into traffic.

For a while after they've left, after the parking lot is empty and Oliver has seen the end of his obligation, he closes his eyes and imagines another day.

It is a day he thinks of quite often, and he now thinks it will be soon. Maybe a cool fall evening, when the leaves are beginning to run toward their own demise, marked by brilliant shrieks of crimson and gold. His mother and Mary will sit together, on a couch or around a table, and listen carefully as he tells them about watching a stranger night after night. He imagines that he will tell them what he's seen and why it matters. Both of them, his mother especially, will be desirous of what Oliver knows. She will be desperate, finally, to hear all that he has to say.

❖

Oliver parks in the freshly striped lot in front of Alfalfa's, the gourmet market downtown. Wearing oversized sunglasses across the
bridge of his nose, despite the late hour, he is conducting surveillance. For the last six days he has been on the trail of a piece of
that summer twenty-one years ago. The glasses, which he picked
up in a thrift store, are big and heavy on his face, just like his
father's were when he tried them on as a kid. These, however, do
not make the floor buckle and swoop beneath him; they remind
him of his purpose. Fact finder. Sleuth. He likes to look the part.

He slumps in the front of the Ranchero, watching intently.

It's been so many years since he's played dress-up or pretend
that he can hardly remember what it's like to be somebody else.
Even for a moment. He's nearly thirty now, for God's sake. But
hunched in the car truck, wearing the glasses, watching, he has
the sense that his life is finally coalescing into something else.
Or simply becoming clear, complete. If someone were taking a
time-lapse film of his life, these would be the end shots in which it
all makes sense. The small drops of water form an icicle, the flower
finally blooms or the last of millions of grains of sand completes an
enormous anthill.

Oliver has plenty of these images on his hard drive. They come
in handy for his work. Mourning a husband, a father, a sister? On
screen, a pretty rose unfolds in the dawn. And your loved one's
face smiles at you from a million rose-colored pixels.

He is drawn to these images. As sentimental as their effect
may be, he cannot help finding some deep resonance among them.
He envies the mechanism that manipulates time in order to reveal
the truth about the way things become what they are. In his mind he

refers to this phenomenon as a widening. He knows it is, technically, an acceleration of time, but its intent is to widen time, to offer a different perspective on reality. Speed it up in order to slow it down. Fast-forward in order to rewind. He wishes he could apply this technology to select moments of his own life. The beauty of time-lapse is its ability to reveal how much and how little can change in a day. Our infinitesimal becoming is so often missed precisely because it is happening all the time. But here outside Alfalfa's, Oliver perceives this becoming. The widening is unfolding before him as though he were watching it unfold on a screen in the dark.

It's been a week since he first spotted his target pushing a long line of carts through this parking lot, the afternoon sun glinting appropriately off of all that metal, catching Oliver's eye. He's an unforgettable kid most people would never even see.

Of course, Oliver is practiced at seeing. There have been other suspects throughout his life, all of them with some version of a red birthmark stretching like a vague arrow from just below the left ear to a narrow point below the jaw. But none of them has been the correct combination of age and gender. There were some much older, or boys just barely entering adolescence. Each of these encounters would cause Oliver to stop, catch his breath, and struggle to move on, reluctantly conceding the person was not who he had hoped. Now Oliver feels certain that he has finally found the one person he's always been looking for.

There are bins of Vidalia onions outside the market, lit this evening by a bright floodlight. Oliver checks the ashtray for change. At a dollar forty a pound, he could probably get a couple of small ones for three bucks.

Curling his fingers around a pile of change, Oliver hesitates. He can see the boy inside the store. Not so much a boy anymore. He should be nearly twenty-one now. He's wearing a thin cotton T-shirt, so thin Oliver can tell it is one of his favorites. They've started selling them that way—well worn, looking old, the deterioration hurried up somewhere in Asia or South America by a commercial-grade washing machine filled with special stones.

But this boy, Jared, is not someone who would pay for a factory somewhere to change a shirt from new to old. Oliver can just tell he's not a kid who worries about his clothes or his hair or his attitude. He looks every customer in the eye, a gesture of goodwill. Bagging their groceries, he's careful, not sloppy. Amenable, not petulant. There's no irony in this job for him. It is a paycheck and a place to be. The toughness around his eyes, in his wiry arms and jagged teeth, is authentic, not a pose, not cultivated for cool's sake. His birthmark fits him the way Oliver had been unable to imagine it fitting anyone.

From where he sits, Oliver can see the lights of the houses spread across the quartet of hills beyond town. Their twinkling glow could be a cluster of bright stars, an unfamiliar constellation, if he didn't know better. If he didn't know that those four steep hills raise the horizon, invisible at night, by hundreds of feet.

Twenty-one years ago, when Oliver was seven, those hills were known colloquially as the Wilds, interesting only to hikers and children. Without much else to do, some of the older neighborhood kids would gravitate there, where the cacti made them feel untamed and the huge boulders and pop-berry bushes provided obstacles for tag or some other game. But now the four hills have been graded and surveyed. They cradle dozens of expensive glass houses built right into the sides of them. The driveways are long, gradual descents for luxury sedans; their aluminum window casings provide a cascade of reflections for the setting sun. There is still open space—living amid an unspoiled landscape is part of the attraction—but it is combed and marked with paths and benches.

Oliver wonders if anybody living up there now knows about the girl whose body was found at the bottom of the northernmost hill twenty-one years ago. That hill, Bear Peak, is the one that Oliver tends to look at, sometimes even blame, as though it were responsible for everything that happened that summer.

Would it have made any difference if someone had found her sooner? Could a few seconds or minutes or even hours have prevented her death? When the paramedics unloaded the backboard from the ambulance there had already been a vulture circling. At least that's what Mary told him she'd heard—or maybe what she made up. The vulture, he thinks, could have been prevented. Maybe more than that. The time between one heartbeat and the next can be stretched. Can be abnormally long and still, there is survival.

Because, really, people don't die in a single instant, do they? It's not like the Clapper—lights on, lights off. The body is a complicated system to shut down. Sure, the heart may stop. No pulse, no breath. But this is not the actual death. The body goes on. Deprived of oxygen, without electricity flowing between synapses, the blood rushes—falls really—then pools around the edges of the body, making the skin bulge.

He hasn't seen death's progress documented this way—

gradually, like in the nature videos—the building of a bird's nest piece by piece. The flowering of blood vessels and fluttering of muscles are the imperceptible changes that create a new reality. The workings of life become those of death. You would see those processes if you could just manipulate time. Life on fast-forward, played back in slow motion. Change deciphered. Time widened.

And in that widening is the hope for reversal. The possibility of undoing this change. Doctors, then, must be experts at the widening, at understanding and locating those places where they can step in and stop death's progression.

There must exist clinical, medical coordinates that are a testament to the widening. Pathologists, including his father, have mapped these places, retracing death's initiation and destination to find exactly where the end was foretold. Where it became irreversible. Such signals and signposts were certainly imprinted in Oliver's father's neurons, memorized for his medical boards and used almost daily.

That expertise died with him. He may have been retracing the route of the girl's untimely death, counting red cell clotting rates even as the bright kitchen light spun above him, even as he was unable to call for help, unable to tell anybody about what was happening inside himself.

Four to six minutes of oxygen deprivation is the outside limit for a brain's survival. Oliver learned this in his lifeguard CPR training ten years ago.

There are exceptions. A child once lived after seventy minutes submerged in frigid water. Oliver's father would have known these exceptions and the complicated physiological circumstances that allow for them. A layperson might call it a miracle, but there are scientific explanations for this kind of widening. Governed by unseen forces, hidden beneath our skin, it is the realm of biology and chemistry and chance.

Sitting here in this car truck, Oliver has been studying hard, figuring out Jared's name first, then his shifts, and finally his habits. He's followed him home, to an apartment complex covered with weathered wood siding, and watched him emerge with a giant basket of dirty laundry. He's followed him to the Laundromat and waited while Jared waited.

The best place for this surveillance, however, is here in front of Alfalfa's, where the fluorescent bulbs burn brightly and the plate glass windows stretch cooperatively across the front of the store, allowing Oliver an unobstructed drive-in-theater view.

Oliver pushes the glasses up onto his head. He abandons the change he's gathered for the Vidalias and rethinks his entry into the store. There is something missing in the plan he's been formulating.

The night's earlier events seem to be giving him pause. The way his mother's face changed when Oliver asked about his father dancing has unnerved him. Behind her agreeable eyes, she seemed to be locking a gate, denying him entry.

Oliver knows what he lacks: a point of entry. He needs to produce a dossier of emotional evidence to illustrate his case. A slew of photographs that might offer a glimpse of their common loss— it is just the sort of artifact Oliver is paid to create. He makes his living on other people's pasts, but he's never thought to fashion a portfolio of his own.

For now, Oliver catalogues another of his subject's habits. Between bags, Jared cracks his knuckles against his own chest, as if he's pushing himself back, trying to shove his ribs toward his heart with his fist. Oliver tries to imagine the hollow crack this makes. Sometimes Jared will wince unknowingly, unaware that the pain has crossed his face. But Oliver sees it. He has made it his business to watch carefully for the mannerisms about a person that would be second nature if you'd grown up together, in the same house, as brothers.

In order for Jared to step into the childhood he should have had, Oliver will need to widen time. He will manipulate time for both of them. He will assemble shreds of an invented past in order to convey the truth of what might have been.

❖

Betsy rolls down her window and leans, just barely, into the breeze.

"Hot?" Martin asks from his place behind the wheel.

"Just a little stuffy," she says, gazing at the darkened corners of downtown. Alleys and vestibules give her a feeling of longing she cannot explain. She smooths her chiffon skirt out along the seat beneath her.

"I thought it was a great success," Martin says, loudly so that his voice carries over the noise of the open window. "You were really something."

She smiles at him. "Likewise, dear," she says, and then looks back out the window. She nearly expects to see Oliver out on the roadside, gazing at her with his imploring eyes, his tripod over his shoulder like a shovel. He wants too much. Or what he wants is wrong. Her grown son is like a stubborn child who's given an entire buffet and won't eat anything but peanut butter crackers. He wants only the pain.

What she didn't tell Oliver is this: that his father didn't think he had the patience for dancing. That Betsy had wished, often, that he would take her dancing, guide her across a dance floor and fix his eyes on her for the duration of the music. It was even a pivotal moment in each of their favorite movies. For Betsy, it was a requirement of courting. How could he not want to dance with her? To hold her waist and caress her cheek and breathe in the scent of her?

She'd actually asked him once. They were already engaged; she was waiting for his residency to end and their life together to begin. His fatigue was real and oppressive, but he still took her out whenever his schedule allowed.

They were in his apartment that he shared with three other medical students. The kitchen smelled of coffee and rotten fruit. It was a dark apartment, a sleeping cave; they kept all the blinds drawn and the only fixture with a light bulb in it was in the bathroom. Usually, if Paul was awake and not working, he came over to Betsy's, but they had stopped by his place for a change of clothes. With her hands on her hips, she watched him look for a matching pair of socks. Finally, she stomped her little black flat against the wood floor and said she thought it was about time he took her dancing.

Paul smiled. Locking his hands around her waist, he bent his head so that she could feel his breath on her ear. Even and regular, he just held her, letting her own breathing slow to match his. Almost imperceptibly, he began to sway. Was he humming? Or was that the sound of the ceiling fan above them? Betsy felt the way his arms held her, their every point of contact on her body, and she followed his slow, deliberate movement.

Within seconds, before she'd even let her head rest on his shoulder, Betsy felt him stiffen against her navel. Simultaneously, he stopped his swaying and let his lips touch her ear. "See?" he said, his voice full of false defeat. "Impossible. Dancing is for patient men. I am not."

There had been a stripe of daylight that was breaking through the edges of the roller shade behind him, like a golden frame of the moment. She held him within it even as he continued to hold her, undressing her without ever releasing her.

And later, when the children were small and it seemed to her that his patience had improved significantly, he would dutifully hold her close, more of an extended embrace than a dance, doing his best to assuage her nagging doubts. To remind her of a time when she had none.

"Well," Betsy says now, as she rolls up the window.

"What's that?" Martin asks.

"Oliver actually showed up," Betsy says, wishing that she weren't surprised.

"Mmm. Maybe he's finally growing up." Martin stops at a four-way intersection. "It does happen, I've heard." He glances at her, his face pleasantly mischievous. "Even at twenty-eight."

She smiles.

He tries again. "They say thirty is the new twenty. So, what does that make us? Sixty going on fourteen?"

She laughs, but wonders, silently, if Oliver will ever grow up. Will he ever accept what happened and move on? "I guess so," she says, reaching over and placing her hand on Martin's arm, coaxing herself back to the present. To what's real.

2

Oliver's office is the second of two bedrooms in his six-hundred-square-foot rental house near the university. On the door to this second bedroom, he has a homemade sign which reads IT'S KIND TO REWIND. This is the name of his business. He used to spend his days driving a city van between the four libraries in the county, delivering books and supplies and occasionally reshelving the materials he delivered. But six months ago, budget cuts eliminated his position. Without a paycheck or any prospects, he taped an OPEN sign to the door of the second bedroom, and never removed it. It hangs like an invitation beneath IT'S KIND TO REWIND, exhorting Oliver to always be open for the business of finding things that are lost—memories, keepsakes—and placing them, logged and labeled, into a permanent bin he can sift through.

He has also installed a lock on the door, not so much for security reasons—it might slow a burglar down a bit—but for its symbolism. It lends the heft of authority to his endeavors. The feeling of the key in the lock of Oliver's second bedroom is an essential part of beginning the workday.

Inside, there is a corner desk with computer equipment and on one wall a bookshelf jammed with videotapes, blank DVDs, a big stack of CDs and a tissue box. Where there might be a bed there is, instead, a sofa and a coffee table. A blackout shade on the window conceals daylight. Oliver turns on his computer, the tape decks, speakers and a mood light next to the sofa. Shazam! The office is open.

He has only one project on the books right now. Nearly finished, it has become his favorite. Sure, he'd rather make his own tricked-out videos of existential angst all day. But Oliver is just grateful that he does not have to work retail or wait on tables to pay the bills. And occasionally, he feels there may be something akin to art in what he does. He'd never say so out loud; the presumption would intimidate him. Like touting wine lists and sushi.

Most of his friends who still live in town go through their day or night jobs having completely dismissed the dreams of their youth. All through high school and college, they made their own skateboarding flicks and haphazard video installations that played on a screen over the football field, formed bands that sold out local venues, and seemed to be cool without any effort at all. They once thought they'd be the proprietors of their generation's culture, dictating the whims and jokes for a broader audience the way they had at school. The promise that this celebrity would continue, if not grow, seemed like a sure thing. Really, just screwing around was something they thought they could live off of forever. Now that most of them are about to enter their thirties, they are becoming bitter and poor, with receding hairlines and pot bellies that could never be famous. They live for the moment when their workday ends and they can drive through Taco Bell, go home to turn on the TV, and watch sitcom actors do the stupid shit they themselves used to do but were never paid for.

Oliver, though, always aspired toward something a little bit different.

He sits in front of the computer and pulls up the bin that he's titled *Not a Day Longer*. As he sometimes does when the footage inspires him, Oliver has made two cuts of this project. A director's cut suitable for his archives, his own personal collection that he shows only to Mary, and a theatrical release suitable for the family and their purposes. The difference between the two is usually in the pacing.

When cutting a memorial video for a family, Oliver keeps the pacing slow, thoughtful, lingering on—sometimes even slowing down—the shot of the smiling face, the wave, the kiss. Those actions defy death by rendering it unreal, impossible. There are lots of fades and dissolves between images. No hard cuts. It should be soothing, melodic, rhythmic. Like a lullaby. Or a hymn.

The director's cut, however, is more atonal. Instead of music that the family has chosen (typically ballads or instrumentals), the soundtrack is a recording that Oliver has made. This time it's a mix of sounds from his backyard at night. Crickets doing their thing, moths swatting against the bare porch lightbulb, birds rustling in the trees, a howling dog, the scratch of branches against his rain gutter. These amplified sounds are combined with rapid cutting, graphics and special effects so that there are no soft edges. It is a conceptual commentary on the brief flicker that humanity's existence takes up in the natural world. Using hand-drawn lines to connect the blurred images of Nonny when she was three and wearing saddle shoes to the old-woman shoes she wore until her death late last summer, Oliver wants to convey something about change. This is his theory about the widening, about death being not instantaneous but gradual, always happening. If only we could figure out how to see the relativity of time for ourselves without digitizing footage and playing it back at different speeds. Couldn't Nonny's death, in fact, be seen in those little girl's saddle shoes? And, couldn't her daughter, the microscopic egg that would be found by the microscopic sperm, also be beginning right there with those saddle shoes? He adds a layer to the timeline on his computer, drawing an egg and a sperm uniting in the glossy patent leather of the shoe.

Oliver has never shown a director's cut to his clients. But there is something about Nonny, the dead old woman, that makes Oliver certain she would approve. Even in her old woman shoes, she has the look of youth in her eyes. There is no weariness, no impatience, no readiness for the end.

Her father, who had been a screenwriter in Hollywood, took grainy 16-millimeter images of her, beginning in the 1920s. She seemed to have the same ebullient regard for life at three years old as she did at eighty-seven.

There is one bit of film that is so lovely, despite its scratches, that Oliver has slowed it down and given it lots of screen time in the theatrical cut. Nonny is crossing a small footbridge with a toddler in her arms. She must be nearly thirty. There are low-hanging branches stretching out over the water and near the bridge. Their slender arcs are shaded by foliage and blossoms. The toddler, probably Nonny's own daughter, the woman who brought Oliver the boxes of film and photos, reaches out for the tree. The footage is black and white. Oliver cannot tell what kind of tree it is, but the blooms are small, like a Bradford pear. The child pulls a single, perfect blossom from a branch and holds it up to Nonny's mouth, wanting to feed her.

Nonny is wearing a hat, which is tied with a thick ribbon under her chin, and a tailored dress and heels. Church clothes. The formality of life in that era creeps into frame, unavoidable. Ladies with gloved hands and gentlemen in bow ties lurk in the background.

Instead of gently pushing the child's hand away, which is what one expects from this elegant woman, the black and white figure opens her mouth wide and lets the child place the bud right onto her tongue. Nonny envelops the blossom, closing her lips in a big smile. Then she turns toward the camera and opens her mouth again. There, in the center of her mouth, is this perfect little flower. It's as if she'd grown it herself, from the thickest part of her tongue. Closing her mouth again, she chews and swallows, then shows both the camera and the child her now superbly empty mouth. The child giggles wildly, clapping her hands. Nonny curtsies at the camera and then turns, walking away over the bridge, utterly distinguished. As though true ladies eat trees whenever they are offered.

Oliver wishes he could find a place for this scene in his own cut. In fact, he wishes Nonny could watch his cut and tell him how to portray her without sentimentality. Because she is devastatingly beautiful. And sweet. And the way she humors the child is heroic to Oliver. She invokes in him a sense of wonder that seems old-fashioned, but also fresh. Hers is an essence that would instantly change the tone of his piece. From dark to light.

Oliver is captivated by her light, but unable to see its relevance to his director's cut. Or to his own life, for that matter. How does it fit?

Her hold on life is fierce. And yet. One day last fall, in a room on the back side of her daughter's house, in a bed that had been her father's, she gave up that hold. That is how she fits; how everyone, eventually, will fit.

We all die. Oliver gets that much. But what he doesn't get is why it's hidden. Why it's folded into medicine cabinets and hidden under sheets, and in the uncomfortable silence between everyone. This is his own sentimentality. He possesses an irrepressible longing to revisit and reacquaint himself with what's been, and to immerse himself in the consequences of what is lost. Nonny, he suspects, would be unafraid to encircle him with every aspect of her death. And her life. And each vanished pear blossom. She would speak of all of it, both what was lost and what could be found.

But it's her daughter who will come to pick up the DVD, writing a check to It's Kind to Rewind. She will take it home and what? Shelve it until the first grandchild is born? Or will she watch it every night, unable to resist having the specter of the woman in the house with her again? Oliver would like to ask—would like to truly know—how it is that this video will be used, but this question always seems intrusive.

He does not advertise his services and relies entirely upon word-of-mouth referrals. The local funeral home has begun to allow him to place a stack of business cards in their consultation rooms, but this has not yet generated any paying clients.

A couple of people have called wondering if he would video-tape the actual memorial service, either graveside or in the church. It would be easy enough money, running camera, but Oliver prefers eating ramen for a month to becoming a funeral photographer.

He offered the callers a package. He would agree to record the funeral if they would let him commemorate the life. Give him photos, video, poems, music, and he'd create a montage of all their fondest memories of the life, with the memorial service and burial tagged on at the end. For a flat fee.

But each caller refused, saying they only wanted a videogra-pher. Not a documentarian.

Both requests bothered him for days. What generates the urge to capture a funeral service rather than a life?

Good-bye and good-bye and good-bye again? A factual account-ing for posterity?

Even wedding videos are inane to Oliver. Without any footage of the courtship, the misunderstandings, the revelations, the pas-sion, the proposal, what does the wedding mean? The life together makes the love story. Not the ceremony that makes it instanta-neously official.

Nobody has yet asked him to shoot a first date, a first kiss, a first fight. Nor have any of the callers from funeral homes been interested in anything but the funeral.

Day by day. Night by night. In small undocumented moments the truth of loss, like the truth of a marriage, happens over time. Slowly, you discover what has changed and what has not. You realize that the way life used to be will never be again, even when you wear the same clothes, use the same towel, have the same haircut. People around you still drink coffee and deliver mail and even laugh. Everything is the same. Except nothing is the same.

What about making *that* video: the first days of grief. What shots would he include?

Oliver watches his director's cut of Nonny again, tweaking the sound in places, and decides both cuts are finished. He puts aside this project to prepare for his first meeting with his newest client, Mrs. Wilcox.

❖

She is not a friendly woman. She does not smile first or easily. Many people avoid her, alienated by their own discomfort with her circumstances combined with her surly face. Her jaw is distinctly square and always clenched. With large, heavy-lidded eyes, she watches the world without charity. One can see her judging and blaming each and every passerby's existence for her own misfortune.

Oliver, however, does not mind this bitterness. In his line of work, clients are not often cheerful or talkative. He is not intimidated by grief's expression.

When he greets Mrs. Wilcox at the front door, they shake hands and do not linger on niceties.

Oliver brings her into his office and invites her to sit on the couch. He sits in his desk chair but spins it around to face her. In her arms she has a photo album.

"We didn't do video," she says, first thing.

"Didn't do it?" Oliver says, lamenting the endless dissolves that will be required.

"I'm not sure why. Neither of us really . . ." She glances around the room as if she can't be bothered to explain herself.

"Okay. It's not a problem. But we will need other elements to make the video dynamic. More than just a photo album," he says, gesturing to the book in her lap.

"You probably told me on the phone," she says without apology.

"Right. We talked about music, spoken word, other images that you could actually go and videotape now. Like favorite places or views or . . ."

Mrs. Wilcox looks blankly at him.

"Would you like me to show you some sample work, Mrs. Wilcox?"

"You know that you look just like your father, don't you?" It's nearly an accusation.

Oliver blinks. "Yeah, I've been told." Normally, Oliver doesn't pass up an opportunity to talk about his father. But this is different. He's not sure he wants to talk with her about his father. About what his father did for her.

Instead, he turns around in his chair and fires up the monitor just beside his desk. Oliver inserts his demo reel, of pieces from different videos he's made for clients. It begins with a black screen and the sound of a piano playing a Bach sonata, not very well. Soon, the black dissolves into a portrait of an elderly man, smiling at the camera from a piano bench.

"Enough," Mrs. Wilcox says. "I'm not interested in other . . . people's . . ." She cannot come up with a word.

"Videos?" Oliver stops the tape.

"Yes. That."

"I just wanted you to know the kinds of things I can do."

"Oh, I know what *kinds* of things you do. Pathetic, really. Isn't it? Old women like me. All of the men die first."

There is an awkward pause, but neither of them fills it.

Looking down at her hands clasped around the album, she continues. "As girls we swoon over the older boys. They make us feel so safe, so cared for. And then they all die. Their provisions are tools we know nothing about and closets full of useless neckties." She finishes with a forced laugh, neither humorous nor cheerful.

"I'm sorry. I think I've misunderstood. I thought this video was to be about your daughter."

"That's right," Mrs. Wilcox says impatiently. Her voice is so gruff it is hard to believe she's ever cared about anybody. "My daughter. Now that Roger's gone, I have no one. Nobody who knew her to help me remember. So many parts of her, suddenly gone again when he died. The worst is to forget."

Oliver nods. He is also afraid of forgetting, of letting the handful of memories he has fade even more.

The thick shade over the window makes the monitor bright and easy to see. But the monitor is black now, and the room's darkness makes their silence acceptable. Breaking it would feel as uncouth as talking in a theater or a chapel, so each stares into the space right in front of their eyes, seeing nothing.

As he often does, Oliver revisits the memory of being in the tree behind his first childhood home, next door to the house they'd soon move into, once their mother married Mr. Nice Guy. The day had begun as another long, empty morning spent sucking at small, tart crabapples and peeling away patches of thick gray bark, bending their bodies to fit the curves of the branches. Just like any other summer morning. One never knows which day will sharpen and scribble your life into two separate columns: Before and After. This was the last halcyon day.

They are plotting, thinking of names. Frederick. Skywalker. James. Percival.

Mary is keeping a list. Her pink spiral notebook is swollen and brittle, having been left one afternoon on the porch and victimized by the powerful spray of the fancy new sprinklers that turn on and off by themselves in the middle of the night.

Oliver, on the other hand, is watching a group of neighborhood kids who've gathered in the yard adjacent to theirs to play hide and seek. They are older than he. Older than Mary. Probably twelve or so. Their voices carry easily, their insecurity masked as confidence that spills out of them like gasoline, flammable and caustic.

They mill around the yard, disorganized and unfocused. Nobody wants to be *it*.

They shove each other, then laugh, intoxicated by this brief bodily contact. Finally one boy volunteers. He will be the seeker. He is fast, Oliver can tell by his compact form, by the easy sway of his shoulders. Will anybody make it to home base? Oliver wonders.

This could be exciting.

Normally, there is not much to see from up here. The neighbors' rooftops all around, their cylindrical aluminum vents spinning like little dancing robots. The decks and porches that stick out from most of the houses are cluttered with rusting lounge chairs, trikes, deflated balls, and big bowls of muddied dog water. Hardly anything exciting ever happens on Oliver's block.

Until now.

All the other kids scatter except for the fastest of the boys, who stands in the center of the yard with his eyes closed. His clenched fists sprout fingers in time, counting to ten.

Watching them from above, Oliver admires the good hiding places—behind the shed, under the deck, in the abandoned doghouse—and rolls his eyes at the conspicuous choices the lesser of them make: behind a slender ash tree, in the middle of a bed of perennials, or, worst of all, just crouching in the grass in the middle of the yard because a voice calls out, *Ready or not, here I come!*

There is one girl Oliver recognizes from the pool, her hair thick and black. Patty Wilcox. Without a doubt, it is she who has found the best place: beneath the barbeque cover that is draped over the deck railing. Oliver would have tried it himself had he been invited to play. She straddles the rail, then pulls her feet up behind her, like she's flying. With one arm, she drags the cover over her, so it's hanging just as it was.

Oliver's own adrenaline begins to race as he sees her disappear. He can imagine what it's like under there, hearing the sounds of the yard, her eyes slowly adjusting to the dark. Her own breath hot and moist and making her sweat.

The boy who is *it* comes frightfully close to her location, the tips of his fingers skimming the barbecue. But he goes on by, unaware.

One discovery after another is made and the found kids scream as they run for home base. None of them makes it and Oliver roots harder for Patty Wilcox each time someone has been found. Soon everyone else has been caught. But not Patty. They've no idea where to find her.

Oliver is suddenly filled with anxiety, certain that any second one of the other kids who are halfheartedly looking around the yard will pull up the cover and scream at her, "I found you. I knew it. I found you."

But this doesn't happen.

He watches the cover closely, trying to detect some movement, some sign of her breathing. But the canvas cover is motionless, as though it's just hanging there with no living thing beneath it. Could she have already slipped out and made it to home base, escaping Oliver's notice?

Then, just beneath the hem of the canvas, Oliver spies the string of her shoelace. She's still in there. But she doesn't move a muscle.

Eventually, the group grows tired of looking for the girl. One by one, without warning, they abandon her—-her exquisite triumph— and like dogs who've found a new scent, they follow each other quickly out the side gate, leaving the yard empty and still.

Oliver's jaw drops open. Can they do that? Just leave her there? The winner? Surely she deserves some congratulations, some acknowledgment.

But the yard is quiet. The game is over.

Oliver wants to yell at the girl, to tell her that she won. Instead, he listens to his sister's voice and the list of names she's still recording.

"Jake. Stewart. Duke. I've always wanted a Duke in the family. It sounds so regal. What do you think, Oliver?"

Oliver shrugs, his eyes still on the yard below. "Jolly good," he says, just as she's instructed him to reply to her whenever he doesn't know what else to say.

The girl does not come out. Does she know her friends have left? Surely, she must hear the sudden quiet of the yard. Has she forgotten the game, curled up in her own darkness? If she doesn't come out soon, she will not catch up with the other kids. She will miss the rest of the day's fun.

Oliver begins to worry. Has something happened to her? Is she sick or hurt? What if she dies under there? What if that is the consequence of not being found? You cannot live unless somebody cares enough to pursue you, to look in every single place, to seek and seek and not give up. Oliver scoots closer to the wall, thinking that he will jump into the yard, run to her and uncover her. Find her. Save her.

Just as he's readying himself for the drop, he sees the cover begin to move.

Slowly, she pushes it away from her body and peeks out at the yard. Her hair has fallen in front of her face, an additional camouflage. But when she sees that nobody, in fact, is looking for her, she seems embarrassed and hops down quickly, brushing off her knees, shoving back her hair, trying to regain her dignity.

Oliver yells out, unable to contain his admiration. "Hey, down there. Good spot. I saw the whole thing. You won!"

For a brief moment she looks up at Oliver, smiles, and blushes. She raises her hand as though she might wave.

Oliver wants her to come up into the tree and see her hiding place from his vantage, but then Mary stands up, interested in what her brother has found. "Who? Won what?" she asks, peering over Oliver's head, her bare feet gripping the tree branch.

As soon as Mary's face appears there between the leaves, the girl on the ground changes her expression. She is older than both Oliver and Mary and suddenly seems ashamed of her solitude and their witness of it.

"Shit," she says, kicking at the canvas hanging off the deck. "What are you two looking at?" she says, her lip curling, her hands on her hips.

"Can't say," Mary says, unafraid of confrontation. "What are you, exactly?"

Oliver blanches, sensing he's caused some dispute. "I was just watching you play. I mean, I was just watching the game. That's all. You had a good hiding place. Great, actually. No one found you." He smiles widely, still vicariously proud of her accomplishment.

"Do you always spy on people? Because it's rude, you know." She shifts her weight, her hands still on her hips.

"Bloody hell!" Mary shouts back. "Spies do the work of kings and queens. Protecting the crown, protecting Her Royal Majesty. Have you never heard of double-oh seven?" Recently, Mary has become a devotee of anything to do with royalty. They've watched James Bond movies and documentaries and even the wedding of Diana and Charles. She saves her money for British tabloids that occasionally appear in the grocery store and, when she remembers, speaks with her best British accent.

Patty takes her hands off her hips. "Freaks," she says, and then she flips her middle finger at Oliver and Mary before running off in search of those distant voices fading somewhere down the street. Later that afternoon, she would be dead.

As he sits now in his office, looking at the deep lines around Mrs. Wilcox's eyes, Oliver thinks of Nonny and the director's cut drawing he'd made on her saddle shoe. We never see our beginnings. One of the many eggs that began deep within Mrs. Wilcox eventually became Patty, and the eggs that Patty was carrying when she fell to the bottom of Bear Peak had been huddled in her ovaries before she was even delivered from Mrs. Wilcox's womb. Oliver's father must have noted those unremarkable white organs during the autopsy.

It was much later that Oliver learned why his father had been called into the hospital on what should have been his day with the kids while their mother went to her sewing club. Patty Wilcox had decided to sequester herself, with a pack of stolen cigarettes, on the top of Bear Peak. Somehow, her fall had ruptured not only the skin across the back of her skull but the certainty that it was an accidental death. An autopsy was required. Dr. Finley would have to be called in.

Sitting on the porch, a deck of cards between them, Oliver and Mary had been practicing their bullshit faces.

"Ace of spades," Oliver says, his lips pulling together, his ears reddening with effort.

Mary narrows her eyes, studying his face. He doesn't look away, as he often does when trying to disguise a lie. In fact, he opens his eyes wider, their green irises the same shade as her own; mimicked by the pine trees that grow effortlessly here in this high country, dropping cones onto their metal roof that then roll down the sloping pitch and make a noise like a tiny drum roll. Often, during conversation, their father will pause, look to the ceiling and say, "Wait for the drum roll," hoping that a pinecone will punctuate his thought.

As Mary studies Oliver's eyes, trying to decipher them, Oliver wonders what color irises the baby will have. Certainly he will not share this trait of theirs. The thought of a different set of eyes both strengthens his affection for Mary's and shoots a ripple of excitement across his shoulder blades as he imagines loving someone new. The baby, when it's delivered next week, will look nothing like any of them. Its size, shape and coloring will be a surprise, will continue to surprise them all their lives. There will be no precedent, no biological destiny toward thin hair, freckles or an allergy to penicillin. The baby to come will be a mystery to solve.

Without warning, Oliver bursts into hysterical giggles.

Mary beams and takes the stack of cards. "Let's hope you're not ever captured by enemy spies. You'd give away all our secrets, Oliver."

He rolls onto his side, incapacitated by his own laughter. He has not had a haircut all summer and his pale blond hair falls away from his face and onto the porch floor. Mary reaches her bare foot out toward him, poking him in the side, finding his most ticklish place. He writhes, bending, trying somehow to fend off her efforts. His laughter attacks her, too, and she wiggles her toes again, threateningly. Oliver throws his card at her. She turns her face away.

"Stop," he squeals, shoving himself away from her, trying to catch his breath. "Stop it."

She stays right where she is but wiggles her toes again at him, taunting and extending their laughter.

"Don't," he manages to say, turning onto his back and staring up at the blue sky above their heads. He places his hands over his face so he cannot see her. "It really was. It's the ace, I swear." His chest rises and falls as he catches his breath.

Mary turns the card over. "Oliver!"

Her dismay provokes their laughter all over again. Neither of them notices their father, who stands in the doorway of the open sliding glass door, his head cocked, staring at them with faraway eyes.

"Mary. Oliver. I've got to go into work," he says, finally, startling them into silence. They look up at him, their mouths open, their cheeks blushed. "Should I call Mom and have her come home? Or do you think you can manage for a little while on your own?"

"We've been working on names again, Daddy." Mary elbows Oliver. "Right?"

"Cricket," Oliver says, smiling, his cheek pressed against the cool cement. "We like Cricket. Or Skywalker."

"Cricket Skywalker Finley? Whaddya think, Daddy?"

Their father stands in the doorway, his hands in his pockets. "Hmmm," he says. "I may have to think about that one. Can you guys make a PBJ sandwich and stay out of trouble? I should be home by six."

"Yep," Mary says, unfazed by his request. She hops up and gives him a kiss.

Oliver is less enthusiastic. "PBJ?" he whines. "I had that for lunch."

"Well, get creative, Oliver. Open a can of tuna. Or melt cheese on a tortilla. Or wait for me. I'll feed you when I get home. Okay?"

Oliver nods. He hugs him around the hips, where he can reach, his father's belt pressing into his forehead.

"Be good," his father says to both of them before disappearing. They hear the Ranchero start up and whir as he backs it out of the driveway.

It is a moment that seems to hang in Oliver's brain, suspended between the vast quantities of silence spanning the dark between him and Mrs. Wilcox.

Did Oliver lose an entire part of himself there on that day? If so, which part? Was it a change that did not occur over time, with subtlety, but rather an immediate, noticeable excision? Like cutting a limb off a tree? Could such a change have been photographed?

"This," Mrs. Wilcox finally says, clutching the album in her lap, "is one of two. I cannot give you both. When you've finished with this one, I will bring over the other."

Oliver nods. "It won't take long," he replies, "I just scan them into the computer. A day or two is all—"

"Call me when you're ready." Mrs. Wilcox stands, leaving the single photo album on the couch.

Oliver walks her to the door.

"You're well equipped, I suppose," she says, pausing only for a moment on his front porch. "For this job."

Oliver nods. "The wonders of technology." He realizes only as he watches her walk away from him that he has misunderstood her meaning.

He spends the rest of the evening scanning pictures of the Wilcox girl into his computer. First, the baby, small and scrawny in a pink bonnet, her eyes staring somewhere off beyond the camera. Next, the toddler, balanced on a rocking horse, her pigtails blurry with motion, her mouth wide with glee. Through each milestone she changes, but Oliver recognizes the newborn face hidden within her. He carefully replaces every photo in the album. The upper corners of the pages are disintegrating, the paper thin and gray from so much handling.

3

Missy Rolondo is a well-kept woman of thirty-five. She lives with her husband and their two boys in a great big stone and metal house with a view of the western sky. The glorious sunsets are the reason she insisted they buy the house. It is possible to lie on a raft in the fifty-foot lap pool and stare at the great expanse of sky as it shifts from blue to orange to purple and finally to black. Lately, however, Missy has been afraid to put on her bikini and leave the kids in front of the TV while she drifts across the water with one hand dipped in.

Afraid, she tells Mr. Scrap, because of everything that's happened. Plus she's simply exhausted. She doesn't sleep at all anymore. And she feels threatened.

Andy Rolondo, whom she married on the beach in Santa Monica after the three most romantic months of her life, may have relapsed into a cocaine addiction that he told her he'd taken care of in a facility in Wyoming when he was twenty-five. He owns a chain of gourmet restaurants well positioned across the country. Traveling from location to location, he has always maintained a casual presence in the house. For the past six years, Missy did not mind this routine. Or lack thereof. There were sitters when she needed a break from the children. And his absences kept her eager for his return. The house became more lively, more glamorous, more seductive whenever he was home.

This is her story.

She dressed herself carefully each day, never knowing if he might come home a day early just to surprise them. She looked forward to the times he would arrive and bring with him some token of his affection—jewelry or fresh lobster or once, even, a fur coat.

Always, he brought toys for the boys. The baby didn't notice. Only giggled when Andy tossed him into the air, farther and farther into the dead space of their two-story foyer. But Andrew, their older boy, had become accustomed to what Missy called the longing. Fits of hysteria or melancholy struck without warning, requiring her to explain to the boy that this is the way love sometimes feels. He mostly thought the trade-off was worth it, she told herself. His closet full of electronics outweighed a few missed T-ball games or swim lessons.

Andy wears clothes beautifully, walks with a kind of assured grace, and has an easy smile that makes his brown eyes soften and the room brighten. He could have been a theater actor or a Hollywood celebrity.

He tires of cars quickly, loves new shoes, new sunglasses, is always altering his taste in music and movies, and can never make up his mind about art. But, when he proposed marriage on the interstate between Phoenix and Denver, he assured Missy that, like his instincts for chefs, he had a surefire instinct about her.

She had been well aware of the extensive dating life he'd pur-
sued before the day they met—he in the dental chair, smiling, she
hovering over him, scrutinizing. She felt grateful that he had chosen her as the one permanence in his life.

She was reliable, consistent, the antidote to all of his drama
and his excess. Their life together would be as brilliant as his entre-
preneurial life because he knew how to decide upon partners. Any
chef who could choose a menu—and produce it night after night
with exquisite consistency—had a permanent job with him.

So, too, would Missy. Mrs. Andy Rolondo would require the
same sort of dazzling consistency, calm under pressure, and ability
to keep unusual hours as a five-star chef.

Missy, who had never before been commended for her depend-
able nature, thought that the purpose of her whole life had been
revealed. After so many dull, unremarkable years broken up only
by the forty-five-minute increments of removing plaque from
around the gum line, she was suddenly in the middle of more
excitement than she'd ever imagined she was destined to enjoy.

Andy let her choose the house—he'd never bought one of his
own, preferring to rent luxury penthouses in a variety of cities. She
chose this mountain resort community because of its quiet, rather
lackluster downtown that would not distract her husband when he
was at home. And that she would fit into when he wasn't.

The climate, she felt, was sensible, allowing children an opportunity to know four distinct seasons. But most of all, it reminded
her of her grandparents' home in Colorado near the top of a mountain at the end of a winding dirt road. As a child there, she had
collected beetles and lizards and studied the particles in the dirt—

flakes that looked like silver and gold, seeds from ancient times and pinecones too small for growing. These things are stepped on and paved over in other places.

Missy told all of this to Mr. Scrap as background.

So frequently, with background, one never knows where to stop. How far back to begin. How deep to dig. Suddenly, when you're sitting in that chair across from the attorney, it becomes clear that your entire life, from the time you were first swaddled, has led to this moment.

She could tell Mr. Scrap how Andy's eyes looked while he listened to her little stainless steel tool click against his enamel, her gloved fingers holding steady on his lips, her hygiene mask covering her own nose and mouth. How she didn't notice that he'd stretched his fingers across her forearm until he pressed gently, perhaps from discomfort. Unable to speak, to charm, he held her eyes with his own and pressed more firmly only when she looked away.

Mr. Scrap has heard a million stories. All the same, really. All unhappy endings. That's his business.

This part of the initial consultation has become the most tedious, tiresome part of his day. But it is often more valuable to his clients than the alimony he can arrange or the percentage of their spouse's retirement he can secure for them.

He is able to force himself to sit attentively through these preliminary sessions because he knows how close he himself once was to an unhappy ending. Not divorce, but unrequited love.

He is grateful, mostly, for the sheer dumb luck and perfect timing that delivered him from that ending. But in the quietest part of himself, he is also afraid.

Every day, he tries to atone for the wish that came true. The death he had hoped for and then witnessed. He knows, however, that this attention to his clients may not be enough. That it may not matter at all.

His ability to listen to the doubt, heartache and anger of people for whom he has no secret agenda, no ulterior motive, no desperate longing, is a quality that has set him apart in his field.

He is a premier divorce attorney; his wealth is sizable. There is almost nothing that he's wanted that he cannot acquire. Except, perhaps, the love of his stepchildren. But that is a mythic complaint, echoed by friends and acquaintances, and he has come to accept it. He certainly cannot blame them; his own life shifted from bleak to hopeful on the day their father died. That he is a calming, sensible, savvy counselor for people who mean nothing to him—surely this chore, this penance, has repaid his debt.

Mr. Scrap works in an office tower that has an underground parking garage. As a tenant in the building, he is given an automatic pass through the pay booth in the form of a small, magnetized card. At five in the afternoon, however, there is always a line of cars waiting to exit. Even in the Tenant Only lane.

Today as he waits with the radio off and the windows rolled down, he turns over in his mind the travails of Missy Rolondo, whom he accompanied to her car just across the deck from his.

Her husband has become dismissive of her requests that he spend more time at home; his part-time commitment is growing old and stale. She has become dissatisfied with her choice, realizing now that it was a fantasy to think she could sustain any intimacy with somebody so different, so distractible, so absent. And a mistake, she said, tearfully, to bring children into the world with a father who would not change his life for them. What kind of man would not be flattered by requests for bedtime stories and seduced by footed pajamas?

Then there was the drug habit. Hard to tell when or if he'd ever been clean. Missy assured Mr. Scrap that she had married a sober man. But Mr. Scrap has been witness to enough of these kinds of splits to understand that people's perspective can shift. What before might have seemed like a charming indiscretion suddenly becomes a reason for divorce.

For Mr. Scrap's purposes it doesn't really matter. He will file a petition for sole custody and temporary alimony and child support until there can be a hearing. Meanwhile, he has instructed Missy Rolondo to change her locks and agree to communicate with Mr. Rolondo only through their attorneys.

Unfortunately, clients cannot be trusted to follow his advice. He suspects that the next time Andy Rolondo flies into town, she will take his call, allow him to come to the house just for a drink, accepting whatever exorbitant gift he brings with him. Looking on with relief as he carries the baby upstairs, asleep on his shoulder, she will wonder if maybe she hasn't been hasty, harsh, mistaken. Hope is a powerful aphrodisiac.

Regardless, Mr. Scrap has paid his penance for the day.

He inches his car forward. He is nearly at the front of the line.

A squealing of tires prompts him to glance in the rearview mirror. He sees Missy Rolondo in her oversized SUV blocked by a ridiculously small black sports car. She is crying.

Mr. Scrap slouches a little in his seat, not wanting to be turned to for help. He is nearly out of the garage, on his way home.

The cement walls of the garage make the air feel hollow and Andy's incredulous voice echoes. His hands are in the air, gesturing in mid-conversation.

"What? What are you doing, Miss? I get a voice mail that you're seeing a fucking attorney? Since when is this the way we do things?"

She's put her head down now, so that she cannot see her husband.

"Look at me," he screams. The traffic stops completely. The driver in front of Mr. Scrap turns and stares past his car, right at Missy and Andy Rolondo.

Missy lifts her head from the steering wheel. Her bottom lip is quivering. "I didn't know what to do, Andy. You've been gone for weeks . . . I can't get you on the phone. . . ."

Her husband takes a deep breath. Mr. Scrap can see his shoulders heave beneath his blue broadcloth.

"Okay. Listen, leave the car here, let's go have a drink. We'll sort it all out."

But Missy shakes her head unconvincingly. She looks away. "I'm not supposed to do that," she says, as though reading lines from a cue card, her eyes fixed on Mr. Scrap, his window still down.

Andy's eyes follow hers. He sees who it is that she is looking at. Mr. Scrap turns his eyes away, busies himself with a file folder on the seat next to him and wills the cars in front of him to start moving again.

Andy points. "Did that guy tell you what to do?" He turns his body toward Mr. Scrap's car. "Did he tell you not to see me? Not to have a drink with your own husband?"

Missy Rolondo looks at him again. "Don't, Andy."

Andy doesn't pay her any attention. He smiles winningly at the cars in front of and behind Mr. Scrap as he strides across the space that separates them. He even holds up a finger, indicating that their business will be finished in just one minute. Then he leans into Mr. Scrap's car, his hands gripping the open window. The two men's faces are nearly touching. Mr. Scrap looks unflinchingly at Andy Rolondo's eyes, hoping this shows he is not intimidated.

More quietly than Mr. Scrap will remember, Andy says, "Are you the prick that is telling my wife to leave me? So that you can charge me five hundred dollars an hour for her to cry on your shoulder?"

Mr. Scrap knows that an answer is not wanted, but he finds himself saying, "Divorce is never the first option, Mr. Rolondo. Perhaps the two of you should see a counselor—"

Andy Rolondo cuts him off. "Watch your fucking back, asshole," he says. His cologne is subtle but distinct.

Mr. Scrap turns his head forward again, staring straight ahead, watching the brake lights of the car in front of him intently. He's never been so close to another man's face.

Andy sniffs the perspiration on Mr. Scrap's hairline. "I could roast you," he says. His breath smells of stale cigarettes.

Mr. Scrap moves his eyes so that he can see the perfectly trimmed hairs along his opponent's temple.

As though he can sense this furtive curiosity, Andy Rolondo

opens his mouth and snaps his jaw closed. His teeth crack together like a firework right next to Mr. Scrap's ear. Then, pulling a lighter from his pants pocket, he ignites it just beside Mr. Scrap's jaw. He holds it there, steady, and fishes out a cigarette, which he lights without moving the flame. Exhaling a deep draw of smoke into Mr. Scrap's face, he says, "You would cook faster than a game hen." Even after he's slowly pulled his head away, his hand remains on the door. He flashes those perfectly polished teeth at the surrounding cars again, then loosens his grip on Mr. Scrap's car and carefully presses the lock with his thumb.

In a rather loud voice he says, casually, "You better lock your doors, mister. Safety first, I always say."

Waving apologetically at the cars around them, he returns to Missy's SUV, where she is covering her own mouth with her hands. Her sobs are too heavy to hold in.

Mr. Scrap tugs at his ear, the heat still traveling under his skin. He loosens his tie and then grips the steering wheel so that his hands will stop shaking. His eyes burn from the cigarette smoke as he follows the line of cars in front of him. With a quick glance in his mirror, Mr. Scrap witnesses Andy Rolondo lean, once again, against Missy's door, before the scene is swallowed by the sudden appearance of daylight.

❖

On this lonely dirt road, there is nothing that dates Oliver's 1972 Ford Ranchero. The long truck bed attached to a two-seat sedan is like a farcical experiment from the welding yard. With no shiny models to compare against its matte paint, no new designs to foil its clumsy car-truck shape, it may as well be straight from the factory—just a silver car driving fast around the curves through a lush, green forest beneath a blue summer sky.

And the driver? He, too, could be circa 1972. Wearing a maroon turtleneck and houndstooth check trousers, his full beard a bit shaggy where it meets his sideburns, he hangs one arm out the window. The stark white bark of aspens glares in the sunlight.

Oliver lets his hand drag on the airstream, imagining a girl named Betsy next to him. He would've met her in 1969 during medical school, when he was thankful for anybody who would allow him to appear on a Saturday evening, drink two beers, perform an abbreviated, exhausted coupling and then sleep through that night and the entire following day and night.

While he slept, Betsy would go on living around him. Even straighten up the room around him. Open the shades, flush the toilet, turn on the stereo. These gestures would filter into his dreams, but she would never wake him or condemn him when he did stumble out of bed, eat a plate of eggs and dress in the green scrubs she'd taken to the Laundromat during his slumber. His gratitude for this acceptance of his god-awful schedule would be seductive to them both. And also deceptive.

Is this right? Oliver goes on imagining he is his father, trying to inhabit the man he was.

Oliver's father would find himself married with two children before he realized he had married somebody about whom he felt only a genuine and deep appreciation. The way he might regard a particularly helpful resident. Or a maid.

Oliver's mom was the one who doted, who treasured their father's very presence in the house, while their father always seemed happy to see her, grateful for her longing, but not nearly as certain of his own emotions.

She could be lovely, from the right angle, when she wore her hair down around her face. Her figure was slender and graceful; her embrace strong and earnest. But on an afternoon like the one Oliver imagines he is driving through, when his parents took a rare outing by themselves, there would be little conversation. His father would surely look at his mother with admiration, her hair tousled by the open windows. He might even reach across and put his hand on hers, holding it gently. Trying to emulate love.

Oliver looks over at the passenger seat. The upholstery came a little torn and he has yet to fix it. His father's Ranchero was sold long ago, so on a fluke Oliver bought this vehicle from a gentleman who'd advertised it in the newspaper. He painted it with silver metallic paint and added the red racing stripe like the one his father often fingered absentmindedly as he drove, one arm hanging out the window.

Oliver doesn't mind that this actual car belonged to a stranger. The vinyl bench seat feels familiar, and the generous cargo space is convenient for hauling boxes of the mementos and photographs, videotapes and music his clients load him down with.

If Betsy *had* been sitting there next to his father, she might have asked him to stop the car so that she could take a snapshot of the view. Right?

Oliver's father would smile at her impulse to capture nature. A photograph of Out West to send to someone else. Such a dubious undertaking. Politely, though, he would agree. He would even agree to pose when she wondered if he wouldn't stand just so, there by the car.

This beautiful magic of recurring summer, which happened twenty-five years ago and still happens now, allows Oliver to step back in time. He's sure his father knew this road and how it looked on a day like this.

This road is a point of entry to a history that might actually have been.

Oliver pulls the Ranchero over to the side of the road, parking it on the dusty shoulder. He has loaded the back with his equipment: tripod, camera, a remote trigger.

In a pouch on the front seat are a few items from the wooden box he keeps in his closet at home, full of things he never knew he might really need. They've been untouched for years, these personal effects sent home from the hospital instead of his father's body. They'd been attached to his body. His bow tie. Wallet. Watch. Tic Tacs. Birkenstock sandals.

All of his father's biology, however—his fluids and hair, his nails—were left at the hospital. Then transferred to the morgue. Then buried in a cemetery not far from this place. All of this was completed by men who wore dark jackets his father would have scoffed at, refusing to wear them even to weddings or dinner parties. These middle-aged men of the mortuary with small black nametags pinned to their lapels didn't smile much, but they tilted their heads to the side as you spoke, like old dogs hearing familiar words. These were the guys who placed his father's body into the casket. Who trimmed his beard and combed his hair. Straightened his glasses and tightened his belt.

As a child, Oliver couldn't understand why, if they would relinquish all of the things in his pockets and from his office, they wouldn't give up the body, too. Let Oliver and Mary cradle it and bury it in their own backyard. With the hamster. And the neighborhood cat their father had buried when it was hit by a car. Instead, his father was suddenly off-limits, a part of the system of death that somebody else presided over.

After their father's death, Mary read to Oliver a passage from an anatomy book that explained hair and nails. They were dead cells, it said. A collection of strong, dead cells. If the beard was already dead, had been dead when his father was alive, why couldn't they keep it? It wasn't newly dead, requiring burial so that it could rot properly.

Even if claiming it had been allowed, Oliver would have left the beard on the body; his father wouldn't have been his father without it. Besides, now Oliver can grow the same beard himself. It's taken only a week or so to turn out a nice full one in preparation for these photographs. The idiosyncratic difference in color between his father's head hair and facial hair has been replicated in Oliver. His head hair is blond, nearly white, and grows close to his scalp, thin and straight. His beard is a deep lumberjack red. This morning Oliver trimmed it with the miniature scissors that once belonged in his father's bathroom drawer.

Despite what his mother thinks, Oliver is not morose. He wears his own houndstooth check trousers, his own slim turtleneck. The seventies are back. He cuts an impressive figure. He could go downtown this evening dressed just this way. Find a girl to take home with him who herself is also dressed in some form of plaid. Play disco music, or soft rock, electric jazz; he has all of the albums.

But not while wearing his father's watch, carrying his father's wallet in his pocket, the license to drive the original Finley Ranchero long expired.

He had called Mary a year or so ago when he saw this identical car listed in the classifieds. "Wasn't it a 1972?" he'd asked her, breathless. "The one that Dad had?"

Mary yawned into the phone. "I'm just back from a forty-eight hour layover in Miami, Oliver. What *are* you talking about?"

"His car truck. Dad's Ranchero."

There was a silence on the line. "Oliver," she finally said, her voice taking on the tone of concern and exasperation that she reserved for these conversations. She worries he is stuck between letting go and moving on; he thinks she is afraid to be still.

"You're doing the voice," he'd said, reminding her of their agreement.

The line was silent.

"Don't you remember?" Oliver began again. "He'd let us ride on the hood . . ."

She sighed, then, and gave in to his nostalgia. "What *was* he thinking?"

"And Dad would drive, probably five miles per hour, but it felt like we were racing." Oliver treasures this memory as it is one of the very few.

"We'd have bugs on our teeth because we couldn't stop smiling."

Mary was smiling now, he could tell. Her top lip curving asymmetrically, the same as his.

"We were laughing. The whole way up the hill, Mare."

"And the engine would get hot on our backs."

"What did we even hold on to?" Oliver asked, already knowing the answer.

"Each other—for dear life," she said.

"It worked."

"Yep," she said, "it did."

"And the sky looked like it was getting farther and farther away. Remember? We'd think we were sinking into middle earth. That's why it was so hot, we thought?"

"*You* thought that, Oliver."

Oliver laughed.

"So, was it a 1972?"

"Yeah, that sounds right."

"There's one in the paper."

The line went quiet again. "Oliver, don't," she sighed. "That's just creepy."

"Why? Why is that creepy, Mary?"

"It's a dumb car, Oliver. And a dumb truck. A dumb car truck. Not to mention gas mileage."

"I don't drive that much."

"How 'bout date? Do you date much, Oliver? Because that car will reduce your pool of possible dates by about ninety-five percent."

"It'll screen out the shallow ones, who care about what kind of car I drive."

"You're calling me shallow?"

"I'll let you ride on the hood."

"Not interested," she said, coldly.

"We loved that car, Mare."

Once more, the line was silent. Oliver knew she was taking a deep breath, trying to summon patience from the chasm between love and disapproval.

"Sure we *did*, Oliver." She meted out the words.

"I'll bring it by. We can sit in the passenger seat, squenched together like we used to."

"I have to sleep now, Oliver."

"Okay. I'll take a picture of the front seat and leave it in your mailbox."

"Perfect," she said and hung up.

Cheerfully, he did photograph the front seat and drive it over to Mary's apartment. Right away. The blinds were closed and he was careful to move the hinges quietly on her mailbox. He hesitated for a moment before dropping it in. It was the first picture he'd taken of anything from the past. He loved the melancholy look of it. The authentic, historical quality of his hurried, crooked framing.

There are no photos of his father. None that Oliver has been able to find. He didn't like them, his mother has explained, exasperated. They reminded him of work, the ugly flash in the windowless morgue.

Oliver has his father's eyeglasses in his shirt pocket. When he puts them on, they still make the ground buckle and swoop beneath him, just like when he was a kid. He cannot wear them to drive. But as he sets up the tripod and attaches his camera to the remote trigger, he props them on his head.

He finds a place just wrong enough: a shady patch dappled by sunlight. His mother has always rushed photographs, doesn't pay attention to details. She would have framed her husband's face in shadow, shot into the light, ended up with a glare hugging the edge of the picture.

As he leans against the hood of the car, his own fingers rubbing the slick stripe of paint, Oliver imagines her standing there in the middle of the road, trying to focus. He pulls his father's glasses down onto his face. Everything goes cloudy. He cannot study the scene anymore.

His father would be doing what? Trying not to blink. Trying to be patient. Remarking to himself how much easier it is to photograph a corpse.

Finally, he would grimace a little—his concession to her request for a smile—and that's when Oliver drops his foot on the remote, opening the shutter from afar.

Then it is over.

Oliver takes off the glasses, placing them back onto his head. He is startled by the precision of the beauty all around him. Everything is so clear, so distinct. Each aspen leaf ends and begins just where it should, quivering its own little dance in the breeze, its individual color and shape just as spectacular as the millions all around it.

He folds up the tripod, detaches the remote, snaps on the lens cap and returns his equipment to the back of the Ranchero. Before getting into the car, he also removes his father's watch and wallet and places them back in the pouch. The absence of these two objects—the bareness of his wrist and the emptiness in his back pocket—leaves Oliver fighting the lonely, eerie feeling that only now, at this moment, has his father been truly taken from him.

With his other hand, he covers the place on his wrist where

the watch was. He smooths the hairs and wipes away the memory of the thick metal band.

❖

There is a strange piece of mail in the box today. A thin blue envelope reminiscent of airmail, with no return address. Betsy Scrap sits down with the letter, placing her reading glasses carefully over her eyes. She has time, these days, to read each and every solicitation for juvenile diabetes, each political accusation, every credit card offer. Her mind wanders best when she's perusing a form letter. The full page of italicized print is like a panacea, and she often finds that when her mind wanders, two or three hours can pass without any effort at all. A vast empty stretch of a day is transformed into something else entirely. She'll realize she's skipped lunch and has only a couple of hours left to grocery shop and prepare dinner before Mr. Scrap will be home.

Often, she wonders about Mary, her eldest, flying somewhere over Singapore or Frankfurt or Stockholm. As a gesture to their filial relationship, Mary dutifully provides her mother with her flight schedule each month. She e-mails the itinerary to Mr. Scrap's office—Betsy having no use for computers, and Mary having no use for extemporaneous visits, though her apartment is not more than five miles away.

Such a brainy, curious, precocious girl Mary had been. Her father adored her nature. It intimidated Betsy. The books the four-year-old brought to her from the shelves in the public library, curled up to listen to in the warm afternoon sun, were not tales of Peter Rabbit or Mother Goose, but volumes about astronomy and revolution. What did Betsy know of galaxies and supernovas, espionage and the British monarchy? These subjects, which Betsy didn't think could be appreciated by a child so young, were keeping her daughter awake at night.

Mary had shown no interest in cooking or knitting, sewing or interiors—pursuits Betsy deemed necessary for the kind of happiness she'd found. Happiness could not come, she had reasoned, from a love affair with history or space. Betsy's own exquisite happiness had been with Mary's father. Which, she'd reasoned, was possible because of her ability to make him a home. To help him pursue his happiness. She'd lived through Women's Lib and even burned her own bra one night in college when she'd been drunk at the Spring Fling, but she couldn't see how such unreasonable expectations could lead to any lasting pleasure.

Some time after Paul died, during Mary's adolescence, Betsy realized that her insatiable daughter had become satiated. She no longer carried books to the pool or spoke with a British accent. Much like Betsy, she stared quietly out the car windows as they drove, never asking about the destination, its relevance or distance.

Betsy had been relieved, mostly. For both of them.

Heavens. What she didn't know then. What she couldn't know about life and its surprises. Now Mary is a flight attendant, intent on remaining single, intent on living most of her life thirty-seven thousand feet above the ground, and Betsy is as bored with cooking and sewing as any person could ever hope to be. How she wished she could train her mind to focus on a book, to read some history, to memorize the names of Jupiter's moons. So that at least, while she stirred together a roux for the hundred thousandth time of her life, she might say to herself the beautiful Greek names of another planet's lunar bodies.

Betsy looks at the letter spread out in front of her on the table. It is handwritten in a boxy, unconventional print.

August 10

Dear Stranger,

This is not a letter of acquaintance. I am writing because I do not know you and I would like us to go on being strangers to one another. What, though, really separates us? Distance? Knowledge? Desire? This may seem a rhetorical question, but it is one that haunts me. Certainly if we could follow history and genealogy and biology back to the beginning, we would all be related. From one fateful coupling of the very first romance. Maybe on a plateau or a tundra or in a green river valley. Can you imagine? You and me, 46-millionth cousins. Would we still be strangers if our shared lineage was proven, published in one scientific journal or another, recorded on an ancient piece of brittle papyrus excavated from a cave in Peru?

Or would we send each other Christmas cards and birth announcements, besieging the postal service with our infinite connections?

I have a couple of cousins I don't really talk to. They are my father's sister's kids and they live in Reno and like to build stock cars and dress like TV wrestlers. The tight red shirts that hug their bellies proclaim them "Captain Pain" or "Master of the Mat." They could not be more strange to me than you, certainly. Though, as I said, I don't know you at all. Perhaps you also favor this style of dress, which would be fine for our purposes. If I didn't know my cousins, they would be much more interesting, for they would be cultural icons or anthropological case studies. Instead, I've ridden with them in a Toyota Celica across the Las Vegas desert in order to visit our grandmother—the woman who raised their mother and my father in the same house, sharing a single bathroom and meals every day for fifteen years, even though, from what I can tell, they seem to share nothing anymore— and sat next to them as they gleefully threw a box of Cheez-Its out the window, onto the highway where it cartwheeled from corner to corner until another car flattened it. There it lay on the asphalt, red and orange, like roadkill. At that proximity, my cousins were no longer interesting in their otherness.

I have your street address because I picked it out of the phone book the same way that as a child I would spin the globe, eyes shut, and place a finger on the place where I'd be sure to meet my husband. Mozambique or Brazil or Syria. I still haven't found him and the realities of language, religion, culture and money have long since rendered these ideas fantasy. I've only crossed the Atlantic once, for a short stay in London, where the fog was so thick I could not have seen my future husband if he'd taken my hand. So, it is still possible that the man I'm meant to marry is waiting for me, toiling in a café in São Paolo or cultivating olive trees in the hills outside Damascus. Do you think that's naïve? Probably. But I'd rather be naïve and full of hope than sophisticated and full of despair.

This is a hopeful project. Its goal is for me to truly see you. The film in my camera will record you as you are, without pose or pretension.

Art, too often, is full of trickery and effect. Forget about art! Even life itself is full of trickery and effect. For one brief stretch of time, you can be honest and I'll catch you being honest. Which means, if you'd like to participate in this artistic endeavor, sometime between 9:30 and 10:00 on August 18th, leave the light on in a room that faces the street. Just flick on a light and go about your life, whatever it is that is your life that evening. I will send you a proof of my photograph before I include it in any public showing. However, if you are not interested in being seen but prefer to keep the dark corners of your life dark, please turn off the room light or close the curtains. I will abide by and accept your desire obediently.

But please do not come bounding out of your house and think that we can become acquainted first and then you can run in and pose for me in the light. I do not work that way. I cannot truly look at you if I know you even just a bit. A mere handshake changes the lens through which I see. It distorts my vision, subjectifies it and pollutes it. I am not interested in a pose. I've answered my own question—my own rhetorical question: what separates us, what keeps us apart, is our own dishonesty, our own desire to hide and obscure the truth of life.

Sincerely,
M. K.

Betsy holds the letter in her hand, reading it once, then folding it back up, forcing herself to laugh out loud, good-naturedly, looking around to see if Oliver is videotaping her reaction. At first she thinks it must be a prank, a way for him to goad her. She is accustomed to his peculiarity and has come to expect that he will always be trying to unearth her. He conceives of her as a solid stone that will never turn over—whose underside is coated with slow-moving secrets and hidden terrain full of answers about why life wronged him and took his father prematurely. If she could answer this, if she were privy to that kind of secret, certainly she would share it with her baby boy. Her only son who still retains some tenderness of childhood, some softness in his brow and in his hands that is juvenile. Here in her solitude, with an artificial smile still bending her lips, she can admit that his fragility sometimes evokes her pity and sometimes her disgust. She is perplexed at his inability to move on, grow up, get tough. Certainly, she's had to.

Of course, she's the mother, she reminds herself. She's the one who willfully brought Oliver into this world, knowing its dangers and sadnesses. Still, it isn't fair that she has had to acclimate and he has not. She has had to model for both her children how to love another, make a home with him, live in another house, let go of the past and find a new present that was not planned or desired, but is simply the result of plans and desires that were long ago extinguished. Oliver watched and studied her and her example and, ultimately, rejected both. In fact, the youthful passion that Betsy disapproves of in Oliver is exactly what drives his disdain for her pragmatism.

Well, why would he write this letter, this concoction? What is this talk about a husband? Does he want her to think he's gay now? Why? But, then, why, too, would he buy the same kind of car his father used to drive and grow a beard so that he looked like a dead man walking?

Simply to upset her, she supposes. She vaguely remembers that during her first semester of college, she chose to bleach her hair blond and start smoking French cigarettes so that on Christmas Eve, standing by the luggage carousel, waiting, she would see her mother's eyes pass right over her, then slowly darken and close with disgust as she realized that she'd sized the girl up as a floozy before recognizing her as her own daughter. They'd driven home in utter silence but for the carols playing on the radio.

Heavens. But Betsy had been eighteen. And her self-righteous satisfaction of that moment, along with its devastation, came from proving just how conditional her mother's love was. Why she counted this as a victory is still a mystery.

Oliver is nearly the age Betsy was when she had to sit at the pink Formica table in the overly cooled office of the fat funeral director. The man's brow was splotchy and damp and his tie hung morosely short, just skimming the table as he helped her choose a coffin for her husband's body. And a headstone to mark the place where the coffin would be buried, in the old cemetery she had never before visited. Words on a headstone—their size, their shape, their meaning—made her nauseous. More than the ringing of the telephone or the stacks of casseroles in the refrigerator or the bright summer sun, shining, still hot, still cheerful, unyielding to death.

Her own mother had come. Suddenly capable and unconditional. She'd stayed in the hotel downtown and arrived each morning to scramble eggs for the children, fold laundry, answer the phone, warm up the casseroles, select the hymns and the flowers and, finally, choose the words on the headstone. When she saw them, Betsy recognized the Latin phrase from her grandparents' headstones: *ad astra*.

Betsy looks once again at the letter in her hand. Did she take care of her son? Did she ever do those things for Oliver that her mother had done for her? Clearly, she'd been unable to care for herself after Paul died. She'd stayed in bed as much as she could, his shoes beside her on the floor, his clothes, still smelling of him, in the hamper, his razor still on the sink. Her mother fixed sandwiches and arranged play dates. Combed Mary's hair—life's retribution had subdued the girl's aversion to the comb—and clipped Oliver's fingernails. Readied them to bury their father. Something Betsy could not do.

Taking the letter to her rolltop desk, Betsy reads it again. Her suspicion that this is one of Oliver's endeavors wanes and she begins to think it may be sincere. An honest request from some "artist" who has nothing better to do than photograph strangers.

Well, all right, then. Maybe her own image will hang on a big white wall in some museum or gallery and mean something to someone. Someone will see her face and know her soul in the way she'd always imagined somebody might. The viewer could find, as if studying an atlas, the sea of unhappiness around the corners of her mouth that fall into a frown whenever she's relaxed; the plateau of hope that stretches across her forehead, even now, with its deep lines of possibility; the reservoir of disgust that is the loose skin around her jaw and neck, which she battles every evening with expensive salves. She could be important in an art photograph. Suspended in life, vibrant and permanent, not fading out the way she feels she is now.

Of course, Martin would find it comical to stand in his navy blue suit amidst the artist types all dressed in black, holding his wine glass tightly and observing her photograph with irony. Not that he doesn't adore her; he quite clearly does. But he is not comfortable with spectacle. He would find her glossy portrait an affront to the quiet life he's cultivated. He would not know how to react other than to chuckle and call her his little masterpiece.

He might even buy it, if it were for sale, simply to get it out of the public space. He'd lay it flat, face-down, in the trunk of his car and then drive home in silence, his hand on hers.

Her mind drifts back to Oliver once more and she wonders if he will make her a video, some maudlin remembrance, when she's gone. Will he think he knows her simply because there are photographs and video? Using his footage of her life—the swing dancing he documented without any knowledge of the experience—can he concoct the moments that are never seen, and certainly never photographed? The long stretches of days when she does absolutely nothing but worry about her children and how she's equipped them for life? She glances at the letter again. *What separates us is our own dishonesty.*

Betsy picks up her pencil and writes in her date book: *August 18, 9:30 pm, Lights on.*

4

Oliver sits outside of Alfalfa's in the Ranchero, looking at the photo of himself as his father. He is as convincing as his photography is accomplished. So accomplished that anyone might believe that it's a real artifact of his father's existence, created twenty-five years ago, not yesterday. It has an aura of expectation—the golden tides of aspen leaves and his father's hesitant grin. Oliver wants more, at least a handful more, so that when he introduces himself to Jared, he can also introduce Jared to his father.

Oliver looks up from the photograph and sees a girl standing in front of his car. She is blocking his view of the store. In fact, now that he's looking at her, he realizes that she is leaning on his car, one dirty sneaker propped up on his fender.

He rolls down the window, sticks his head out. She doesn't budge. "Hello?" he says, finally, unnerved by her indifference.

She turns around, revealing a small digital camera with a big lens cradled in her hands.

"Yeah?" she says, looking at him without any congeniality.

"Um, you're leaning on my car. It's just, I kinda . . ." He finds that he can't articulate his complaint.

"And, *um*, you're on my beat. So, one dirty trick deserves another."

"Huh?"

She doesn't respond. She has turned away, busy with the camera.

Reluctantly, Oliver puts on his dark glasses, opens his door and steps out. "Excuse me," he says, thinking now that she's probably crazy. "Would you mind just not leaning on my car. Okay? That's what I was trying to say. I just, could you please move?"

The girl is probably twenty-five. A wrap skirt stretches around her wide hips, a T-shirt with a smiling ketchup bottle on it is fitted across her slender torso, and she wears skating sneakers on her feet. Her face does not appear crazy. Her hair, maybe, twisted into two short, stubby pigtails streaked with colors of blond, red, and brown. But her eyes are clear and thoughtful. She has skin that looks gossamer thin, as though it might tear for its delicacy.

"Sure," she says, glancing briefly at him. She's shuffling through images on her digital camera. With her foot that's on his bumper, she pushes herself off of his car, holding her leg up behind her for a moment, like it's part of a dance. Then, just as gracefully, she places it on the ground. But she doesn't move away.

Her figure is lovely in its fullness, Oliver thinks. All of her in proportion—sturdy, unflappable.

But he remains aggrieved and perplexed by her position in front of his car. Looking over her shoulder, Oliver can see the images on her camera. They are all candid shots of people coming out of Alfalfa's. She moves through them fast. Once, then again, and then a third time, Oliver sees Jared in her photographs.

"Hey, what's he doing? Why are you taking his picture?" Oliver asks.

"Whose?" She shuffles to another one of Jared.

"There," Oliver says, putting his finger on the viewer.

The girl pulls her camera away. "Whoa," she says, "don't touch my equipment. This is my livelihood." Her voice is forceful, serious, but then she turns her head and looks at Oliver, winking suggestively.

"Sorry," Oliver says, putting his hand by his side. "I totally understand about equipment. I have my own. I'm picky about it, too. A girl's livelihood is definitely not something I want to touch without invitation."

"Okay, that's weird. Loquacious flirting. Whatever. You sort of have that nerd thing going for you."

Oliver feels misunderstood. Was he flirting? Is he a nerd? He can be relaxed, succinct. But not now. Not when she has pictures of his almost brother on her camera. "But, *who* is he?"

"Don't you know? Isn't it obvious? True, you look as though perhaps you live in retroland, entertainment-wise, but this is a photograph of the very current, very hip Stub Coops, the Anglo hip-hop artist whose first single went platinum and who has been dating Tom Cruise's ex."

Oliver closes his eyes. A smile creeps up from his nervous stomach. He beams at her. "Are you for real?"

"Wanna touch me?" she says, holding her arm out for inspection.

Oliver places his index finger on her forearm. "That is not Stub whoever. That guy is so not even a celebrity . . ."

The girl pulls her arm up and away from him. Intently, she is readying her camera.

Oliver looks to the store, having forgotten, for a brief moment, while his finger was on her skin, that she was blocking his view. *His* view, *his* subject, *his* future.

All of a sudden, there he is. Jared walks out, his limbs lanky.

"Stub! Over here. Hi, Stub. How's Penelope?" She shouts these entreaties as though she and Oliver were standing among a crowd of thirty other people, all hollering for his attention. Really, there are only two other people in the parking lot: a mother loading her toddler into their minivan. The mother turns to look, does a double take when she sees Jared, and then goes back to buckling the child.

Jared, in turn, casually bids his paparazza hello with his fingers in the peace sign. A rock star gesture or a signal that there is nothing at all strange about this turn of events?

He must see Oliver standing next to her in his dark oversized glasses, but his face is placid, unfazed. He doesn't answer her questions about Penelope or their new Pomeranian and soon looks away from her altogether, toward the perimeter of the parking lot.

Oliver begins to wonder. Could he really be a celebrity? Some white rapper with a bagging job at Alfalfa's? What does that mean about his relation to Oliver? Is he actually just another stranger?

The fear and disappointment that he's gotten everything wrong paralyze him.

The girl's camera becomes quiet as soon as Jared places his hands on the first stray cart.

She looks at Oliver. "Good get, eh?" she says, quickly shuffling through the batch. She leans toward Oliver to show him one she especially likes.

In it, Jared is acknowledging the camera only begrudgingly. His baggy clothes, sloppy hair and tattooed arms really do make him look famous. There is something about the quality of her framing, her angle, that turns the candid photograph into a tabloid shot.

"You're not really paparazzi, are you? And he's not really named Stub, right?" Oliver's disbelief is fueled by hope.

"Could you please respond to the photo?" she demands, ignoring his question.

Oliver shrugs, unable to do anything but follow her instruction. "It's nice. He looks like . . . he looks like he could be famous."

She beams at him. Her two front teeth have a slight overlap. "Exactly. He could be. Anybody could be. So, if he looks it, who's to say he's not it? Isn't perception reality? I mean, who says he might not be the next boy toy?"

Oliver hears the sound of carts being pushed across the asphalt. At the helm, Jared slouches over his load, pushing mightily.

"Boy toy?" Oliver says over the din of dozens of wheels.

She also has to raise her voice to be heard. "Okay, so not here, he doesn't seem to be. But imagine you are at the newsstand. You see the photo in a glossy and, boom, it's real for you."

"So, he's not some superstar?" Oliver feels a grin spreading across his face.

"No more than you are," she says, raising the camera again, this time focusing it on Oliver.

Indulging his vanity, he places his glasses up onto his head to tame his hair. He has so recently photographed himself that he thinks he knows precisely what she sees through her lens: the red beard; his eyes close together and a golden shade of green; his hair, which his sister has told him is his best feature, falling onto his temples in jagged points.

If he doesn't try, he looks overly sincere and eager. When he arranges his forehead in a furrow and purses his lips, he looks like a self-centered philosopher. When he smiles, he looks like an adolescent.

He goes through these faces, enjoying her attention.

"Okay, you need some coaching," she says, holding the camera at her side. "But—" she looks at the viewer again—"I think if you lose the facial hair, you could pass for a Chris Martin. Or a Paul Bettany. See, look." She beckons him to come near her.

He studies the picture of himself on her camera. His brow is furrowed, his mouth pursed. In the picture, it looks as though he's reprimanding her: shameless photographer invading his privacy. But he also looks more certain than he's ever felt. It's as though she's put a filter on the camera that casts a veil of assurance over all of his features.

"Paul Bettany was in *Master and Commander*, right?" he says, impressed with his look-alike.

She shrugs. "Dunno. But he's married to Jennifer Connelly and *she's* A-list."

"So if we found a girl around here who could pass for Jennifer Connelly, we'd be in big business? I don't usually have the beard. It's temporary. For a project I'm working on."

"I love projects. Can I see?" she glances toward his open car door. "There's an Alfalfa's in Santa Monica that looks remarkably like this one. I keep sending the photos to groups in L.A. Agencies. Gossip rags. Nobody's bought one yet."

"Why not just move to L.A.? Where there are *actual* celebrities?"

"Oh, I'm not going to be part of that racket. Those are real people's lives they're interfering with. Publishing photos of their kids, their houses, their grocery carts. Ugh. Jared doesn't mind that I take his photo. He's on board. I would never really ambush somebody coming out of a grocery store. Do I look like that kind of a person?" Her voice rises with this question.

Oliver shakes his head emphatically. "Absolutely not."

"I want to undermine the system. Show it for what it is. The augmentation of simple humans into godlike status. A circus of absurdity based on the commercialization of people. The hierarchy of certain beach-house living, stiletto-wearing, yoga-practicing cells. It's smoke and mirrors. Pixels. And if I could *show* that. Really illustrate it by getting a fake into the glossies—*that* would be killer. Couldn't you just see all the *Teen People* teeny-boppers clipping the candid shot of Stub Coops for their wall, when really they're hanging up—worshipping, no less—a picture of Jared? Our local grocery bagger?"

"Jared," Oliver says under his breath, having momentarily forgotten everything about his own life. He puts his shades back on, reminding himself of his purpose. "And what about the birthmark?"

"Incognito for a reason?" she asks him, ignoring Oliver's mention of the red stain on the left side of Jared's face.

Oliver shrugs. "Um, yeah. It's sort of complicated."

"You really *are* Paul Bettany?"

"Could be. Just slightly rearranged, right?"

"I'm Miranda Knack," she says, holding her hand out to him. "A.k.a. anybody else in the world, totally rearranged."

Oliver shakes her hand. "Oliver Finley," he says. "You definitely seem like one of a kind to me."

She stares at him, seeming not to have registered the compliment. "Okay. And about that." She gestures at the side of her own face. "Everybody has a good side. Everybody turns to show the good side when they see a camera coming at them."

She looks at Oliver's face, studying again. "I'd say that's your better one," she says, pointing to and nearly touching his right cheek. "So, hello to your better side. This one is mine," she turns to show him her profile. "Now that our better sides have met, we can say good-bye. We are saying good-bye, aren't we?"

Confused, Oliver shrugs. Nobody has made him feel less articulate since his sixth-grade English teacher. "Dunno . . ."

"'Cause they kind of stress me out. Good-byes, I mean. I say good-bye to people and then I imagine their car crashed into a telephone pole or a knife squeezed into their back while they're at the ATM. And worry that I'll catch a glimpse of the news and realize I didn't even say good-bye and maybe the five-second differential our good-bye would have created could have saved their life. And then I'll feel unable to live my own life because I failed to save theirs. It's a really bad habit. I try to train my mind against it. But I also want to say a proper good-bye, which requires being aware of what is always possible on the other side of the good-bye. You know?"

"Too well. I know too well what is possible on the other side of good-bye." Oliver shakes his head. "But, I'm a stranger. You're not in charge of chaperoning me or saving my life."

"But maybe I am. None of us know our true purpose, right? What it is that makes us useful or unique in this complex system of organisms."

Oliver shakes his head again. "You honestly think that your role could be to protect me? After confessing that you'll be thinking of my body splayed out in a pool of blood the minute I drive out of here?"

Miranda blushes, the pinkness of her cheeks making her eyes look even more brilliantly blue. "It won't be a happy thought. That's exactly why I hate good-byes."

"You should have had my childhood. You'd be accustomed to them."

"Mmm. One of those?" she says, furrowing her brow, looking more closely at his face.

"Yep. Loss and abandonment issues. Full disclosure."

"Doesn't scare me," she says, putting her camera into a canvas bag.

"Really? It does me," Oliver says, thinking of the photo on his dashboard. "I'm a total basket case."

"As we all should be, eh? Look at the risks we take. Reckless drivers, gun crime, secondhand smoke. It's a fucking miracle that anybody survives."

"True." Oliver chuckles. "Like the gambling man that I am, I'm going to get in my car and go to work now. So, this is the proper good-bye, here." He stretches out his hand again. "Very nice to have met you, Miranda."

She takes his hand in hers, nodding. "Yes, Oliver. It was lovely to make your acquaintance."

"Okay, so now you don't have to worry, right? 'Cause the thought of you thinking of me lying in a pool of blood is starting to freak me out."

"Right. Sure. It's all taken care of now." She points at her temple and makes a clicking noise, turning off a switch.

Oliver slides into his Ranchero and starts the engine.

"Unless, of course, I've just created a five-second differential on the other side of fate and placed you right in the path of some oncoming semi." Her voice follows him through the parking lot, then fades.

5

Please ensure that your seat belt is fastened, your seat back is upright and your tray table is stowed in its upright and locked position.

Mary doesn't even know what the words mean anymore. They're just a series of comforting sounds, like the benediction that a priest gives to his congregation day in and day out. She knows this song; these are her people.

If she's at home, however, and unable to sleep, jet-lagged despite her best efforts and still smelling of cabin pressure, the words are not comforting at all. Instead, they taunt her, cycling through her head.

Seat belt. Seat back. Tray table. Up. Right. Locked.

Sometimes she has to sit up and turn on a light, look around her small bedroom for a piece of life with no connection to air travel, some object upon which she can focus.

Tonight she sits atop her exercise ball, gently bouncing, staring at the picture Oliver gave her just before her surgery last year. He'd wanted to walk, once more, down memory lane, to a destination that Mary had long ago abandoned.

Such relics of her brother's memory are not the distraction she needs. To avoid the photograph of his new Ranchero's bench seat, she turns out the light and gets back in bed.

There are six exits. Two in the forward cabin, two over the wings and two in the rear cabin. Keep in mind, the closest exit may be behind you.

Her fingers rise above the bedsheets, pointing automatically: forward, middle, rear, forward, middle, rear. Bedpost, closet doors, fish tank. The refrain runs faster in her mind, trying to wear her out, trying to find its own exit. Her hands flail through the air, striving to keep up. The bed begins to spin, like horizontal turbulence.

It'll never end, she thinks. Always half-packed. Always between trips. Always in midair.

But the alternative—the semblance of a life you believe to be grounded, stable, continuous—is actually also just moments away from disaster. Death, disease, disillusionment abound and there are no emergency plans, no flotation devices or security measures.

Remain calm. The captain has turned on the Fasten Seat Belt sign. Forward, middle, rear.

Often, if Mary can stop her hands from moving, then the words will stop, too. She places her hands on top of her breasts, a reprimand and a change of subject. Look, girls, she says to herself, look how lovely you are. She does love them, firm and substantial beneath her own palms. Well worth the chunk of money it took months to save. Well worth the pain of recovery and the loss of sensation around the nipple.

*In the seat pocket in front of you you'll find more safety informa-
tion for this aircraft.*

If her father were alive, he surely would not approve. This is
what Oliver intimated when he drove her to the hospital before
dawn on the day of the surgery.

"It's *elective* surgery, Mare. You're *asking* someone to cut into
your body. And not in a life-saving capacity. Dad always said that
the hospital is not the place to get well."

"That's your assessment." Her eyes were closed, her hands folded
in her lap. She didn't expect that he would still be trying to talk her
out of this on the way to the hospital. Why had she asked him to
drive? The city bus would have been more relaxing than this.

"Don't they make lingerie that could do what you want? I
mean, they're going to saw into your flesh, through muscle, through
nerves." With his free hand, he made jabbing motions in the space
between them.

"That's enough, Oliver." Mary opened her eyes and looked at
his hand. "I'm the one who went to med school. And you're right;
they are going to do all of that. If I die there on the table, getting
my breasts enhanced, you will hate yourself for talking to me this
way. So shut up. Now." She put her head back against the seat
and closed her eyes again. There was no point trying to convey to
Oliver her desire for buoyancy.

Oliver placed both hands on the wheel and drove quietly into
the parking garage. He carried her bag for her as she went through
the myriad locations and paperwork of admission. He sat silently
next to her as the nurse finally inserted the IV and he kissed her
dryly on the cheek when he was told to leave. Already a little groggy,

Mary looked at his face as he stood over her, lingering. It seemed to take great effort, but he said, "You'll be just fine, Mare. Nothing to worry about. Jolly good, then."

She's seen less of Oliver ever since. Partly because she's upped her transatlantic flights. But partly, too, because she's lost her patience with him and he's never forgiven her for growing up, for propelling herself beyond that night in the old kitchen, when they both stood over their father with wide eyes and sunken hearts.

That, and the subsequent weeks in which a baby came into the house, held onto each of their fingers, then left. This, too, has receded from her. She's relinquished it to the past.

She gave up detective work long ago, along with becoming British, climbing trees, and wishful thinking. These preoccupations could have doomed her to chasing the same phantoms Oliver is after. Instead, she learned to practice detachment as a way to exist while floating above the pain of life. She paid even more attention to facts. School work became her favorite companion.

With so much information, she hoped not to be surprised by life again. Not knowing what else to do, she went to medical school, pushing herself through one excruciating year during which she disappeared into the intricacies of anatomy and its diseases. But when the day came to begin the second year, she got on a plane and never wanted to get off, seduced as she was by the limited space with its forward-facing seats and clear, simple rules illuminated overhead. Its speed—with which it could create instantaneous distance from its point of departure, turning the small picture into the big picture in a matter of seconds—launched her into duty.

Her own disappointment with who she'd turned out to be

vanished whenever she was en route. The day was split into finite chunks of time between departure and arrival, during which she could be part of a team with a clear and common goal. Mary enjoyed the good-natured banter with passengers, the ability to take care of immediate needs like thirst, anxiety, cold and hunger. Slowly she let go of that year's worth of medical facts, leaving them behind in cities all over the world.

Her old personality gradually returned at thirty-six thousand feet, far removed from the sorrow that her brother had dug his heels into.

When Mary told Oliver she was planning an augmentation, he insisted that their father wouldn't have approved. But what Oliver doesn't know, what he can't bring himself to imagine, is that a lot of the well-meaning, Birkenstock-wearing guys from the seventies—men just like Oliver and Mary's father—are flying first class now, wearing Rolexes and sipping Merlot.

If we can do anything to make your flight more enjoyable, please let us know.

Sometimes they'll buy her a drink or dinner in their layover city. Maybe they're wondering about more. Maybe they think it's all sewn up. But Mary disdains stereotypes; she did not have a breast enhancement for the attention or affection of men. She is not interested in spending evenings wrapped in a scratchy complimentary robe, standing in the window of a glass high-rise Hilton in Miami or San Francisco, listening to the other end of a phone call home. A man stretched out in his briefs on the bed, sipping on wine and nibbling shrimp from room service while complaining to his wife that there was nothing on the plane to eat but peanuts.

Saying that air travel is becoming a glorified bus system. Saying all of that even while the extra robe is being used by a flight attendant with a boob job.

Instead, Mary wanders the halls of the hotels, trying to stay on her time zone. Often, she thinks of the videos that Oliver has shown her—the ones he makes for himself. They sit together on the couch in his office and Mary dutifully watches the disjointed soliloquies that open up like small windows into his own existential angst. She is his undecided voter, he is the candidate's best huckster, and his is the exact angst that she has been determined not to elect.

When Oliver first told her he was making a video, Mary was thrilled. She'd thought he meant that he was using his skills to tell a story, something entertaining and witty. She'd even appeared on his doorstep with popcorn and root beer.

"Movie night," she'd said when he opened the door.

"Right on," he'd said, munching the popcorn and sipping soda while Mary watched the screen buzz and moan and whistle.

There were children doing cartwheels, old men playing piano, and ants swarming a fallen bird. It was not entertaining. There were no stunts, no jokes. She sat on her hands, eyes wide, heart pounding. As the monitor went black, Oliver turned to her with his eager face.

"So?" He licked the salt off his fingers.

"Oliver," she said, trying to rally some disdain. "That's not a film. What is that?"

He shrugged. "Dunno. But, please, contain your enthusiasm."

"No, I mean. Obviously, it's accomplished. Technically. I just don't know what it is. What I'm supposed to think." Mary never wanted to encourage Oliver to live inside his head more than he already did.

"You're *supposed* to think whatever it *is* that you think. This is not a test. Tell me what you think." His face was open and pleading.

Mary turned toward him and sighed.

"Yeah, okay. I got it." He stood up and turned off the monitor.

"Oliver." She wished she knew how to respond. The truth is that she felt the end of her nose and her lips were buzzing, as though she'd been shaken. But she didn't want him to know this.

Nearly everything Oliver did drew on some thread from that summer. Though she could not see it there in Oliver's darkened office, the thread unmistakably pulled her back to the moment in which she'd stood in the kitchen, holding Oliver's hand as they watched Mr. Nice Guy bend over their father, her own heart beating impatiently with the curious combination of dread and hope. So her response was to sit on the couch, trying to untie the video and detect its purpose. But all she understood was the overwhelming urge to see it again.

"I don't know what it is either," Oliver said before she could revise her opinion. "It's just me goofing around." He smiled and took another swig of root beer.

She glanced at her hands. "What are you going to do with it?"

Oliver looked at her cross-eyed. "Put it in the drawer. Any ideas?"

"No," she said, quickly, relieved that there was no ulterior plan. When he was fourteen he placed an ad for their would-be brother in the Lost and Found section of the local newspaper. She did not care for his eccentricities to be made public. "I did like watching it, Oliver."

So he continues to show his films to her, whenever he finishes another. She sits on his couch, holding a pillow, mesmerized again and again by what she sees. But she never reveals to him her complete admiration. She never tells him that remembering these images sometimes makes her want to throw herself out of the aircraft at thirty-three thousand feet just to be able to feel something. His videos, if she let them, could make her a believer again in the gorgeous possibilities of life. It seems to her that he is bottling up the contents of his heart and mind, shaking them all around and decanting them into a slender, graceful cup.

When she's on the road, unable to sleep, she thinks about these videos. She admires them again in her mind. And her own mind wanders to the infant boy that they gave away.

Lying in bed now, as wide awake as ever, Mary breathes deeply. She thinks of her favorite window at the airport hotel, how outside the sun glints off the puddles after a rainstorm. As planes take off and land, moving people to and from their lives, she always reminds herself to be only in each day. She is bolstered by the swell of her breasts. The small pouches of silicone planted inside are proof that biology is not destiny.

Your seat cushion may be used as a flotation device.

❖

There are footsteps somewhere in Mr. Scrap's sleep. They echo, the hollow din becoming louder as they get closer. Where is he? In bed? Or has he fallen asleep in his car? Yes, it must be the parking garage. Somewhere above him is the whine of tires turning on the slick concrete. If he could just wake up, he could drive away from the danger. This dream is trying to rouse him, protect him.

But he cannot force his eyes open.

Now there is silence. But his dream is not over. Of that he is sure.

He waits for the next move. Before he recognizes the sound, he hears it. A scraping of flint. The ignition of a flame, its hissing close by. Then the smell of fuel. A delicate and terrifying trickle. The first piece of fire licks his sideburns like a hot breeze. His arm jerks, pushing it away, and this movement wakes him when nothing else would. He only had to raise his arm.

How many other mistakes has he made?

In a cold sweat, he fingers his ear, touching the bristle of his sideburn.

Mr. Scrap sits up and rubs his eyes, wipes the sweat from his brow and neck. His wife sleeps soundly next to him. Her face has not changed much in twenty years. Though her hair is different, short now instead of the long, sloping curls that her first husband preferred, her skin is still tender, unlined, placid. There are small galaxies of freckles at the tips of her cheekbones.

Where was he when those freckles were born under the deep summer sun? Probably reading joke books, unaware that there would ever be a girl, the sight of whom could both comfort and pain him. A girl who would grow up and love another man, marry him even though she knew he didn't love her the same way, have his children and then bury him, holding her grief close to her like a valuable package. And when he could stand it no longer, Mr. Scrap would offer her refuge, allow her to hold onto her sorrow, even as she became his wife.

She loved him a little bit less than he loved her, but it didn't matter. Mr. Scrap knew that they had this in common: asymmetrical love.

Perfectly reciprocated love was not necessary at all. She let him love her the way her first husband had allowed her to love him. Like an adored kitten in the hands of an overzealous child, she let him throw her over his shoulder and whisper in her ear, even though.

Whenever he awakens like this, he can reach over, stroke the curve of her forehead, the slope of her nose, cheekbones and chin, run his finger down her throat, between her breasts, across her stomach and the thinning fuzz between her legs. She will not even flinch. Not even open her eyes to check. She is accustomed to his habits, his nocturnal desires.

He lets his hand rest on the inside of her thigh, its warmth reassuring. Closing his eyes, Mr. Scrap thinks he will sleep again. But as soon as he's alone in the darkness of his head, he again hears the slush of gasoline. He opens his eyes and listens closely.

Perhaps there's a faucet running somewhere in the house. Or the dishwasher has gone kaput again. But now that his eyes are open, he cannot hear anything.

Frustrated, Mr. Scrap gets out of bed and walks across the cool wooden planks to the French doors. He checks the handle to make sure it is locked. But the handle turns easily in his hand and he opens the door. He looks back at the bed, his wife sleeping soundly next to this unlocked door.

Did he forget to check it before bed? Did she unlock it sometime during the night? Has someone else been in the house?

Out on the deck, the only sounds are the swarms of summer crickets singing in unison. The elevated deck stretches around two sides of the house, providing a view right into the treetops of the smaller fruit trees in the backyard. An apricot, apple, pear and fig tree all face him, their fruit sweet with the aroma of ripening. On the apple and pear trees there are still a few wilted blossoms. Somewhere in their anatomy, new fruit is beginning.

Mr. Scrap follows the perimeter of the deck, his hands clasped behind his back. When he has turned the corner, he can see the road in front of his yard. A streetlight down the hill casts a small yellow circle on the asphalt, the only bright spot of the entire block.

There is a wide, bushy hedge of untrimmed boxwoods across the front lawn whose leaves shine even in the predawn haze. When Mr. Scrap planted those scrawny little perennials, the doctor next door had chided him.

"I like a man who's not afraid to make a statement with his horticulture," he'd said, playfully.

The little green shoots had looked absurd dotting the front of Mr. Scrap's enormous lot. But he just chuckled good-naturedly, not wanting the doctor to know how much he resented him and the ease of his life. A man like the doctor didn't plan. His life just happened. He had married a kind, pretty, tender woman without really trying. And she clearly adored him. It's what first made

Mr. Scrap notice Betsy. The way she loved her husband. The way she placed her hand on him when she addressed him, looked deep into his eyes.

Bushes and shrubs and perennials and weeds were concerns the doctor didn't bother himself with. She did. The doctor's life went on wonderfully.

Until it didn't.

And when it ended, not only was there no life insurance or sufficient savings for these circumstances—there were no photographs or any other tokens for his beautiful, devoted wife.

Now the shrubs that line the edge of Mr. Scrap's property are majestic and robust. He stands on the deck looking out on them, conjuring the memory of the doctor's tall stature, the square glasses framing his green eyes, the thick red beard that was a striking contrast to the pale blond hair atop his head, like a genetic mistake.

It was a mistake repeated in the son who never appreciated the security provided by his mother's remarriage. The kid has deluded himself out of a life because he has held on to a grudge. About a newborn baby, no less. A baby his mother never wanted and was not obliged to care for by herself.

Of course, Mr. Scrap has had his own doubts about that decision. But at the time it was not his to make.

Only in retrospect could Mr. Scrap know that the little wailing infant had been his one chance to be a father; only in retrospect could he know what he didn't on that dark summer night as they swaddled the boy and delivered him to a less desirable address. He had rerouted the baby so efficiently, supplying him with a different path, a new home, another set of voices talking over him while he slept. Finding an alternative family for that newborn had granted him a role to play, an intimacy he thought he otherwise could not have attained. How could he have known that he did not need to win her heart or her affection, that she would marry him as certainly as she would accept a drink on a hot day? Polite, sensible and thirsty, she was far more attainable than Mr. Scrap had imagined.

A sudden wind brings with it the previous afternoon's smells. Fresh cut grass, roses, coolant, chlorine—all of summer's bounty in one breeze that blows through the thin cotton of his pajamas. But then he feels goose bumps ripple across his shoulders at the whiff of something else: cigarette smoke. Mr. Scrap looks around for an early-morning dog walker, a high school kid out until dawn. But there is nobody on the block that he can see. Who, then?

He looks over the deck at his own front door, where the porch light is casting a hard, bright light onto the threshold. This sight haunts him. If it were a painted still life, there would be a menace outside the frame.

Mr. Scrap walks to the edge of the deck, looking through the wooden slats beneath his feet. Is the smoke coming from below? The wind blows again, further confusing him. Are any of those rustlings unnatural? A tin can cartwheeling, a plastic bag inflating suddenly, heavy branches rubbing against one another, or footsteps on the pea-gravel pathway beneath him?

The gust of wind subsides, as do the rustlings. But the smell of cigarette smoke is just as strong.

Should he call out? If he thought it were a common thief down there, he would announce himself and startle the criminal back out into the night. But Mr. Scrap does not for a moment think that the cigarette smoke wafting up through the boards of the deck is that of a random delinquent. He is certain as he stands there in his bare feet, with the night's dream fresh on his skin, that Andy Rolondo has come to intimidate him further.

Without a sound, Mr. Scrap kneels and then stretches out on his stomach. He presses his forehead against the wood, fixing an eye on a space between two floorboards.

There are a couple of old bikes, two shovels and a bucket his wife uses to collect weeds. Nothing seems disturbed. But Mr. Scrap cannot pull his head away. If he watches long enough, surely he will see some movement, some evidence of a trespasser.

Perhaps the cigarette smoke and the footsteps are figments of his paranoia. Perhaps there is nothing at all remarkable about this predawn hour. Then the wind blows again and once more the surroundings become a refrain of ominous, indecipherable stirrings.

With the summer breeze casting about, Mr. Scrap falls asleep right there, with his eye in a crack, waiting for some proof of his suspicions.

His wife will find him later in the morning, having walked through the open French door with a trepidation that quickly turned to dread as she saw his body laid out on the deck, looking so much like another loss.

❖

With his equipment slung across his body, Oliver hops over the fence of the community pool just as dawn is about to emerge. The pool is officially closed and the brilliant blue water, stretched out in a seamless rectangle, is dizzying. As a kid, Oliver would have wished for an opportunity like this, when he could be the one to break the water's edge with his feet, to submerge himself beneath the surface alone and listen to the hollow sound of nothing. But this morning, he is in character: a married, thirty-nine-year-old pathologist with two kids.

He sits by the side of the pool in his swim trunks, his goggles around his neck. A grin stretches wide across his face, as he catches something outside the frame. It is his children frolicking in the pool. His son and his daughter, swimming through the legs of mostly forgiving adults, are what he thinks of as he remotely triggers the shutter.

As he smiles, the aperture clicks shut, like a door closed tight. How sad his father would be if he knew all that he had missed. All the chaos he caused by dying. That his death orphaned the little boy he'd been so anxious to save, so anxious to know.

Watching the sun's light throw long shadows across the pool deck, Oliver decides that looking in on life after you've left would be cheating. Like Orpheus looking back at Eurydice because he can't stand not to. Or, Oliver thinks, like being told about the ending of a book before you've read it all for yourself.

Oliver, for one, would rather leave off in the middle of the good book, when everybody is still alive. If it falls behind the bed, gets buried under a pile of junk mail, then he'd rather never hear how it ends. He'd rather the beginning remain suspended in his mind.

Oliver imagines his father on the kitchen floor. Slam. The book is shut before he's finished reading it. No harm, no foul. His father, at least, is safe from the tragedy.

But the book still exists. Even if no one is reading it. The pages fill up in a whirlwind of melodrama: his mother rejects the adoption, marries the next-door neighbor and pretends this new life can replace the old.

There is a crabapple tree arching over the pool and as Oliver stands to put away his equipment, a branch drops two of its red fruit into the water. They bob on the surface like perfect little buoys. Scarlet warnings.

When he was a kid, their bitter taste didn't matter to him. Just eating fruit he could pick himself was joyful, regardless of its flavor and tough texture. He ate the crabapples off the tree in the backyard all the time. Or, rather, he chewed them and sucked on them as he perused the adjacent yards.

Later that afternoon, after Oliver had seen Patty Wilcox hide beneath the barbecue cover, did he and Mary hear sirens? He doesn't remember. When his father was called into work, Oliver climbed back into the tree, picked a crabapple, and looked about, hoping to spy something as exciting as he had that morning.

But it's not as fun being in the tree alone. He's headed in to ask Mary to join him when, to his surprise, he finds her stretched out in a plastic chaise on the deck, making notes.

"What's going on?" he asks, holding the crabapple against the inside of his cheek.

"Bad business, old chum." Her accent is back on. "That girl"— she points to the tree—"that girl from this morning. The one you found. Patty Wilcox. She's missing. Since noon. That's all I know. Tina Farnsworth told me." She shrugs. "Everyone's round the bend trying to find her. Even the police. Maybe she ran away." Her eyes widen with the idea of a crime. "Or got kidnapped."

Oliver races back to the tree. He climbs it effortlessly and stands on a branch high enough to see over the wall. He looks at the barbecue cover in Mr. Nice Guy's abandoned yard, still draped over the railing just where she left it. She's hiding again, he's sure, waiting for Oliver to find her.

"Mary," he calls down to her. "I'll bet you anything she's hiding under there again."

"Why's that, Oliver?"

"Because I just know it. Come on. We've got to hurry." He shifts from one foot to the other, anxious.

"Right," Mary says, compelled by his urgency. She follows Oliver up to his branch, then they both place their feet on the high cement wall separating the two yards.

"Is he home?" Oliver asks, looking at the big windows of the house next door.

"No. He's a lawyer, Oliver, remember? They're never home."

"Oh," Oliver says and is the first to jump. He lands well, but too close to the flower bed and flattens a large iris.

Mary lands nearby, without crushing anything. "We've no time to waste. We must find the queen."

Oliver looks at her quizzically. "Huh?"

"Oh, you know. What's-her-name. Come on, then."

"Jolly good," he says, assuming a hunched position to match Mary's. They tiptoe through the grass straight to the railing. Oliver lifts the barbecue cover, but nobody's there. Mary's head swivels, checking for enemy spies. They search other places, under the deck, behind the shed, along the side of the house. Nothing. The yard is empty. They're sneaking around, though, moving through the strange yard cautiously, as though it were the darkened alleys and cobblestoned streets of imaginary London.

"Blast it," Mary says, turning around to face Oliver. "The trail is cold." A siren wails somewhere in the distance.

"Blast it," Oliver repeats, picking up a stick on the ground.

"Back to home base, then, chap?" Mary asks, pretending to dial up her phone. She speaks to the boss, telling him that they've lost the queen.

"He says we've got to come in for a briefing. Hot water for us, chum."

"I'd say." Oliver twirls the stick in his hand. "I thought for sure we'd find her. Do you really think she was kidnapped?" Oliver imagines the girl tied up in the back of a van.

"Dunno," Mary says, walking back toward the wall. She leans against it. "Um, Oliver. I think we'll have to go around."

She's right. There's no way to climb the wall from this side. It's entirely too high.

A couple of branches from their crabapple tree extend plaintively over their neighbor's yard. They've dropped their fruit here, dozens of crimson orbs that freckle the grass. Does this make him mad, their neighbor, Mr. Scrap? Does he wish they would cut back the branches, pick up the fruit? Or is it a fair exchange for the swath of shade that covers the back corner of his yard?

Oliver shrugs and follows Mary out the neighbor's side gate, into their own front yard, through their side gate, and into their own backyard.

With the stick in one hand, Oliver walks toward the porch, thinking of yet another peanut butter sandwich. His mother is still at her sewing club and his father has not yet come home from the hospital. As much as he wishes his father had not been called into work this afternoon—they'd had plans to go to the pool—there is a freedom in this circumstance that is unusual.

Oliver feels something crunch beneath his bare foot. He hops away and looks down at the grass. The offending object seems like a piece of trash. He reaches his stick to it and turns it over. It is not trash. It is an egg. Bright white, speckled with gray, cracked. He nudges at it with his stick again.

"Hey, Mare," he calls. It is more than cracked. An entire side is missing, as though half of the shell has been cut away to create a diorama.

"Mary," Oliver shouts, panicked now by what he sees. "Come here. I need you."

Oliver can't take his eyes from the nearly formed bird, all pink and gray and bare. Mary now stands in front of him, assessing the situation with clinical eyes.

"What is it?" she asks as she kneels next to him. She has a fresh piece of watermelon bubble gum in her mouth. Its smell is strong and sweet.

"I don't know. A bird, I guess."

"Wow. It's like a perfect little body," Mary says, taking the stick from Oliver's grasp. "Look, it could be human," she says, pointing at its miniature folded arms and legs.

"Birds don't have arms," Oliver says. "Is that why it died?"

Oliver's eyes are big and worried and hopeful that it is not he who killed it. "It had arms and it shouldn't?"

"They'll turn into wings. Put some feathers on there and they're wings." Mary stretches her own arms out and flaps. "It was close to being alive, though. It's almost fully formed. Maybe it *is* fully formed," she says, poking the point of the stick on the small, flattened beak of the bird. "I think this is how they hatch. Just like this, with wide beaks that grow into a point—it makes it easier for the mom to get the food into there."

Oliver watches Mary, her blond hair falling forward in front of her shoulders. She presses the stick into the bird. The underside of the shell cracks a little more.

"Hey, cut it out," Oliver says, grabbing the stick from his sister.

"It's already dead, Oliver. I can't hurt it."

"How do you know? You don't know everything about how the world works." He wipes the bottom of his foot through the grass.

Mary rolls her eyes and sucks a big purple bubble into her mouth. "When you die, you die," she says proudly.

"But what about its spirit?"

"Also gone. To heaven," she says with a trill in her voice, her arm extended gracefully skyward. In that pose she freezes, as if for a photo. "Or to hell," she says suddenly, her voice low and her arm stiff, pointing at the ground. She bows her head, waiting for applause.

Oliver looks away. There is always this with his sister: drama. She wants to be the most captivating thing in any situation. And, usually, for Oliver, she is. Until she begins performing. A part of him hates her for thinking that she should be more interesting than a little dead bird still curled into its shell, the slivers of pink feet tucked into the abdomen like it's been shivering. How could she ask for Oliver to adore her even more than he already does? "Stop it," he whispers.

The bird looks so fragile and withered in its egg, as if it has been caught dead at the end of life, not the beginning. Its beak is wide and flat as though collapsed from overuse. Its skin is wrinkled and thin, the eyelids baggy.

Mary sighs heavily next to him, smacking her gum. "Okay. So, should we bury him, then?"

"What if he's not a baby? What if he's already lived his whole life? And this is like his—what is it called?" He is thinking of the big book from the King Tut exhibit on his parents' bookshelf. It would be better if the bird had lived a long life, not died before it'd even sat in the nest or caught a worm, or stretched its wings out and flown. Oliver would feel a whole lot better if the bird were old and tired.

"His sarcophagus?" Mary looks at him with her nose crinkled.

"Yeah, his sarcophagus. We could place treasures around him, like breadcrumbs and earthworms, and dig him a tomb."

Mary shrugs.

Only her imaginings get any play these days and they always involve something about being an adult. And British. Not dead and Egyptian.

"Did it fall out of its nest, Oliver?" Mary looks up at the crab-apple tree they had been sitting in earlier.

Oliver uses his stick to rock the shell back and forth. He is no longer thinking of the bird, but of his brother. The baby they will adopt in another few days. The one his parents spoke about only in hushed voices for weeks before sitting Oliver and Mary down on the couch and telling them they would soon be a family of five. His mother solemnly reminded them how much work a baby is, how much help she would need. His father's face, on the other hand, was smiling, carefree, ecstatic. Oliver makes a silent promise to this little brother yet to come, whose name is somewhere in the notebook Mary has nearly filled, that his imaginings will get plenty of play.

"I know what to do," Mary says suddenly, heading for the house. "Wait there," she calls out to him, her voice purposeful.

Oliver squats and studies the bird's translucent skin more carefully. He doesn't want Mary to think he killed the bird. He doesn't want her to tell on him. That his foot crushed a nearly perfect baby bird. The damage, he knows, is done. Whatever Mary is inside figuring out will not include resurrecting him.

There are chirps and squawks all around. Robins, doves, sparrows. They are on nearly every branch of the crabapple, looking down at Oliver just as he'd looked down on Patty Wilcox. The birds' black eyes shift uneasily as he tries to look into them. There is no warmth in their gaze. They despise him. They are staring at him with reproach.

Mary returns and spreads out a dishtowel on the weathered wooden picnic table on the porch.

He crawls up on the picnic table beside the dishtowel, leaving the egg behind in the grass. "Mary?" he says.

"I need you to get me the egg, Oliver." She has the Swiss Army knife held tightly in her hand, one blade open.

For an instant the cloth on the table looks like a placemat and Oliver has the horrible thought that his sister might be preparing to eat the bird.

"You cannot eat it, Mary. I won't let you." He runs back to the egg and lifts it from the grass, cradling it in his hands.

Mary stands facing him, the knife still in her hers. "Relax, Oliver. I'm not going to *eat* the bird. What kind of a spaz do you think I am?" Her mouth twists into a grimace.

Oliver looks down at the bird. "Why do you have the knife?"

"It's a scalpel," she says.

"Huh?"

"We're going to do an autopsy, Oliver. Like Daddy does. We're going to find out what happened."

Oliver hears her, but what she says does not reassure him the way she seems to think it should.

"Hello? Did you hear me? I need the bird," she says, reaching out her hand toward his.

Oliver steps back. He transfers the egg to one hand and wipes at his eyes with the back of his other hand. "I don't get it."

"An autopsy, Oliver. We'll figure out why this happened. If it was foul play."

"But we don't know how. We'll just ruin it." Oliver turns to look at the crabapple tree, the eyes he knows are watching them still.

Mary puts her hands on her hips.

"I got instructions from headquarters. This could be just the break we need to solve this case." She snaps out of her accent for a moment and speaks in a terse whisper. "We'll show Daddy when he gets home. It'll be a surprise. He can help us dictate the notes afterward."

Mary stares at her own bare feet. She looks back at her brother. "Okay?"

Oliver shivers. The egg barely has any weight in his hand. He imagines his father's careful hands. "Okay," he says, finally.

"You can set him down," she says, motioning to the picnic table. Her cheeks are flushed.

Oliver carries the bird over to the dishtowel and places him in the center, wishing that his hands could convey some apology. Not knowing if this is possible or not, he simply holds his hands around the perimeter of the egg for a moment, creating a shield.

"Not like that," Mary says, laying a plastic magnifying glass on the table. "Hold it still, but leave me space. Maybe we should take it out of the shell first. Here," she reaches her hand out, but Oliver pulls away.

"I'll do it," he says.

"Carefully, be gentle."

"Don't boss me. I know how to do it." He cautiously holds the egg in one hand and with the other peels back the portion of the shell that seems to be attached to the bird. The shell chips off in small pieces, some of them jabbing the skin beneath his fingernails. They are coated with small bits of feather and dried blood. Oliver keeps working, though, until the bird is completely exposed. He is surprised that it doesn't feel warm or particularly soft. Without the egg beneath it, its body seems to flatten against the shape of Oliver's hand, which he holds out so that the creature is just below his sister's face. "See?" he says.

Mary nods.

Oliver looks in her eyes. "Done."

"Good job, old chap. Lay it down, now."

Oliver does as he is told. He keeps a thumb on either side of the body while his sister pokes her small blade at the base of its throat. When her knife finally cuts through, she lets out a hollow little shriek.

Oliver also screams, not knowing what has happened. Then they look at each other and giggle.

"Nervous Nellies, we are," Mary says, nudging Oliver with her elbow.

She guides the knife down to the place where there are two miniature legs, crossed like sticks.

"We're in," she says, wiping the knife on the dishtowel.

Oliver watches her close the blade and open the small scissors. As she slips them into the incision and cuts away the flimsy skin, there is suddenly a smell that tightens Oliver's stomach into a coil. It is almost sweet, like wet dirt or an old blanket. Mary doesn't move. Her scissors hover over the hole she has made.

"What do you see?" she asks, her voice quiet and stern, like a teacher's.

"Nothing," Oliver says, rather loudly, trying to cover up the nothing. "Nothing at all, Mary. There's nothing there. You've just made it worse." He sees a tiny pale pink sac surrounded by slivers of darker pink strings. And yellow. "There isn't any blood, even."

This last observation makes Oliver think that maybe the bird wasn't dead; maybe it was still alive when Mary cut it open.

She places the scissors on the dishtowel and wipes her hands on her cutoffs. "Okay, Oliver, now is not the time to freak. This is just the beginning. We have to be able to see something. We can't see anything if you're yelling at me."

"But there is nothing to see. It's the inside. Nothing else. We knew the inside was there before you cut anything." He doesn't know why he is so angry.

"Calm down. We're looking for something wrong with the inside. Got it? Something wrong that made him die."

"What's wrong with the inside is that it's there," Oliver says, pointing at the little desiccated bird on the picnic table. "Now it's not inside anymore. It's outside for us to see and that is what is wrong."

"This isn't wrong, Oliver. This is what Daddy does. This is how he helps figure out why people died."

Did his father really do this? Cut dead people open and let their insides out like Mary has just done? And then come home and hold Oliver's hand while they walk to the end of the drive for the evening paper, whistling?

A fly lands on the scissors. Oliver watches it. Mary shoos it away. It buzzes around their heads and then lands on the bird. Its wispy legs crawl over the bird's eyes and then down to the opening in its abdomen. Mary shoos it again. It lands on Oliver's cheek and he permits its legs to deposit some microscopic bit of the bird onto his cheek, just as the bees do in the plant book by his bed, releasing clumps of pollen from their legs onto the petals of a flower. Pistil. Pollen. Stamen. The way plants stay alive, make babies, continue.

But whatever granules the fly has transferred from its legs to Oliver's cheek will not keep anyone alive.

Mary is casually poking at the pale pink sac again with her knife when both of them hear the garage door. Their father is home.

Just a few years before, they would have run inside to catch the first sight of him in the house. Still intent on confirming that objects continue to exist even when they are no longer visible, they would wrap their scrawny arms around his legs and marvel at his return.

Daddy goes away, Daddy comes back. A thrill each time, well into their toddler years.

At seven and nine, however, the concept of object permanence is solid. They no longer need it proved.

It will haunt them in the years to come, especially Oliver.

But now they are only worried about being found out.

None of this would be approved of, Oliver is certain. Not the bird on the table, not the knife or the scissors. They are in big trouble.

"Can you put it back together, Mary?" he asks.

She is quiet. The house door opens and closes. The clink of their father's keys as they fall into the bowl on the kitchen counter confirms that he is home.

"No," Mary finally answers, recommitting herself to the bird's autopsy. "Not yet." She bends over further and pokes aggressively into the minuscule stomach with the point of her knife.

Oliver can't watch anymore. "You don't know what you're doing. It was a real bird, you know. It didn't come in a kit and you can't just do this."

Mary stops for a moment to scowl at him, holding the knife up, away from the bird. Its dull blade is right next to Oliver's face so that he can smell the sweet, metallic residue of the bird's insides. He is terrified to leave the bird alone with her on the porch, but also terrified of his father finding them, like this, bent over the bird.

Mary, crouched over, continues to cut farther and farther in. Maybe she will make it disintegrate into nothing. Object impermanence.

Oliver hears the water from the kitchen sink falling into the wide bottom of the teakettle. He knows it won't be long before their father comes out, with a mug of instant coffee in hand, asking them what they ate for dinner. When he sees what they've gotten themselves into, he will pull at his beard, drawing it down with anger.

But there is another noise from inside. First, a glass falls, shattering on the linoleum floor. A curse word, then a groan, like his father is absorbing a kick to the stomach.

Then the distraught look on Mary's face, her knife still inside the bird as the kettle begins to scream.

Now, in the quiet of this morning beside the pool, with his father's beard still on his own face, his father's glasses propped on his own forehead, Oliver looks once again at the collection of crabapples on the surface of the pool water. Slowly, one by one, they are sinking and it is relief Oliver feels as they succumb to their own weight. The liberation their defeat affords them is its own kind of reprieve. If only Oliver could allow the weight of himself in the present to actually matter. Instead, he is tethered afloat to these photographs, and to the fullness of his desire for a revised ending of that afternoon twenty-one years ago.

Now that he's found his brother, the need that's driven him for so long will soon be met. He dries off his feet, pulls his corduroys on over his swim trunks and steps into his sneakers, leaving the pool. In a new ending will also be a beginning.

❖

Driving back toward town from the pool, Oliver stops by his mother's house. From the front driveway, he can see the crabapple tree from the old yard that bends its branches over Mr. Nice Guy's wall. Dozens of crabapples still fall there, cluttering his grass with their blotches of red. After his mother moved them in here, carrying their belongings in shoe boxes and suitcases across the lawn, one of Oliver's chores was to pick up the fallen fruit.

He didn't put a single one in his mouth; they no longer seemed like anything but trash. He lugged the half-full bucket to the place under the deck that Mr. Nice Guy pointed to with his gloved hand; they worked in the yard together. And that is where the bucket stayed through the summer and the fall. The fruits softened and rotted. Birds and flies and ants visited often, as did Oliver. Drawn by the putrid smell and the fate of being forgotten, Oliver squatted by the bucket and witnessed it. He saw the way the skin loosened and wrinkled. He witnessed their insides bleed out. A lonely little widening.

This morning, when his mother comes to the door, she looks nothing like she might have riding next to his father in the 1972

Ranchero. Her hair is cut short around her face now, the gray creeping in gracefully. Her reading glasses are nearly always on her nose, so that she has to tuck her chin to her chest in order to look over them. She frowns when she sees Oliver.

He looks like a memory. But she does not say so.

"You coming in?" his mother asks, as usual.

Oliver steps over the threshold into the sparse living room. He can see past the dining area to the wall of glass across the back of the house. Tall evergreens dot the property line, and the lawn is green with well-groomed grass. A large redwood deck flanks the back and side of the house and Mr. Nice Guy is sitting on it, his own reading glasses perched on his nose, a stack of paperwork piled high on the table in front of him.

"Not coming in," Oliver says, though he's already standing in the middle of the living room. "Just passing by." He kisses his mother's cheek.

She pats his arm. "I've got tea," she offers, turning away from him toward the kitchen.

"No time, Mom. I'm picking up materials from my newest client."

His mother's face changes. "Oh. Another?"

"People die all the time, Mom."

"Well, of course they do, Oliver."

"Guess who she is. The new client."

"Heavens, Oliver, it could be anyone. I don't particularly want to start guessing who's just died."

"That's your first clue. They didn't *just* die. It's history. Part of *our* history."

Oliver's mother pulls her glasses all the way off of her face. She purses her lips, intrigued and irritated. "I'm not playing twenty questions, Oliver. Aren't you hot in that turtleneck? It's such a warm day."

"It's cotton. It breathes."

She looks at her son, taller than she, his face and figure so much like his father's. Today, his beard is grown thick and trimmed just so. Putting her glasses back on, she looks down at a stack of mail on the table. "Do you want to tell me about your historical client or not? My tea is getting cold."

Oliver squeezes both hands into the front pockets of his pants. "Mrs. Wilcox."

His mother lets the mail be. She is speechless. She walks to the front window, looking out at Oliver's Ranchero. "Well," she finally says, "what in the world?"

"A memorial. She wants something lasting. Digital. For posterity, because there is nobody else. You know Mr. Wilcox died last year?"

She nods. "I heard. I see her in the grocery, sometimes at the stitch shop. What will she do?"

Oliver shrugs.

"I mean with your video."

"Watch it?"

"Well, that's just sick." Her tone is official. "Morbid. How awful." She plucks a few deadheads from the bouquet on the table under the window.

"Morbidity is in the eye of the beholder, Mom. Some people are comforted by memories."

"Good for them. But in my book, life is now."

"Yeah." Oliver nods. "Yeah, you're like Oprah Winfrey with that book, Mom. You don't even need a teleprompter to sell it." Oliver lowers his voice to the range of a newsman. "*The Book of Now* is flying off shelves. A bit shallow, a bit trite, but readers everywhere love it."

She musters a thin, irritated smile. "Oprah and I have good taste. And we know that the here and now is not necessarily shallow or trite."

Without warning, Oliver walks over to his mother and kisses her blank face before he starts toward the door. Her here and now is everything. She doesn't long for what was lost. Would she even long for Oliver, if he were lost?

"Oh, I almost forgot," he says, pulling a DVD from his backpack. "*Your* video. Swing Night."

She takes the slim case from his hand. "Thank you, Oliver," she says, and means it.

He shrugs again, then bounds off of the front porch. "For *The Book of Then*. Whenever you finally get tired of now."

Oliver's mother can't tell when he's joking. He always has a smile around the corners of his mouth, always a slight levity in his voice.

"You're a pill," she says.

"Trying not to be a bitter one," he answers.

His mother stands on the porch, looking over her nose at him, and throws both hands up in the air in an exasperated gesture of good-bye.

The Ranchero's motor turns over noisily. Oliver hangs his arm out the window, giving his mother the sign of peace. Then, with his fingers resting on the ridge of the red racing stripe, he drives away.

He remembers waking, the sun not yet up, the house overly quiet. There was only extreme fatigue, as though he had been wrestling with somebody much older and stronger. His body knew what his mind had forgotten.

He rubbed his eyes and his face felt cool against the heat of his little palms. Only then did he realize that he was in his parents' bed. His mother and his sister lay on either side of him. Nobody was undressed. Nobody was under the sheets. Getting comfortable in this new reality was an impossibility. And then he remembered.

Dressed in the same denim shorts his father had thrown at him from the laundry basket the previous morning, Oliver tiptoed down the hallway from his parents' room to the den. Through the glass doors, he could see only the outline of the chaise longue and the picnic table on the porch. He unlocked the door and slipped out. The morning air was cool and stung his lungs. The concrete slab of the porch still held the last day's warmth and his feet welcomed this touch. As he got closer to the table, he could see there was still something there. Not the white dishtowel, and not the little magnifying glass, but the Swiss Army knife that his sister had used. It was there, as was the bird—two objects of similar size and color, lying alongside one another like siblings. Like Cain and Abel.

The bird's eyes were more sunken than they had been the day before. Turned nearly onto its side, it looked like a piece of rotten fruit. A half-dozen ants were making their way in and out of the carcass. Its open wound was shriveled and dry.

Oliver put the knife in his pocket. He pulled his shirt off over his head, used it to pick up the bird and then wound the sleeve carefully around it. The tight swaddle, Oliver thought, looked a little like an oversized egg. In the dim light he walked through the grass to the place where he'd first seen the bird in its shell. The dew was cold on his feet.

Setting the bundle down gently, he stabbed at the grass with his sister's knife and pulled out clumps of sod until he finally found dirt. With his fingers he dug out a mound, opening a hole in the ground. The dirt was wet and cool and some became wedged beneath his fingernails. Oliver bit his lip; he tasted blood. When the hole was just big enough for his bundle, he placed it in.

But he wasn't finished. He needed something to put into the hole with the bird. Oliver walked through the house, looking around at the bookshelves and countertops, through toy cars and plastic balls, whistles and clay figurines. He stopped outside his sister's room, squinting his eyes in the dark of the house. Her bed was empty, still made. Her fish tank produced a faint gurgling. Oliver walked into the room and stood near her bed, looking around. There was nothing useful here, either.

In his parents' bedroom his mother and sister slept side by side. He walked close to the edge of the bed and put his head near his sister's face. She always smelled like pancake dough. He knelt by her face and laid his head down and closed his eyes. He could feel her breath on his hands. He wanted to enter her sleep, to be back inside that dark cloak.

Instead, he imagined the birds roosting in the trees in their yard. Their wings fluttering, their heads bobbing. And then, beneath his closed eyes, Oliver saw one of their nests, tucked between two branches. He could see every bit of it. Empty.

He opened his eyes and waited for his sister to scold him. She slept on.

She had a very generous spirit. For example, she'd given Oliver the last miniature pancake yesterday morning. His father's little halfhearted dripping of the batter on the griddle was a phenomenon they both coveted.

Everything could be different come sunrise. He could give the birds this ceremony and in exchange the universe would forgive them. Their actions atoned for, his father would come home and laugh about the hysterics of last night, especially Mr. Nice Guy locking his lips onto his with such vehemence. The chaos and confusion for which Oliver felt culpable could not have been meant for his family. It could still be undone. An offering for the afterlife was something his sister would understand. A piece of her could change the course of the future.

Oliver stood up and reached into his pocket. He opened the blade still caked with dirt and wiped it on his shorts. Then he put the blade away. He wanted the scissors. He wiped them, too, on his shorts, just in case. Then, slowly and with care, Oliver lifted a long clump of his sister's blond hair and clipped it right at her scalp. He held it in his hand and judged that he needed a little bit more, enough to twirl into a single slender nest.

With the two clumps of long hair hanging from his fist, Oliver tiptoed out of his parents' room and back outside. This time, the cold of the dew brought out goose bumps on his bare torso. Oliver wound the hair into a tight coil, placed it on top of his shirt in the hole and then replaced the dirt. As he laid some of the uprooted grass over the exposed patch of soil, he couldn't help crying. These tears, hardly noticeable, slipped out easily, as though they were a breeze coming through an open door. The tears he'd shed for the benefit of his mother and sister the night before had been conjured by the witnessing of his mother's. He had been a child mimicking his parent's agony.

Oliver looked up through his new, quiet tears to the trees on the side of the yard, where he knew dozens of nests were perched. The dawn was suddenly filled with the noise of those roostings. He had never liked apologies, but none, he realized, had been so deserved as this one. "I'm sorry," he said, his voice an insignificant murmur. There was no sign of acknowledgment or forgiveness, but the first wren of the morning descended from her branch and flew past Oliver's head. He wiped at his eyes and dragged his feet through the grass.

Before going inside, Oliver replaced his sister's knife on the table, where it stayed for days.

Maybe not everything was lost. In that dim barely morning, Oliver remembered that soon they would save a baby, a phrase their father had used. Could giving a baby a home, a place to be loved, make up for all of this? Had his father planned it this way?

Oliver swore to himself that when his new brother was old enough, he would tell him about last night. About what they had done to the bird and what happened next. The way the kitchen smelled and the loud buzzing of the fluorescent light. The wail of the teakettle. His father's open eyes, twitching mouth. He would be his brother's history teacher, giving him the details of life and of life's fragility.

Oliver stood in his parents' bedroom, looking around at his father's things. His pants flung over the chair. His stack of magazines by the bed. The bowl of change, overflowing, on the dresser. A pile of hard peppermint candy collected from myriad restaurants. Would they bury all of this, too?

The chirpings of daylight swelled outside the window. Taking a peppermint from his father's stash, Oliver climbed back into bed with his mother and his sister. Pulling the wrapper's ends away from each other, he slid the candy into his mouth and held it on his tongue. The sugar melted and coated the inside of his mouth, dissolving slowly as he waited for the others' eventual awakening.

❖

Though he knows another stop may make him late to collect the second album from Mrs. Wilcox, Oliver cannot help driving by Alfalfa's, just for a glimpse.

Parking near the end of the lot so that he has a straight shot into the checkout lanes, he retrieves his pair of dark glasses from the glove box. The slew of grocery carts stacked inside one another outside the market are like shiny metal confidants.

Forever, it seems, he's been looking for this kid brother. His determination is inscribed on his face—eyebrows always furrowed to a point just above his nose, eyes open just a little wider than most. Even the slight grin he holds his mouth in is not, as some might believe, an expression of carefree happiness; it is his mode of intense concentration, a characteristic that he inherited from his father. For twenty-one years, Oliver has been fiercely studying the world, checking each face for some indescribable feature. Something familiar, something misplaced.

When he was fourteen, he asked Mary to try to remember those weeks she'd worked so hard to forget. Specifically, he needed her to revisit the last of those three weeks during which the baby had become their own, his face recognizing theirs, calming at the sound of their voices, drinking from a bottle held in their own small hands. If Mary could just remember the name their mother had used when she made the phone call. They'd sat in the darkened hallway, listening to her voice quiver, while the baby in between them quietly slept. Or if she could give him the name of the street that Mr. Nice Guy drove them to sometime the next day. Their mother had sat up front, holding her head in her hands. If she could just recall the name and the place, they could both find him.

His ongoing game of hide-and-seek became a habit. Whenever he went home from school with a new friend, he'd check the closets. Without interrupting their game of catch, he'd look under tables, behind curtains, in the broom closet. After taking a leak, he'd open the clothes hamper, the vanity cabinets, pull back the shower curtain. The game didn't end. In fact, Oliver couldn't imagine the game ending.

But now. In his '72 Ranchero in the parking lot of Alfalfa's, Oliver anonymously watches his kid brother bag expensive eggplant and organic spelt. He studies the myriad tattoos stretching from the back of his neck to the tips of his fingers: the small green toad with bright red eyes that sits on one wrist, a pyramid with an eye in the center that covers the other, the length of barbed wire extending past each elbow, an army green star on the inside of his left arm, a red torpedo floating up his bicep and three lightning bolts on the back of his neck. Here in the car with his dark glasses on, Oliver wishes he knew how those tattoos came to be, and what each one means. He would have driven the boy home after each one, in the Ranchero just like their father's.

And then there she is again, Miranda with her camera. Only this time she has a dog with her, too—a scruffy blond mutt that could be a Benji look-alike. Which is maybe the point: Miranda's anonymous, famous-looking dog.

As she crosses the parking lot, Oliver is suddenly reminded of the young Nonny from the video, moving through space not as though she were sure of everything, but as though she were entirely not sure and this uncertainty was for the best. Her childlike look of wonder was actually an untroubled acceptance of instability. Miranda has this same bearing, and Oliver cannot keep his eyes off of her. He almost expects her to open her mouth and reveal the same pear blossom that Nonny picked and put in her mouth sixty years ago.

Instead, Miranda comes around the back of Oliver's Ranchero and peeks into the truck bed. Her hair is down now, not in the pigtails he remembers from before. Though the streaks of platinum and red in her dark brown hair are certainly youthful, on the whole she looks older, more serious.

She continues to walk around the car, then opens the passenger door and looks in at Oliver with a huge grin on her face. "I am so glad to see you," she says. The dog puts his paws up on the seat, sniffing the vinyl.

"Really?" Oliver picks up the folder and puts it on his lap so there's room for them both.

"Yes. Absolutely. You were not hit by a semi or attacked by a mugger or some other horrible thing." She breathes deeply. Then, as if she's known him all of her life but hasn't seen him in years, she studies him and pronounces her finding. "You look good. Really good. What's new with you?"

Oliver smiles, free to study her now, too. "Um, yeah. Things are good. You know, still working, still living over there on Marquette," he gestures with his arm to the south.

"Marquette? Right," she says. "I don't think I've been to your new place. And the job—how's that going? Are you still in pharmaceuticals?"

"Nah," Oliver shakes his head, trying to mask his excitement at playing along. "You know, all the pills and the doughnuts, they kind of got to me. I took a nice severance package—a year's worth of Zoloft—and got the hell out. How 'bout you? You still on the circuit? Still doing the consulting thing?"

"You mean with the baboons? That was eons ago. Oh, no. After every single pair of shoes I owned was peed on by those baboons, I decided to give up on zoology and join a circus."

"Which one?"

"The American Media Circus. I do sleight of hand and a little customer service in the front office." She shrugs. "It doesn't pay the bills, you know. Sometimes you gotta put your passion on hold to go broke. Can't always make a lot of money doing the things you hate."

Oliver's stomach is hurtling, as though he were on the edge of a steep descent. He wants to take a photograph of her, here in his car, her dog licking the glove box. "Stay right there," he says, hopping out of the car and grabbing his camera bag from the back. "Can I?" he asks, sitting back down, the folder resting in the space between them.

"Oh, come on. You've got a million photos of me. Remember that time . . ." She's drawn a blank, doesn't finish.

"You mean at the Swedish bathhouse?"

She nods. "So many pictures. Ay, ay, ay—you must have a stack. But, okay. Add another. Who knows how long it'll be until we see each other again. I mean, what time does your plane leave?"

Oliver checks his watch. "In an hour," he says, turning on the camera.

"Me, too. Where you headed?"

"Anyplace nonstop. I can't stand the landings and takeoffs." Oliver removes the lens cap.

"No way, those are the best part of air travel. Like a little roller coaster there, bookending the monotony of the pressurized air and loud engines."

Oliver takes her picture.

"Oh, now I remember," she says. "The last time I saw you, we fought about the whole nonstop thing. Can't fly anything but nonstop. Wow. Some things never change." Miranda looks at Oliver wistfully.

"Oh, but they do," he says, grinning. He takes another picture of her, then puts the camera down. "Remember—a year's supply of Zoloft."

Miranda laughs. The first real one. Oliver has made her laugh.

"We should pretend to know each other some more," she says.

"What are you doing later?" Oliver asks.

"Later? I have this thing. A thing I'm doing. What are you doing now?"

"Now?" Oliver pulls the folder back onto his lap. "Now? I have this thing. A thing I have to do. I'm already late, actually," he says, thinking of Mrs. Wilcox's stern face.

"Hmm," she says, scratching the dog's ears. "Well, okay. You could come with me. On my thing. I usually prefer to work alone, but . . . since we go so far back, I guess it'll be all right."

Oliver nods. "Yeah, if that's cool. I'll tag along."

"So, your thing—are you doing someone's taxes or what?" She points at the folder he's fiddling with.

"Something like that. Accounting. My new career. I'll fill you in tonight."

"Good. Aren't you going to ask my dog's name?"

"What's its name?"

She scoffs. Then, covering the dog's ears with her hands so that it cannot hear, she whispers, "It's Benji. *The* Benji. Can't you tell? He's very private. Doesn't like to give autographs or anything. So I call him Angelo. Jello, for short. It's a good cover." Miranda winks, then steps out of the car. "Come on, Jello," she says, and the dog jumps out. "Nine o'clock. The corner of Main and Jefferson."

"See ya," Oliver says, wiping his palms on his pant legs.

She hesitates. "Yeah," she says, but doesn't move.

"I'll be there," Oliver insists. "No highway driving, no trips to the ATM, no meat consumption planned for this afternoon. I'm safe."

She bends over and smiles at him. "No meat?"

"Most people choke on meat, right? Hot dogs, steak, meatballs."

"Dunno." She reaches through the open window for his hand and grasps it.

Oliver can't remember the last time somebody touched him with such assurance. It holds no promise, nor any refusal. It is only what it is: her touch. He is smitten.

She lets go. The air outside suddenly feels cool. Oliver folds his hands in his lap.

"You can eat—just chew a lot," she says, walking around the front of the car to Oliver's side. "And now that we've said a proper good-bye, we can let fate take its course, okay?"

"Okay," he says, watching Jello sniff at her ankles. "Fate it is, then," he answers.

She smiles a little, so that her nose wrinkles and her eyes twinkle. "See you later." Miranda turns and walks away, the dog unleashed, following close behind.

Oliver watches their figures retreat, as though they were the last shot of a family movie, with a banjo playing the happily ever after. It's time for the credits to roll.

He holds his camera in front of his face and takes a picture of the two of them. Maybe tonight life turns into something more than a list of what could have been.

6

The community has voted three times, now, against allowing the big-box store into the city limits. But on a Saturday afternoon, when Mr. Scrap drives the five miles on the highway to the closest such monstrosity, the parking lot is full. He is not accustomed to being at discount stores. He is frugal, yes, but also old-fashioned and averse to spending an afternoon among the crowds and fluorescent lights of a retail warehouse. This afternoon, however, it is a necessity. Where else will he find vacuum-cleaner bags, a box of hooks and eyes, and a quart of heavy cream before five P.M.?

Betsy is at home in the false dark of their bedroom—the blinds pulled, the door closed—with one of her occasional migraine headaches. So these errands that she would have been in charge of have now become his responsibility. He and Betsy are hosting a gathering at their house this evening. Just a few friends, two couples, with whom they often play cards or dominoes. It is usually on these afternoons, once the cooking is done, that Betsy claims to have a migraine coming on. He is suspicious of this malady the way he is of an unreliable witness in the courtroom. If he could cross-examine the migraine, he would try to show its patterns of behavior. Isn't it true, he would ask, that you come only when there is something that your host (my wife) is avoiding? And isn't it true that to go away you require silence and darkness, which your host craves on these evenings? Could it be a convenience and not an affliction? You are in partnership with her, are you not? A welcome relief from whatever it is that she wants to escape.

For some reason, entertaining makes Betsy nervous, fidgety and moody. Because she cooks well, makes good conversation and has luck with games, this is something about her Mr. Scrap cannot understand. But he is also beginning to accept that he cannot change it. He has made this trip in the hope that it will assuage her migraine if he gets the vacuum bags, vacuums the living room, buys a new hook and eye for the blouse she wants to wear, and stocks some cream for the after-dinner coffee, all the while leaving her to her dark room.

If he can perform all of this happily, without a cross-examination, there is a chance the migraine will subside in time for their guests' arrival. Otherwise, when the tires stop on the driveway, the car doors close forcefully and the voices spill out across the front lawn, he will be in the awkward position of answering the door, his face in a forced grin, and inviting the Davises and the Coles to come in and sit with him at the table that Betsy has laid and eat the meal that Betsy has cooked beneath the chandelier that Betsy has polished while Betsy herself lies in darkness upstairs, too miserable to join them.

There is an entire wall of vacuum bags and Mr. Scrap has to read the fine print on the back of nearly every package to determine the correct one for his Kirby upright. More than once he is tempted to go home and vacuum the living room without a new bag and without a word about it to Betsy.

Finally, he finds one that says it will fit and puts it into his empty, oversized cart. On his way to the sewing department, he passes housewares and sporting goods. There is a fishing rod that catches his eye and he stops to check the price.

He hasn't thought about fishing for a long time. It was something he loved as a younger man, but once he was married and trying to care for his new family, he no longer enjoyed being alone by the river. He always felt that the children were conspiring against him. If he were not around in the evenings or on the weekends, they might try to convince their mother that they no longer needed him. Perhaps had never needed him and were much better off alone.

Once they were through the shock and the grief and the abandoned, unmoored feeling of a house without a father, they might have reasoned they could do without Mr. Nice Guy, which is what Oliver called him in a cynical, ironic tone of voice. Already, at the age of nine, the boy was as unnerving as his father had been. That particular combination of uneven temper, easy intellect and rigid independence made him very difficult for Mr. Scrap to love. Or even like, really.

Mr. Scrap had always had an easier time with Mary. She was sweet, easy to comfort, but also fiercely independent. Her eyes pitied Mr. Scrap, but he didn't mind that because he didn't believe that she had any reason to. He believed only that she was prone to pitying, that it was her default emotion to be maudlin.

Before he'd married, the solitude of fishing tempered his envy of other people's happiness. Alone on the bank of a fast-running river, with the aspen and pine trees shading the water, he relished the monotony that was so much like his life, the empty hook of his line so filled with promise. Testing his reflexes, he would keep himself alert through the monotony until, suddenly, there was a tug on the end of his line. Just that fast, everything can change; all the discouragement of the moments before would be pulled under by this wriggling, translucent curve of scales. He always moved quickly to reel in his line, afraid of the disappointment that would follow if it was empty when he pulled it up.

Occasionally, he would lose the trout midair, its rainbow of colors like a mirage, a crescent of hope, falling, falling back into the swift current. More often, though, he would reel the fish in, unhook it carefully and drop it into the bucket. He thought it was greedy to fish for another before the first had died. He would watch it flip and flop, with moments of stillness in between that looked like death. Finally, when only its gills were moving and its eyes were fixed on Mr. Scrap's face, he would abandon the bucket for another try.

The most fish he ever caught was seven in two hours. It wasn't the bounty of his catch that mattered, but the existence of a catch at all. The delirious feeling of driving home with something that he had wanted, something that had not been guaranteed.

The evening the doctor next door died, Mr. Scrap at first felt only the flush of panic and adrenaline that is natural in such a catastrophe. But later that night, in the familiar quiet of his house, he couldn't sleep. With the image of the doctor's body—so heavy beneath him, so still beside the kids—he saw the dawn. With the same pre–fishing trip mixture of anticipation and dread brewing in his stomach, he felt the sun stretch across his bed.

As he stands now in the discount store, marveling at the low prices of colorful graphite rods and the slim cork handles and aluminum oxide guides, Mr. Scrap is reminded again of how quickly everything can change. A fisherman is not privy to the life under his rod; he cannot see the stones tumbling beneath the water, colliding, until the moment that their combined mass slightly changes the flow of the river. He cannot see the way that the silt puffs in the water, clouding his bait. Though its prelude may be long and complex, the change comes in an instant. That tug on the line, that call for help from next door, even that threat in the parking garage—all of these happen in single, unexpected moments. Only those people with presence of mind can be ready for the change and adapt quickly to life's new circumstances. This, he reasons, is the secret to his success.

Behind him, perpendicular to the fishing display, is a counter where a group of three or four young men are standing, boisterous in their admiration for the product they're being shown. Mr. Scrap leans a little so that he can see what it is they're handling.

The weapon is small and dull, not quite black. It is hard to believe that this is allowed: such casual perusal of a deadly weapon by young men who look so careless. With their pants hung low, baseball hats turned backward and tattoos all over. Mr. Scrap takes a step back, afraid. He watches, aghast, as the clerk, an older man with thick glasses and a bald head, hands over the weapon, allowing each of the oglers a chance to hold it, cock it, point it.

Mr. Scrap involuntarily puts his hand to his belt, where his cell phone is strapped. Isn't this the moment that stretches out in front of chaos? The moment in which regret lives. The deadly maybes of memory.

Mr. Scrap quietly steps back again, now pulling his phone from its perch on his hip and flipping it open. Every sound is amplified, every second prolonged.

Laughter. He hears laughter. With his sweaty finger on the nine, he looks once more at the scene. One boy is spinning the chamber; the other two have wandered off to look at other guns on display.

Mr. Scrap closes his phone. He wipes at his forehead with the sleeve of his shirt.

Bullets. There were no bullets in the gun.

The gun itself had seemed so dangerous to him, so inflammatory and nefarious, that he'd completely forgotten its deadly ingredient. Bullets.

What a fool he must have looked, this middle-aged man in a button-down shirt, cell phone ready, temples glistening, hidden behind a display of tackle boxes, ready to report the local Armageddon.

He walks away from the aisle, slowly pushing his cart toward the sewing department. The fear that gripped him when he smelled cigarette smoke in his own backyard now seems justified. How silly he'd felt, waking up on the deck, his face creased from the texture of the wood, the birds chirping innocently, the sun rising benignly. But now he's seen how real the danger is. How easily, how giddily, a gun is bought and for less than the price of a new set of tires.

There is no security system that can empty an intruder's gun of its bullets or even establish a perimeter between Mr. Scrap and someone who walks into a big-box store, swipes a credit card and walks out with a weapon. Mr. Scrap looks behind him once more.

The hook-and-eye set is easy to find; then, in the grocery department, he locates the heavy cream. Also, he cannot resist a package of chocolate Popsicles and a snack-size bag of potato chips. When was the last time he ate a bag of potato chips? He is nearly giddy with the thought of eating them in the car, licking salt off his fingers as he drives home. How rarely, he thinks, I indulge myself.

But then he sees the line. Twenty-five cash registers govern the front of the store, but only three are operational and the lines are so thick, they no longer appear linear. Now he understands the trade-off for the variety of goods and the low prices. Instead of driving to three different stores, Mr. Scrap will spend that time waiting in the midst of this horde of people, their carts jockeying for position. Once he's in line, it feels spiritless to give up. To walk away after finding your items is like giving up on your bride because she's twenty minutes late to the altar.

So he waits, unable to avoid eavesdropping on family arguments, whining children, cell-phone conversations, Saturday-night aspirations, and product testimonials. Mr. Scrap checks each cart around him for a gun. There are batteries and bleach and fertilizer and jump ropes and all kinds of other potentially dangerous items. But he does not see a gun.

On the way home it is nearly five o'clock and Mr. Scrap drives fast around the curved forest roads that connect the interstate to his street. For a while, Mr. Scrap doesn't notice the one other car on the road; he's busy with the potato chips in his lap. But when he yields for a big, stubborn crow in the middle of the road and the sports car behind him comes up close—too close—he flinches, certain that impact is imminent. Gripping the wheel and holding his breath, he thinks of the delay of an accident, the tedium of exchanging paperwork, the trips to the body shop.

The crow flaps its heavy wings and caws angrily, skimming Mr. Scrap's windshield. The car behind has not touched him, but it appears to be in his backseat.

"Maniac," Mr. Scrap says, both to the crow and to the windshield in his rearview mirror. He throws both hands up in the air and hits the gas.

Then, beginning the ascent again, Mr. Scrap notices the car is riding his bumper. He edges close to the shoulder of the road, allowing plenty of space for the car to pass. But it won't leave his tail.

Is he being followed? Before he's even completed the thought, his palms begin to sweat. Is it the same make and model as the black sports car that Andy Rolondo burned rubber with in the parking garage? Mr. Scrap accelerates, his eyes glued to the rearview mirror.

The angle of the sun burning just above the horizon has cast his assailant in shadow. He cannot make out the face of the person driving. It's certainly a black car, though. He can tell that.

If he is being followed, he should not go home. Then again, Andy Rolondo may already know where Mr. Scrap lives. In fact, now he is sure that it was Andy Rolondo sitting outside his house last night, smoking. Still, he should not lead his pursuer into a confrontation he is not prepared for.

He could call 911.

"For Christ's sake," he says aloud, fumbling for his phone. A few more curves and he will be just a couple of blocks from home. Mr. Scrap flips open the phone, glancing down to find the numbers with his sweaty thumb. Just as he does so and pushes send, the black car comes around him on the left, passing with an alacrity that is almost more frightening than their near collision.

"This is a nine-one-one operator. What is your emergency?"

Mr. Scrap's heart is racing, his mind unclear about what danger he was in and if, in fact, it has gone.

"Uh, hello. Someone was following me. But I'm fine. He's gone now. Sorry for the call."

"Sir, what is your name and location?" She's adhering to protocol.

"No, I'm fine. No emergency. Thank you, though."

He hangs up and throws the phone into the seat beside him. Wiping one hand and then the other on his pant leg, he takes a deep breath.

What has happened, he is still not sure, but everything feels different, as though he has seen below the surface of the underwater world that deals the fisherman his fate. The bottom-skimming catfish, sifting through silt, combing the water grass just upstream, finds the swollen worm and bites hard, the sharp hook stinging its face and triggering the venomous proteins that flood into the catfish's pectoral fin, which will strike the weekend fisherman as he reels it in, sending him to the hospital, shamed and badly injured by a fish.

Mr. Scrap has seen a menace that he now cannot get out of his mind. To ignore the hovering black car and the reality it has introduced would bring certain disaster. He must adapt to this change.

As he pulls into the driveway, Mr. Scrap glances all around, looking now for peril in his neighborhood. Stealthily, he initiates the automatic garage door to close behind him before he's even turned off the ignition.

Inside, Betsy is standing in the kitchen, a barely awake glaze still covering her eyes.

"Cream?" she asks without looking up to confirm who it is coming into her house.

He watches her whisk together oil and vinegar for the salad dressing. Her knuckles are white with exertion.

"Right here," he says, placing the groceries on the counter next to her.

"And did they have the vacuum bags?" she asks, finally looking up.

"They have everything there." His voice in his ear sounds sunken, as though it is trapped in a cave. Has she heard him? "Absolutely everything," he says again, unbuttoning his shirt, watching her hands as she unloads the cream.

"Well, good. You've been initiated, then." She smiles at him, untroubled, her fresh coat of lipstick flawless.

Mr. Scrap shrugs. He cannot tell her what he knows. Her life has already fallen victim to conspiratorial forces that hid in the channels of her first husband's heart, his arteries narrowing each night as they slept side by side, in peaceful ignorance. Like the fisherman sitting by the river, unaware.

"Not too long in the shower," she says. "I need you for a

stubborn wick." She gestures to the buffet, where a trio of candles has been placed.

He nods, glancing out the window, checking the screen for signs of tampering.

As an afterthought, he asks, "You're feeling better?"

"Mmm. The medication worked today." She shrugs. "Who knows?"

"That's good." He pats her shoulder as he passes by, thinking only of protecting her from things that she cannot see. "What a relief."

❖

After Oliver sees Mrs. Wilcox and trades one album for another, he goes home and tries to work. But he gets through only a handful of scans before he is drawn back to his own photographs collected in the plain manila envelope. There are nearly a dozen and all of them are appropriately varied, he thinks.

Dressed in sneakers, gym shorts and a headband, he'd run around the block three times before he took the picture of himself standing outside the pharmacy downtown, perspiring and flushed as though he'd just played a game of racquetball. He chose the pharmacy simply because it looks just as it did twenty years ago. Same neon sign, same red brick, same bald pharmacist hunched over sleeping pills and penicillin.

For the one of him sitting in an armchair at the library, he'd placed a copy of the *New England Journal of Medicine* from 1975 in his lap. There were other journals Oliver remembers his father reading more frequently, but the library didn't have any archived. He is not looking at the camera, but somewhere off in the distance, his brow furrowed, as if trying to interpret something he's just read.

But there is one more photo Oliver wants. He packs up and returns to the street of his childhood. With this, the dossier will be complete and he will be able to present to Jared a glimpse of the life he missed out on. The father that was taken from both of them. The home that was taken from Jared. Maybe, just maybe, neither one of them will have to get over these losses. They can reclaim them instead.

An adult should be hardened by the things that happened on this street, not softened. This is what he's heard, anyway. From Mary, especially, who worries about his mind and his heart. She was the one who told him long ago that they would not get over it—they would only get through it. She took that glossy, pastel funeral-home-pamphlet aphorism literally, marking each day off on her calendar, anxious to pile more and more time into life's Past column, until she looked at the imaginary spreadsheet and decided that she'd done it. She had gotten through it. The end.

Oliver will not appear in this picture; his freshly shaven face is his own again. He is using a tripod, though, and is grateful to the dusk for the long and emotive shadows it creates. The house they used to live in, just next door to his mother's current house, is a single-story, pitched-roof structure, covered in wood siding that is painted a creamy yellow. The large circular driveway lined with groomed evergreen bushes gently slopes into the street.

The current residents are not friendly to Oliver. He long ago wore out his welcome when they found him, over and over, sitting in their backyard, perched up in the crabapple tree, walking in through the open screen door, standing in the kitchen, looking at the linoleum where it had all come to an end. These people, Mr. and Mrs. Wagner, had at first been sympathetic and often walked him home across the lawn to his new house. Mr. Nice Guy was always waiting there, holding open his own screen door, the artificial coolness of the air conditioner reaching out into the night. The Wagners were young newlyweds who had so far been immune to life's iniquities.

But then Mrs. Wagner became pregnant. Suddenly aware of how badly they wanted things to go right for their own child in this perilous world, they let their sympathy wither. Oliver was bad luck, a token of sadness they no longer had room for in their house.

One day after school, he wandered into their nursery, the room that used to be his—the room where his father had last tucked him in—and stood above their newborn's cradle, drumming his grubby fingers on the edge of it. When Mrs. Wagner walked into the dim nursery with a pile of clean towels in her arms and saw a small figure leaning over the cradle like a pint-size kidnapper, she screamed. Her scream woke the baby and frightened Oliver, and as Mrs. Wagner caught her breath and whisked the baby from its cradle, Oliver hung his head.

She started to say something. She held the baby's head against her shoulder and rocked from side to side. "Oliver," she said, but he wasn't listening.

"We had a baby here, too," he said, almost too quiet for her to hear. "We never really made him a room. He slept wherever we were." Oliver noticed his shoelace was caked in mud, stiff in its bow. When did that happen? Was that mud from school? From the park? From his yard? Or this yard? Oliver's old yard. His real yard. "'Course babies don't need rooms. They're so little at first they can sleep just about anywhere. Portable adorables. That's what my dad called them." Oliver liked to talk about his dad. The funny things he used to say. Nobody seemed to want to listen, though.

Even Mrs. Wagner looked at him funny, her face all furrows. "Oliver," she continued, as though she hadn't heard him. "You cannot just walk in here." Her words were accentuated by the restraint in her voice, by the clear struggle she was having to maintain her composure.

Oliver looked up at her. The baby's little legs were pushed up under his tummy, his bare toes peeking out, pink and minuscule. "Okay," he said, obedient and afraid. Was she doing something to the baby that he shouldn't see? Was the baby sick? Was she worried about germs? Why couldn't he be here anymore?

Oliver knew that he would never hurt the baby, so he figured that she must not want Oliver in the house because it wasn't safe for Oliver. Or good for Oliver. Did she think, like his mother, that it wasn't useful for him to remember his dad? Or their house? Remember his room—the way it used to have a row of puffy stickers in the corner where his bed used to be, that he touched every night before falling asleep?

Or was she worried that Oliver might, through his remembering and revisiting, actually conjure his father or his baby brother? Mary had told him about ESP. Minds could be more powerful than distance. Could Oliver's remembering somehow conjure one

or both of them back here to the house with the long, straight hallway and the big brick fireplace? If Oliver's father returned, what
would be wrong with that? Why should that worry Mrs. Wagner
and give her big unhappy creases on her face?

He looked at the new curtains, the big blue clouds painted on
the ceiling. There were not clouds on the ceiling when it was his
room.

And then he understood.

Mr. and Mrs. Wagner would have to move. If Oliver could
bring back his father and his brother, then they would have to go.
Oliver's father, cradling Oliver's brother in his arms, could return
and say, as he sometimes did at the crowded Sunday pancake restaurant, "So sorry I left my place unattended. We had to make a pit
stop, but we were here—see the newspaper?"

Mr. and Mrs. Wagner would lose this house. They'd have to
move to another house, put their baby in another room and paint
the sky onto its ceiling.

"I mean," Mrs. Wagner went on, still controlling her anger,
"it's just not the way people behave. To walk into other people's
houses like that. If you were a grown-up, that would be criminal.
You could go to jail."

Oliver could hear the birds in the trees, scolding. He put one
foot on top of the other, stepping on his muddy shoelace.

"Oliver?" Mrs. Wagner said, now stroking the baby's bald head,
her voice a little looser.

"What?" Oliver said, wondering if there were really people
in jails who had walked into the house they used to live in, the
house that was just next door and still seemed a little bit like their

own. Did they wear striped suits and eat off of metal trays and live behind thick, black bars? Oliver didn't want to go to jail.

"I think it's a good lesson for you." Her eyebrows were raised as though she was surprised by her own effectiveness.

"Okay," he said, backing out of the room. Small clumps of mud from his shoelace shed onto the floor as he turned and walked out. He was never in that house again. Looking at the Wagners' now, Oliver wishes he had gone back there every day, snuck in the side door without anyone knowing.

The Wagners' baby boy grew to be a bully, pushing down a second-grade girl on the playground and knocking out her two new front teeth. They had to send him to fat camp and then had to drive five hundred miles in the middle of July to pick him up early because he had lit a counselor's sleeping bag on fire. As a teenager, the Wagner boy bought guppies from the pet store just to spread them across the deck of Oliver's old house in an orderly line, watching as the sun dried out their gills and shrunk their eyes into glossy black pebbles.

Now that he's found Jared, Oliver wants a photograph of the house they might have all grown up in together. He also wants a photograph of Mr. Nice Guy's house, where Jared could join them now for Sunday brunch or Christmas dinner.

He places his tripod up on the sidewalk across the street. He wants a wide view: Before and After.

As he sets up the shot, however, he is distracted by the lights that have come on in the After house. Through the large front window, he can see his mother standing with a wine glass, her head cocked to one side, her free hand on her hip, as though she is training a puppy and the wine is its reward for rolling over. She is listening to a woman, Shelly, whose last name has changed four times over the years. In the months after his father died, Shelly came over day after day and pulled Oliver onto her lap, her eyes welling up as she rocked him, saying, "You poor dear. Really, Betsy, your poor children." It made his mother uncomfortable, being pitied so openly.

Mr. Nice Guy saunters past his mother and Shelly, checking each of their glasses. There he is again, Oliver thinks, with his wine bottle and a little towel for the drips so that no one is ever thirsty or dribbled on or left alone.

Suddenly he fears it is only a matter of moments before somebody looks out and sees him with the camera. His mother will look away, pretend she doesn't notice, or if she does, pretend she doesn't know him. Mr. Nice Guy will wave and open the door, inviting him in, like he always does, averse to revealing how much Oliver riles him—how low their mutual opinion is.

To avoid being seen, he pulls up the hood of his sweatshirt and hurries to his place behind the tripod, finds the shot he wants through the lens and snaps it. The two houses, side by side.

In his rush he drops the lens cap. It lands on the curb right on its edge and begins to roll down the hill. He reaches a foot out but misses, then lunges a few paces to retrieve it. He ends up directly across from the cocktail party in Mr. Nice Guy's living room. The plate glass window is like a movie screen. Twirling the lens cap between his fingers, he thinks of Miranda. Could any of these people look like celebrities?

Certainly not his mother, unless she were some sitcom star

from the sixties, like Patty Duke or Sally Field. Her friend, Miss Shelly, who's had a face-lift, could look like Farrah Fawcett or Suzanne Somers with the right lighting. But Mr. Nice Guy?

Oliver sits on the curb and studies him from under the cover of his hood. There is just no way that he can turn him into anybody worthy of screen time. Not even a criminal. Maybe, if it were dark and he were wearing a white sailor's uniform he could pass for the captain of the Love Boat. But in his dark trousers and sport coat, with his reading glasses propped on his forehead and a dishtowel hanging over his shoulder, Martin Scrap only looks like himself.

Just as Oliver begins to stand, Mr. Nice Guy notices his hooded figure. Oliver looks right into his eyes, but for the first time in memory, Mr. Nice Guy doesn't raise his eyebrows in faux delight; instead, his eyes narrow. He's frightened by what he's seen.

Oliver hunches over to maintain his disguise and runs back toward the car, out of sight. He throws the tripod in the back and hits the gas as soon as the engine starts. The Ranchero screeches up the street, backfiring once, like a gunshot.

7

Mary has perfected her ability to talk to strangers. People on air-planes are anxious to reveal their lives, to craft them into brief expositions, with dramatic plot points that usually entail a death, a divorce or an unbelievable coincidence. Really, on any given flight, there are at least three people with a screenplay in their briefcase or a novel in their head. Soon, the whole world will be on TV.

For whatever reason, Mary never tires of listening. Each anon-ymous misery is a tonic, a salve she applies to her overactive mind. She can fill an entire sleepless night replaying the tales of travelers she might never meet again.

In some kind of perverted Zen theory, the process of listening to countless personal sagas enables her to shed her own hang-ups, like so much dirty laundry, like dropping pieces of her clothing into a tub of water in order to watch them become saturated and sink. So that she is both naked and invulnerable.

As she sits in the hotel bar, listening to this latest passenger tell her his marital woes, she accepts it all.

With obvious distress Doug confesses that, really, he and his wife have been nothing more than roommates for over two years now. Whatever romantic spark brought them together has long been extinguished. Their marriage is a result of the pregnancy that began at the end of a bad date with too many drinks and very little conversation. But they had been young. Barely legal.

He smiles at Mary, his eyes a deep brown. His woes are not unique. But his demeanor is. He's way too handsome to be honest, she reminds herself. "You don't really want to hear this, do you?" he asks. "She's a great mom and I'm a decent enough father and we're raising pretty good kids. So," he says, taking another sip of wine, "we trudge on."

"Is she happy?" Mary asks, more curious than she's been in a long time.

He shrugs. "Would you be? The talk show hosts can sell it all they want, but there's no faking love. We've tried. She deserves better."

Mary is suspicious. She's trained herself to be.

"What she deserves," he says, his voice hushed, "is for some-one to sit next to her and feel . . ."

Mary's hands sweat against the outside of her glass as he pauses, his eyes unabashedly studying hers.

"This way. To feel like this one moment could be enough. Just this." His eyes finally look down at his own hands on the table.

Mary is caught off guard. Her head buzzes. She smiles at him. He's a married man in a hotel bar with a woman he's just met. That's a fact. Extenuating circumstances are subjective. His wife probably thinks that he adores her. She is probably expecting his nightly call any minute now, in which he will tell her he misses her. Tell her he can't wait to be home.

"Does any husband feel that way about his wife?" Mary asks, wondering why deceit is always sexy and fidelity banal.

"Or wife about her husband? You're right," he says, nodding. "It's a total gamble. But I do know a handful of people who won the house." He looks at her glass. "Want another?"

"No, thanks." Mary is slightly disoriented. There is no accounting for her jittery stomach.

"I'm sorry if I offended you. It must be an occupational hazard for you. Men losing their cool." But he hasn't lost his cool. Or his cool is suddenly amplified by his acknowledgment of its limitations.

He shows her the photos of his daughters that he keeps in his wallet; their thick hair is combed and sprayed neatly around their cherubic faces. The older one, as a mark of her formidable will, Mary assumes, wears a dime-store tiara.

To Mary, they are not memorable. Just two more faces among the hundreds she sees every day. But it's clear from the way he describes them, the way he smiles to himself as he glances at the picture before handing it to her, that he finds them remarkable. This trait is particularly desirable to her. A man who adores his children.

"You have kids?" he asks her, finishing his second glass of wine.

She smiles. "Just the ones that scream at me all day long asking for more soda."

He nods. "I never thought I wanted any. I mean, God, when they're not yours . . . cute for an instant, maybe."

"I'm sure yours are very sweet. They look sweet," she says, handing him back the photographs.

"They're like any others, probably. You spend most of the day thinking that you'd just like some time to yourself, that they're too whiny and you'd trade anything for some peace and quiet, and then, as soon as they're cuddling their teddy, swaddled in a blanket, peacefully sleeping, you want to wake them up and see them do that one-legged hop again that they were doing all over the house that day."

Mary laughs. He's too charming. Their conversation, which began on the plane and has yet to veer into the where're-you-from or where're-you-headed territory, is effortless. The times when she meets someone with whom everything seems so easy are rare, and for some reason with this guy it is as though she could tell him anything. As though she could count on him to matter. She's tempted to want him. Or at least to entertain the possibility of a singular love that could make the risk of losing it seem worthwhile.

Doug asks for their tab.

The band that has been sound-checking is finally ready to play. He moves his chair around, next to Mary's, so that he can see the trio. A singer, a guitar player and a bass player commence a set of jazz standards.

Mary slips off her shoes and puts her feet up on the chair across from her. There are only two other people in the place and they are sitting at the bar, nursing martinis.

"Dance with me," Doug says, putting his hand on Mary's chair, close to her arm. It is a friendly offering, not presumptuous or opportunistic.

"I just took my shoes off," she says.

"No better way to dance," he says, smiling, and slips out of his own expensive loafers, pushing them up against hers, so that the shoes are huddled there together under the table, like naughty children.

Mary lets herself be led to the dance floor. It has been years since she has danced with a stranger. He puts his arms around her waist and she smells the accumulated scents of his day. Hair gel, garlic, sweat, wine. The music is too loud to talk over. They keep their heads parallel, their eyes staring at opposite walls.

To be so close to him is thrilling. Against the syncopated rhythm, she feels the solid strength of his body beneath his clothes. She lets herself imagine how this could go.

They could spend a night together here, going upstairs, barefoot, embarking upon a series of couplings that would soon make each of them familiar to the other. No longer strangers, their faces would offer the kind of comfort provided by a person you've spent an entire dark night beside. A person who's watched you floss and brush, who's provided the last touch of the day and the first laugh of the next.

Suddenly, he would matter to her. Because his face would become a comfort, its absence would create the complementary melancholy. She would begin to wonder about his life outside their time together: phone numbers, birth dates, favorite foods, his list of charming anecdotes of previous attachments. Those children who did not matter to her would also begin to matter. She would no longer admire his dedication to them, but resent it. Like a betrayal. Then she'd hate herself. She'd be a cliché. Oliver would tell her it was the boob job that had clouded her judgment and led her down this road of regret like a gateway drug. There'd be the inevitable painful detangling from this man, this stranger, leaving her naked self ever more weary and uncertain of its worth.

As the couple from the bar enters the dance floor, Mary wonders if they are strangers to one another. Whether or not they are now, they once were. The bravery, Mary thinks to herself, of ever approaching a stranger and thinking that through time he might become your most trusted confidant is astounding. She is a coward unfit for romance.

"I've got an early flight," she says loudly into Doug's ear. "Thanks for the drink."

Mary walks away from him, relieved that his dismayed face is still a stranger's.

❖

Oliver is late now and nearly out of gas. He parks the Ranchero in his driveway, grabs his tripod and camera from the back so they won't be stolen and jogs the six blocks to Jefferson and Main, where he's supposed to meet Miranda. As he crests the hill, he is met with the strangest sight. Coming toward him, as though he has found the world's end and it is a gigantic mirror, there is a figure just like his, with a tripod over one shoulder and a camera slung across its torso.

He soon knows it is Miranda, and his heart beats with expectancy. They each see the humor in their unusual and identical appearance. She throws her head back, laughing, as she continues to walk toward him. Oliver watches her, his own laughter second-ary to his admiration. As they reach one another, his arms pull her into an embrace that neither of them expected. She wraps her free arm around him and they stand there, in the dark, in this hug that feels like a prematurely happy ending and which eventually makes them both laugh even harder.

"Wow," she says, pulling away only to look up at him, into his face. "You never greeted me like that at the Swedish bathhouse."

Oliver drops his arms to his sides. He shrugs, but the smile on his face is steadfast. "I've never been so happy to see you," he says.

"Well, I'd love to stand around and have a handsome man grin at me all night, but"—she looks at her watch—"if you're coming with me, we gotta move."

Oliver puts his hand to his head in a salute. "Aye-aye, Captain."

"This is not a boat," Miranda says, winking at him, "but I will take your allegiance."

She begins to ascend the slight hill toward the houses in the middle of the block.

Oliver follows, placing his hand on her tripod. "Can I carry this?" he asks.

Miranda looks at him. She hesitates for a moment, then hands it over. "Okay, so here's the deal: If you know a house that I stop in front of, know the people who live there, used to do their taxes, or whatever, just keep it to yourself."

"Are you, like, a PI or something?"

"You watched too much TV when you were a kid," she says, grinning. "I'm a photographer."

He smiles back.

"An art photographer—there, I said it. Artist. I still think art can change the world. Call me old-fashioned, right?"

"In the best of ways," Oliver says, staring unabashedly at her.

"Really? Okay. I have two things I'm working on right now. The one at Alfalfa's I'm calling *Who's a Star?* And with this one—I don't have a title yet—I anonymously photograph people in the privacy of their home, doing whatever it is they do at this time of night."

"Is that legal?"

She giggles. "That's not bad."

Oliver breathes on his fingernails, then polishes them on his sweatshirt, accepting the compliment and extending his hands toward her. "Artist, meet Muse."

She places her hand in his and he twirls her, clumsily. "How 'bout you? What are you working on?"

"A thing. Photographs."

She studies his face. "Obviously," she says, gesturing to his camera.

He shrugs.

"Okay. Tight-lipped artist. You'll show me soon enough."

"No, but really," he then says. "Is it legal? What you're doing?"

"You worried you might get arrested with me?" She nudges him with her elbow. "Dangerous is the new sexy, right?"

"There's another title for you," he says, nudging her back, lingering in his touch.

She raises her eyebrows and nods.

"I've gotten permission," she finally says. "I send them each a letter, explaining the project and asking if they'll agree to be photographed. If their lights are on, curtains open"—she points to a flat-roofed house up ahead with a light on in the front and its drapes pulled back—"then they've given their signal of compliance."

Oliver follows Miranda to a place on the sidewalk directly in front of the house. He unfolds her tripod for her and steps back.

She screws her camera onto the tripod and attaches a long lens. Before looking through the viewfinder, she eyes the lit window.

Her subjects are sitting across from one another. An old, hunched, shell of a man sunken into a wheelchair sits knee-to-knee with his caregiver. A young woman in cross-trainers and pale pink scrubs, with a rolling tray beside her, dips a spoon into what looks like a jar of baby food and offers it to her charge. Dutifully, he opens his mouth, accepting nourishment this way. There is a glass of water on the tray as well, with a straw bending, defeated, toward the man, who struggles to get it between his lips. The young woman holds the straw for him, angling it just so.

As he drinks, the old man looks out the front window. His eyes squint, searching the night for his date: the unknown photographer.

There she stands, watching him as he watches her, as Oliver watches all of it. Miranda snaps the shutter, capturing this searching glance full of expectancy. The gentleman not only wants his photo taken, but also wants his life examined, turned over, looked at and revived. The indignity of being fed baby food by an hourly worker does not seem just. He was not meant to get old; he should have been shot down half a dozen times during the Second World War. Out in a blaze of glory.

He lets the straw fall away from his lips.

Now, every day is filled with the fear that he will survive another. He is too weak at this point to end it himself, too alone to have someone else do it for him. End this, his face says to the window as he stares out into the darkness. Take this life and end it.

Then the spoon reappears, refilled. The nurse holds it in front of his mouth impatiently, even nudging a bit at his unresponsive lips. Obviously overpowered, he opens his mouth obediently, still gazing out the window.

Miranda's camera continues to work—open, shut, open, shut.

Then, quite suddenly, she replaces the lens cap, unscrews the camera and hangs it around her neck. Oliver steps forward to help her with the tripod. She allows him to fold and carry it, and they wordlessly climb the slight hill of the block. Her eyes are solemn. Oliver is in awe of the photos she must have taken.

"Did you know that he—"

"I never know anything before I go. I choose addresses from the phone book. That's all." Her voice is flat.

"That was just, I can't even . . ." He cuts himself off, resisting the impulse to clutter their experience with his thoughts.

She appreciates this gesture and takes his arm. Were it not for the digital technology around their necks and the parked cars scattered on each side of the street, they might be promenading through a distant century, their bodies in a traditional courtship.

It's several blocks to the next address on her schedule. Oliver never dreamed that he might find a girl who would be happy traipsing around in the dark, carrying a camera and tripod. He always thought that one day he'd simply compromise, accept a life of wandering aimlessly through the mall holding packages while the girl he'd decided to love amused herself. But now, all of a sudden, he feels as if a part of him has planned all of this. A part of him must have known that through the search for his brother, he would find something else worthwhile.

This is not luck, he tells himself as he looks at her walking beside him. This is the result of being true to yourself.

Slowly, she has slid her hand down Oliver's arm so that now it is folded through his own. The crickets are chirping loudly, emulating the beating of his heart.

"Here it is," she says, quietly, gesturing for him to place the tripod on a piece of sidewalk opposite another house with a front window lit brightly, its covering pulled back. It's a bedroom window, smaller and higher.

"I usually bring a ladder, but I loaned it to my neighbor to fix his swamp cooler," she says, then bites her bottom lip in contemplation.

After a moment of thought, Oliver links his fingers and offers them to Miranda. She beams, then places her foot in his hands, gratefully. He boosts her up into a tall ash tree just behind them, her camera still hanging across her body. She settles on a big low branch. Oliver then passes her tripod up to her and she stabilizes it with its legs straddling the branch she's sitting on. She looks through the viewfinder and then down at Oliver, imploringly.

He climbs effortlessly up to where she is. "What is it?" he whispers.

She gestures for him to look through the camera. The only things visible in the viewfinder are the countless, scalloped green oak leaves hanging from a branch. Oliver laughs. He climbs to a limb above the offending branch, and from there he lifts it so that its leaves disappear from her framing. She gives him the thumbs up.

Oliver lies on his stomach, holding the branch below him with two hands. This time, the person in the window is a young man lifting weights. He has brought the dumbbells to the window and he stands perpendicular to the window so that they can see his profile as he goes through the circuit of biceps curls, triceps lifts, overhead extensions, squats and lunges. His face is serious and committed.

Oliver grows tired of watching him. He rests his cheek on the branch and looks down the hill at the ample glow of downtown. As a boy he loved a chance to see this view at night—the neighborhoods surrounding his own lit up in little clusters of luminosity. He'd studied them, knowing that among those lights his lost brother might be found.

On the drive to one of those neighborhoods, his mother's voice had been shrill and loud from the front seat. "Please, just don't touch him. Heavens."

Oliver closes his eyes for a moment, still holding the tree branch, his arms tiring. The baby is crying—howling, really. His eyes are closed, his mouth open, his little pink gums nearly red with anger. The red and purple birthmark on the side of his face seems to throb with fury. He barely breathes in between each scream. Their grandmother christened him Brandon before she flew home, but Oliver and Mary call him Baby Bee. Short for Baby Boy.

Oliver and Mary have tried to amuse him—Mary holding his hands and moving them back and forth in a little dance while Oliver performs a ridiculous beat box and makes the little stuffed gray monkey hop frantically from side to side. Usually one of these tricks will distract him. But not today.

"It's not much farther," Mr. Nice Guy says, both hands on the wheel. "Does it say to take a right or left here?"

Oliver's mother wipes the tears away from her eyes and holds the directions close to her face. She yells in order to be heard over the baby's cries. "I can't see a goddamned thing, Martin. I just can't."

Mary looks at Oliver, her eyes wide. He can tell that she's afraid. Up until now, he'd thought that she had a plan; a way to get them out of this mess. Some formula by which they would drive home with their baby brother still between them and their mother, grateful, eventually, for their perseverance.

But at this moment, looking at Mary's eyes and unable to see his mother's, Oliver is terrified. Not just of giving away their baby. But at how easily the world can be dismantled. What if his mother died, too?

He doesn't want to be an orphan, driven somewhere in the backseat of Mr. Nice Guy's car late one evening like this and left.

The car comes to a sudden stop in front of a small house with a BEWARE OF DOG sign on the side gate. A woman is standing on the flagstone walkway leading up to the front door. She looks older than any mother Oliver knows and she is wearing long blue jeans with her plastic summer flip-flops.

His mother does not get out of the car. From her seated position she acknowledges the woman with a brave smile, but then she turns away, unable to watch the transaction.

Mary grabs the car seat, as well as one of the bags of clothes and diapers they have packed. She directs Oliver to bring the other one and she gets out of the car, the baby still howling. Setting his car seat on the walkway, Mary quickly unbuckles him, anxious to soothe his hysteria. She picks him up, expertly cradling his head with her hand.

"His neck isn't very strong, yet," she says to the woman, just as they were told only weeks ago. "We brought clothes and diapers. And he hates that thing," she adds, kicking the car seat gently with her bare foot.

Oliver sets down the bag he's carried from the car and places the scrawny velvet monkey on top of it. Mr. Nice Guy, jiggling the keys in his pocket, reaches out his hand to the woman in jeans. The new mother.

"Glad to meet you," he says, though there have been no introductions.

"Same," she says, shaking his hand.

The baby has quieted now and is worn out from his struggle. His head rests against Mary's shoulder. Oliver strokes the back of his neck, its downy fuzz too short to hold on to.

They stand there together, siblings facing an uncertain future.

And then, the inevitable and the unthinkable: the woman slings the bag of clothes over her shoulder and reaches her arms out toward Mary and Oliver, toward their baby. They are just children themselves. The workings of the grown-up world baffle them.

There is a momentary, silent rebellion. Oliver rests his hand on the baby's head proprietarily.

"We waited all summer for him," Oliver says to the trio of

adults who've arranged this. The woman and Mr. Nice Guy nod, registering his complaint. His mother looks down at her lap. Mary kisses the baby on his tear-stained cheek, her lips lingering near his ear.

Dutifully, however, Mary relinquishes her hold. The woman accepts him without flourish. In order to manage all of her new assets, she arranges the baby back in his car seat and picks it up, swinging him at her side as he resumes his howling.

Mary holds Oliver's head in her lap as they drive home, their own tears quieter, and just as useless as the baby's had been.

Miranda has taken a dozen or so photographs and now she signals for Oliver to drop the branch. He lets it go, and the deep green leaves move easily back into place.

He climbs down to where Miranda sits, shuffling through the images on her camera of the boy and his weights.

She looks at Oliver and shrugs. "One more stop tonight."

"Ready and willing," Oliver says, flexing his subtle bicep.

"Are you for real?" Miranda asks him. Her glasses are askew from being pressed against the viewfinder.

Oliver straightens them, then rests his fingertips against her jawbone. He holds her face, like this, gently, wondering as he does so why it seems already like his own. He can feel each delicate corner of her mandible hidden beneath her smooth, sturdy skin; this is as sexy as anything he can remember.

He kisses her there in the tree, tentative and mindful of their precarious equilibrium. Then, eyes still closed, he holds his camera out to the side, capturing their first kiss from midair. The flash illuminates the tree for a moment and makes both Oliver and

Miranda smile. The scandalized murmurs of a few drowsy sparrows descend from somewhere above their heads.

"Damn paparazzi," Oliver says, still holding Miranda's face close to his.

"Nothing is sacred," she replies.

Oliver drops his hands from her face and rests them on her legs. "That picture is," he says. "It will be. To me."

She nods. "The beginning," she whispers.

"Of everything," he says.

They sit on the branch high above the ground a moment longer, their foreheads touching. Then Miranda hands Oliver her tripod and she makes her way down, her camera still swinging from her neck. Without any effort, they have become necessary to one another.

8

While Oliver printed his own photographs last night, Miranda went out again to work. This morning, before dawn, she let herself into Oliver's house and settled into bed beside him. He woke slowly as she flipped through the night's bounty on her camera.

"Look," she said, showing Oliver a woman, not much older than he, standing in an enormous glass window wearing a bikini, a terrified expression on her face. The water from the pool below is throwing silver waves across her bare skin.

"Did she not know you were coming?" Oliver asked, wondering why she'd look so afraid if she knew she was being photographed.

Miranda glanced at Oliver. "I don't know. The light was on. That's what I go by." She shrugged. "But . . ."

Oliver finished her thought. "She thought you were someone else. Not an artist, but a stalker."

"Shit," Miranda said, scrolling through the other photos, each as worrisome as the first. "If she's so afraid, why is she standing in the window in her bikini?"

"Trying to be brave," Oliver said, rubbing the sleep out of his eyes. "To stand you down."

Miranda set the camera aside and spread herself across Oliver's torso. "I don't know about you, but I'd never wear a bikini if I wanted to feel brave. More like a cape or something."

"Perfect," Oliver said into her neck. "I always had a thing for Wonder Woman."

They spent the rest of the morning in bed. Finally, the noise of their empty stomachs had to be addressed. Oliver told Miranda he would like to take her on a real date and she disappeared into the bathroom to tidy herself up.

Now they round the last wide curve to the expensive gourmet restaurant with the fried artichokes and raspberry pie. Oliver has the deposit from Mrs. Wilcox in his wallet and is ready to part with it. He is ready to celebrate. Not just Miranda, but the completion of his set of photographs, too.

Miranda holds his elbow as they walk together into the sedate, quiet dining room.

"Very lovely, Mr. *Fine-ly*," she says, smoothing her hands across the tablecloth.

"Just wait," he says, pointing to the bread basket between them.

"Ah-ha," she says, wrapping her fingers around an oven-warm roll.

"So," Oliver says, watching her pull apart the brown bread. "I'm finished. I printed last night. I'm ready to give it to Jared."

Miranda's eyes widen. "That's great. You finished. By the way, this bread is my new best friend. And since you introduced us, I'll ask that you not become jealous of our bond." She smiles at Oliver, her eyes full of good-natured mischief. "But," she continues, "why give the photographs to Jared?"

Oliver looks at her blankly. "That's why I did all of it. Pictures of my father so that he can know him a little. Start to understand."

"So that *he* can know him a little, or *you* can?"

"What do you mean?"

She shrugs. "I mean, the photos are about you, more than anything. Jared's problems are bigger than a missing set of portraiture."

Oliver stares at her as she chews.

"They're not a gift or a documentation or anything else. The photos you took are called something else, Oliver."

"Like what?" he says, stunned.

"Three letters. Begins with *A*, ends with *T*, rhymes with *fart*. Plain and simple. Your own personal vision of what's real. Or important."

Oliver shakes his head. He'd thought that he didn't have to explain this to her. He had believed that she understood. "No. I'm not like you. I don't have a reason to do anything unless it's about this."

Her face is placid. "Yeah?" She says. "Precisely."

"No. It's not about me." Oliver feels his heart racing.

"Why?"

"It's just not."

The bread basket sits between them, its contents cool now. Miranda chews what's left in her mouth.

"Hmm," she says, resting her chin in her hand. "So you really took those pictures just to show them to Jared. Just because you think he's your brother and you want him to . . ."

Oliver nods. "To see." He fixes his eyes on Miranda's. She does not look away. "To see," he says again.

"Okay," she says, also nodding. "But he could be *anybody*. There's no way to know that he's actually that baby. You know that. Yours is an impossible quest. Right? Is that the way you like them? Impossible to complete? World without end?"

From the forceful look in her eye, Oliver understands that it is a genuine question. A question she's willing to fight about. But he succumbs to his own frustration and looks away from her, rubbing his eyes. "Seriously? I thought you understood," he says, the quiet of the restaurant suddenly like a rapidly flowing river, its current rushing past his ears.

"I do. I do," she says, her eyes still bright, still searching his.

"But you're saying I should walk away from the kid I've been looking for all of my life. So, no, I don't think you understand."

"A kid who could be a famous rapper and you wouldn't even know the difference. That's the point."

"That's *your* point, Miranda. Not mine."

"So, what is your point, Oliver? To pass off your photos as souvenirs for a guy who probably won't even give a shit?"

Oliver feels his hands slide to his sides. "We are not doing the same thing, you and I. This is not an experimental concept. This is my *life*, Miranda. Not art. Finding my brother is what this is about. And I have. I've found him now. The photos are for him. The end."

Miranda leans closer to Oliver, her chest hitting the edge of the table. "Okay, Oliver. I get it. I get it," she says, flicking a crumb his way. But her eyes stare him down, not at all matching the conciliatory tone of her voice.

"What?"

"What?" she says back, her hands now folded on the table.

"You don't think he's my brother. You think I'm wrong about everything."

She shakes her head. "No. Not everything. I think the world is bigger than you'd like it to be. I think you're living small in a very big world."

Oliver looks away from her. "What the fuck is that supposed to mean? Geez. He *is* my brother. I'll prove it to you and everyone."

Miranda shrugs, glancing down at her own lap.

Everything is spinning. Oliver is overcome by the dreadful sense that Miranda is just an ordinary girl who is happy to eat bread while telling him everything about him is wrong. Though he hates to be a cliché, he cannot stop himself. "I'm done," he says as he puts his napkin on the table and walks away from her.

He gets in the Ranchero alone and drives back into town, trying to outrun the sense of dread and regret that are following him.

❖

Why did I always feel that I belonged elsewhere? *Because you did.*

Why have I always felt abandoned? *Because you were. Twice.*

Who is my real family? *We are. Me and Mary and Mom.*

Will anybody ever really know me? *I already do.*

Looking at the manila folder next to him, Oliver notices how innocent it appears, how commonplace it is on the seat beside him. He will walk into Alfalfa's just another guy, a stranger, and walk out with a brother.

That is the plan.

❖

Jared steps outside and lights a cigarette. There is a brilliant pink ripple in the western sky. Oliver wants a photograph of this, too—the sun setting, his brother's silhouette walking through its color—but he leaves his camera in the car.

Oliver jogs a few steps until he falls in with Jared's slow, steady stride. "Hey," he says.

Jared inhales his cigarette and nods at Oliver, not bothered, it seems, by this sudden and unexplained company.

"My name is Oliver. Oliver Finley." As soon as he extends his hand, he realizes it's the wrong gesture. A handshake? What the hell is wrong with him?

Jared nods his head at him in acknowledgment.

Oliver drops his hand to his side. "I have some things I want to show you."

Jared takes another drag on his cigarette.

Oliver nods. "Okay. So this is just really awkward and you probably think I'm some crazy person, but . . ."

Jared just keeps walking, his pace unaffected by Oliver's voice.

"We're brothers." These are the words Oliver has wanted to say for twenty-one years.

Jared looks at him with one eyebrow raised.

"I know it may seem odd, out of the blue and all of that, but it's not, really. I've known for a while—actually, forever. I've known about you forever. And, then, once I found you, I just wanted to do all this." He holds up the folder. "This is for you to see, to understand something about him. About us . . ."

"What. The. Fuck." Jared has stopped walking. His voice is low and calm.

"Yeah, I know. But it's true. I'm for real."

"Who the hell are you? Do I need a lawyer?"

"No, no. Shit. If you do, I do, too." Oliver laughs nervously.

Jared does not.

"Seriously. It's nothing like that. Look, I know there's no subtlety in this, in the way this is happening, but that would be a waste of your time."

Jared's expression is like a reader who knows exactly what's going to happen next because he's skimmed through this part before.

"So, I'm pretty sure that we adopted you. Briefly. My family. We had the stuff—the bottles and diapers and some clothes—and we were waiting for you and thinking of names. The whole thing. And then my dad died. He just up and had a freakin' heart attack. You came anyway. And Mom couldn't cope. So we gave you back. Or passed you on to the next family in line. Like giving somebody cuts. You, go ahead, take him, we're waiting for our life to return to normal."

"What do you need? A buck or something?" Jared begins to dig into his front pockets. "Helluva story for some spare change, dude."

Oliver shakes his head. "No. I don't need any money. For Christ's sake, I'm telling you the truth."

Jared flings his cigarette butt past Oliver's shoulder. The two of them stand there, facing each other like two pawns on a chess board.

"And I'm going to inherit a million bucks, right?" Jared's smile is weary. "You don't have to be on TV to get punk'd. The whole punk'd thing came way before TV."

"I am so not messing with you. Here." Oliver hands Jared the folder. "Look at these photos. This was my father, the way I remember him. The way he was when he signed up to raise you."

Rolling his eyes, Jared takes the folder from Oliver. "Is Miranda in on this with you? Is this a part of her 'art' or something?" He bends his index and middle finger on one hand into quotation marks.

Oliver shakes his head. The mention of her name has made his throat swell, his stomach drop. "Miranda has nothing to do with this. Nothing. It's just about you and me."

Jared raises his eyebrows. "Oh," he says, dubiously. "Really? You sure you're not looking for my celebrity self?"

"This is *not* an art project. This is life. Real life. I did not make this up." He cannot keep his voice from shaking with emotion.

"Hey, relax. I get it. You think I'm somebody. That's cool. Whatever." Jared is accustomed to assuaging troubled loiterers at the grocery. He knows what it means to live entirely in your own head. He opens the folder and starts looking through the photos.

Soon, his gaze has become less dutiful and more genuine. Oliver can tell that something about the photos has captured him. It can't be recognition, obviously, but maybe some kind of nostalgia for a father who looked that way. A father with deep set eyes, a high forehead and a big red beard. Hands that were warm and certain, hugs that smelled of soap. A father whose promise of a bedtime story was always kept.

"Dude, this looks like *you*," Jared says, finally, looking from the photograph to Oliver and back again.

Oliver shrugs, ignoring the shiver that is spreading down his arms. "Yeah. We look a lot alike, I guess."

Jared closes the folder. "Okay. So, what now?" He takes a deep breath and hands the folder back to Oliver. "I'm going home. Do you have someplace to go?"

"You think I'm crazy?" Oliver asks, terrified.

Jared shrugs. "No more than anyone else, man."

"What can I do to prove this to you? Do you have parents around? You *were* adopted, weren't you? Could we talk to them, see if they remember us, me and my sister?"

"I'm not in touch with them, man. Haven't been for years. And I certainly don't need a dead father."

"But it's not just about him." And here Oliver stops. There is a long, heavy pause.

Jared looks at him, his eyebrows raised, waiting for him to finish his thought.

"We would be brothers, see? All my life, I've thought of you and about what might have been. I have a sister, Mary. She's great. My mom, too. We would have been a family. The four of us."

Jared's eyes narrow. "Why are you so sure I'm the guy?"

Oliver cannot help it; he does not even realize he is doing it:

his eyes move to Jared's birthmark. The stretch of purple that Oliver first noticed a month ago.

Jared puts his hand to his cheek. The birds in the tree above him startle at something and fly away noisily. "This? You think this makes me your guy?" He is losing his patience. "Yeah, well. Woulda, coulda, shoulda, right? No going back. Your baby with the ugly birthmark is gone, Oliver. I'm this guy now. Not anybody's little brother or an orphan or anything else. I'm on probation for shit that I did. And I'm trying to stay clean now. I'm just bagging groceries—that's it. I'm not looking for anything else. My day is done, and I'm going home. So, don't fuck with me because I'm really tired of people fucking with me." Jared clenches his jaw, steadying his emotion.

Oliver nods. There is the smell of freshly cut grass on the breeze. "I get it. I know this is way out there and I forget that you haven't been living with it—that you don't know how it all went down. But I . . ." Oliver hesitates for a moment. The mention of himself suddenly seems grotesque and petty. Was this always just about him? Was Miranda right?

Of course. Yes, it *is* just that—grotesque and petty and all about him. Oliver realizes this in the awkward silence he's created. We each end with a fizzle of electricity as our heart ceases and the world is instantly finished and unfinished. Our own world ends and the whole world ends with us. But it also goes on, undeniably capable of continuing without us.

Oliver closes his eyes for a moment and sees the baby, asleep on his sister's lap. The bright red mark stretches across his jaw. They're sitting on the floor of Mary's room together, her bed unslept-in and unmade. Their mother and Mr. Nice Guy are in the kitchen, warming a bottle. Their tense voices carry down the hall.

Mary begins to hum, not a lullaby, but the song they've listened to on her cassette player all summer. Oliver chimes in and they sing together.

> *Young man, there's no need to feel down.*
> *I said, young man, pick yourself off the ground.*

They know the lyrics by heart, have been singing them for months. Their heads bounce along as they sing and stare at the baby's sleeping face. *Young man*, they sing together, over and over again. Oliver hears it in his head, even now.

He opens his eyes and finishes his thought. "I just want to know you. *He* wanted this," Oliver points at the folder to indicate his father. "And I wanted it, too."

Jared nods, his jaw still clenched. "Yeah, well, there's this other person in the equation, isn't there. Besides you and your dead father?"

Oliver shrugs. "Fair enough. Completely fair. You didn't ask for this, true. But it is an option. There's a house at the top of Hillcrest Drive that would have been your home. There's Mary, who's much more fluent with the concept of moving on than I am." Oliver puts on a grin that he's sure would have been charming to any other observer. "And then there's our mother—who's flawed in many ways but she adored our father and she makes birthday cakes and brunch and can sew just about anything. Ornaments, tablecloths, swimsuits."

Jared seems caught off guard by this last bit of information.

He looks once more at the folder in Oliver's hand. "I'm writing you off," Jared says, miming his signature in the air between them, "as a head job. A nut case. And I'd appreciate it if you'd stop sitting outside of Alfalfa's. You've shown me the pictures—I'm sure your dad was great—but now you need to leave me alone. Got it?"

He's speaking to him in a voice that is both tentative and aggressive, intimate and cold.

Oliver cannot move. This is the one moment he'd wished for and waited for across two decades and now it is ending. He can still smell the cut grass on the breeze as the darkness settles around them like a punishment.

If he'd let Jared be a stranger, just a guy with a birthmark that anyone couldn't help noticing, then they might, right now, be revealing a little of themselves to each other—the way people do who sit next to each other on the bus or on an airplane or in a doctor's waiting room—instead of using the kind of voice that people use who know each other too well.

Later, much later, he could have told him that they weren't just great friends. Or he could have left it at that. Great friends would have been enough. He could have shown him the album of his father as an aside. As a piece of fucking art.

Oliver nods. What else can he do?

This: he pushes the folder of pictures into Jared's hand. "Take it," he says. "Toss it or burn it or give it away. I don't want them anymore."

Jared cannot refuse. The human hand wants to reach out. "Your call," he says and turns away, placing the folder under his arm like a schoolboy.

A cricket begins to throb somewhere in the bushes. The birds are quiet, all nested down. Oliver cannot help himself. He hollers out, "We really wanted you. That's all. We really did want you."

Jared does not change his pace; he does not turn around. He gives no sign that he's heard, except that his head falls forward so that from where Oliver is standing, it appears as though the terrain has changed and now he must study the ground beneath his feet.

9

There aren't many streetlights on Hillcrest Drive. In the mid-August darkness, an old borrowed Pinto moves slowly up the road, its driver straining to identify the house. It takes two passes. In the distance, at the top of the hill, walking away from these houses, is a solitary figure in silhouette. A lop-sided, wingless creature in a skirt. She soon reaches the corner, turns and leaves the street empty.

Jared turns off the motor, which has been running loud since there's no muffler on the car. The windows are down and a breeze blows through, bringing with it the smells of leftovers and automated sprinklers.

He is impressed with the house, a sprawling yet reserved split-level without any ostentation. There is a shallow front porch and a wide deck that extends along the second floor; marigolds on the front steps, their deep orange hue illuminated beneath the porch light. This is the kind of house he and his adolescent friends would have egged.

He can see the unsung beauty of such normalcy now. Family dinners and carpools and games of freeze tag. Bedtimes and curfews and table manners. If this had been *his* home, the place where he grew up, then his souvenirs of childhood might be different. Instead of the addiction that clings to his jawbone and the bump on the bridge of his nose caused by one too many fistfights, he might have a shelf of swimming trophies, a framed college diploma and Sunday dinners here at this house on Hillcrest Drive.

It's far too late for dinner tonight, but through the big front window he can see a woman with her reading glasses perched on her nose and a glass of wine in one hand. She is standing so still, he almost wonders if she's real. Like a mannequin in a store window, she looks distant and resigned, as if she is posing for a portrait. But then she quickly turns, the answer to somebody's question. A man walks toward her and empties the last of the wine bottle into her glass. She smiles faintly and lets him walk away without speaking.

There is nothing particularly maternal about her. She is angular and controlled, all cheekbones and brow bones. She is just some woman, like any other woman whose groceries he bags. She is a stranger who doesn't mean anything to him.

This woman in the window who gave him up had merely passed him on, from her arms to someone else's. Like what people do standing around at a party. Here, now he's yours. You take him. Aww, cute. Here you go.

What he would like to know is why the woman who conceived him and carried him and bore him walked away. The typical refrain of any adopted child. But, why? But, how?

He doesn't blame the woman in the window for this any more than he blames anyone else. As he watches her, he can tell she's not entirely untroubled. Even in her big, wide house, even with her cold white wine and polished fingernails, there's something just beneath her skin and tight around her eyes that is pulling and tugging. Could *he* be what's troubling her? Does she wonder about what happened to him after she passed him on? Does she wish, maybe, that she hadn't?

Oliver didn't mention that anyone else was hoping to find him.

Jared lights a cigarette, hoping to burn out this melancholy brought on by ridiculous thoughts planted by some head case named Oliver Finley. Jared doesn't need a brother, and certainly not a brother whose ass you'd want to kick, whose earnestness would wear thin after about third grade.

A light turns on upstairs just as Jared takes the first drag. He checks the living room—the woman is still there, but she has sunk down onto the couch, where she sits, straight-backed and vacant. He can see a silhouette in the upstairs window and assumes it must be her husband. Oliver's stepfather. A man willing to take on another man's family. A man whose rival is long dead although his plaid pants, bushy beard and solemn eyes taunt them all. His youth is eternal, his death mythic.

Jared pulls hard on the cigarette. This is not his family. He tries to imagine himself as a five-year-old in a polo shirt on a shiny red tricycle with a three-speed already propped up in the garage, the expectation of success and growth a luxury this family can afford. But his DNA is not arranged for this kind of life, the kind spent meandering through the circular drive, eating Popsicles and egg salad. His muscles have always been strung tightly, prepared for struggle and deceit, cramped spaces and forced entries.

Even if he had grown up here with yearly vacations and summer camps, nightly stories and dutiful embraces, he would still be an addict. And maybe already dead. Because there would have been enough money to quicken his fate. The woman in the window and the man upstairs were right to pass him on. He would only have brought them more tragedy.

She's still sitting there, unaware of his presence. His would-be mother and her would-be son are separated by a patch of green grass. Jared wonders where the artists are now. Paint this picture. Snap this photo. Capture this moment.

He'd like to soothe her. He was not a terribly lovable child and she would have resented him, no doubt.

Jared could tell her this with confidence as the moths flicked in and out of the porch light. His words would matter to her. Her face would relax. Her grip would loosen on the wine glass.

Maybe then she'd tell him what she knows of his mother. The real one who couldn't bear to take him home, or who maybe didn't even have a home to take him to.

This conversation, though far-fetched, is motivation enough for Jared to get out of the car. He will walk onto her porch and ring the bell. When she opens the door, his birthmark will announce him to her.

❖

The Ranchero's headlights ignite the dark with dizzying beams of yellow. Boxwoods and pine trees burst into view and then recede quickly into darkness as Oliver passes them by. Stray soccer balls left for another day, trash cans waiting patiently for tomorrow's truck, even the occasional litter in the gutter shines in the lights momentarily, like lost treasure. The glint of a soda can, a cellophane wrapper. Each bush and ball and stray object is swallowed by darkness as his speed increases. There is the sensation that he is passing judgment, looking at the world under the bright headlights of an old car and then discarding it. He carries on this way, numbing his mind with the high-speed game of now-you-see-it, now-you-don't.

Soon, the road narrows and bends, indicating his ascent to the Wilds. The landscape changes as he climbs. Now the headlights reveal juniper bushes and agave cactus that stay lit as he passes; a world-renowned landscape architect has installed lamps to highlight their shapes and shadows. There are no sidewalks, no gutters, no litter. The lights of houses twinkle demurely above, like suspended clusters of stars.

For a moment Oliver thinks of his job—the digital clips on his computer that wait for him to impose on them the form and rhythm and music to invoke the sentimentality that Mrs. Wilcox desires. Though he cannot see it against the night sky, Oliver knows which peak is the one that took her daughter. He and his father had climbed it a couple of times, looking for lizards. Once, he even found a silver dollar on the top.

Along with many other unbelievable truths that summer, Oliver hadn't been able to fathom that such a dusty, rocky, empty place could have killed anyone. Had he and his father been in danger there, too? Or was Patty Wilcox just unwise? Oliver knew how girls could be—lugging things around, packing treasures into purses, backpacks and satchels. Mary always carried a book with her; a pen and paper; fairy dust in a crystal vial; a magnifying glass; three acorns; a flashlight; a red pencil; a mirror; and, carefully wrapped in toilet tissue, a cicada shell. These she would sometimes unload at the diner Sunday morning and line up on the table across from their father as he sipped his coffee and watched with a smile hidden behind his beard. Had Patty Wilcox lost her balance because of some object she was trying to collect?

As Oliver hangs his arm out the window and looks now at the place where he knows the mountain to be, he grimaces at the thought of her fall. Seventy-five, maybe a hundred and fifty feet, and at the bottom, only a scattering of boulders and gravel. Her body was brought to his father in a bag, which was then unzipped and gazed upon scientifically. Hers was the last human body his father would ever touch.

Oliver has this girl's final school photo in his house right now, scanned into his computer, smiling at him with the forced, inauthentic smile of picture day that renders every child robotic. It is his job to possess her in this way, to be concluded with an invoice he'll deliver once the video is done. It is also the face his father gazed upon in his own lab, doing his job. This girl is an unlikely bond between him and his father.

If Patty had survived that summer and Oliver had not, would his own name still come up for her? Would his death be folded into everyone's choppy memories of 1982? More likely, he'd just be forgotten. Perhaps Jared would have replaced him in the family photos, accepted as an adequate substitute. Perhaps nobody would wonder about what might have been.

That, after all, was Oliver's purview.

A series of steel and glass rectangles are lit from inside by thick white balloons of chandeliers. Like a punch line to a joke, the last frame in a comic strip, there is a child in a red cape screaming noiselessly behind the glass of one of these. He is red-faced and alone in the middle of a sparse living room. As Oliver maneuvers the Ranchero into a tight K turn in order to descend out of the Wilds, a woman appears and lifts the child, still screaming, onto her hip.

It is a woman Oliver recognizes but can't immediately place. The child fights her with the determination of three men, but will he even remember this moment of fierce struggle? Will he remember the tantrum or the cape or his mother's patience? Or will it be lost to his other, less banal childhood experiences, a memory kept only by his mother and never spoken of, because to do so would be to chagrin her son and boast of herself? Oliver watches the two of them, the tantrum's crescendo and depletion, the charity of the mother's hand on her tired child's head as he sobs into her blouse, smearing her, certainly, with tears.

As she gazes out the window, her figure swaying slightly, Oliver knows why her face is familiar. This morning feels like an eternity ago, but he remembers Miranda's smell as she climbed into bed—the scent of dew and asphalt spread across the sheets. This woman that Oliver watches now is the woman who was so afraid in the photographs Miranda had shown him. She thought she was being stalked.

Looking again at her face, he doesn't see any fear. She looks tired, maybe, but relieved and grateful for her son's surrender.

Oliver wonders what this woman would look like now through

Miranda's lens. Immediately, his loneliness is magnified, as though he himself is in a photograph and it is fading; he is watching himself disappear.

He drives slower, now, back down the hill. What will become of him now? He's thought of this day for as long as he can remember. Never did he think he would feel so foolish and so angry at himself. Never did he think that the despair he felt about this historic loss could be matched by the loss of a girl.

The moon is the thinnest of crescents tonight. Oliver studies it in his rearview mirror. He wonders if Jared has given their encounter a single thought or if he ever will. Miranda was right. Oliver has made his life into an art project without any medium. He is one big concept with zero expression.

A dog lazily crosses the road in front of the car, stopping right in the middle. Carelessly, the dog turns and looks into the bright headlights.

Jello.

Shit. He honks. The dog looks at him, then trots on across the street, his nose to the ground, searching for a fresh scent. Abandoning his own despondence for the moment, Oliver hangs his head out of the window, beckoning the dog with a whistle. Without any streetlights, the dog disappears into the darkness of the shoulder of the road. He could be anywhere. Oliver's whistle becomes more urgent. Nearly his entire upper body is hanging out of the car now, straining to see what he cannot.

He reaches the next curve just in time to see Miranda with a tripod on her shoulder. Wearing an apron-length black halter and jeans, with her hair down around her face and tortoiseshell glasses framing her eyes, she looks incredible. Her composure is visible on every inch of her.

Oliver hears her voice call out, "'Mere, boy. C'mon."

Right away, she winces from the headlights. Oliver stops the car in the middle of the road, its beams revealing the moths and gnats that hover in the thin night air.

Miranda puts her hand to her forehead, trying to block his beams. But Oliver cannot cut them, not yet. The sight of her, illuminated, has taken his breath away. She's smiling, a big, unabashed welcome. He feels an unmistakable surge of hope in his heart.

Her smile turns to a frown. She takes her free hand and swipes it across her throat, indicating her impatience with his lights in her eyes. Reluctantly, Oliver turns them off. She falls away into the darkness of the street.

Oliver is out of the car in a second, getting to her in three long strides. Jello is wagging his tail, standing in the soft sand on the side of the road. He barks twice as Oliver wraps his arms around Miranda.

He holds her there, in the middle of the street, trying to form an apology.

"I had the raspberry pie," she says before he speaks.

"Shit," Oliver says, mortified that he left her there alone. "I can't believe I did that. You must hate me."

"I have not excelled at interpersonal relationships. For whatever reason." She stands on her toes and whispers in his ear, "I'm a freak." Then, in a normal voice, she goes on. "But that doesn't keep me from thinking I'm an expert on certain human fundamentals. I still maintain that you're bigger than you think. You're trying to live on this small patch of the past. It won't sustain you. You can drive off forever, but there is no road to way back when."

Oliver looks at her face. It is open to him in a way he cannot remember anyone ever being open. He bends down and plucks a dandelion from the side of the road, presenting it to her with his head bowed.

As though written in some cosmic script of a video made by the universe, Miranda takes the bright yellow dandelion from its stem and smears it on the tip of her nose, painting the skin yellow. Then she twirls the short blossom between her palms and uses it again to mark her cheeks, her forehead and her chin.

She paints her face with the pigment of the dandelion, and in his mind Oliver sees a golden bloom emerge from her mouth.

"I want to show you something," he says.

She nods. "Sure."

They drive the short way to his house and Oliver fires up his hard drive. Miranda stands behind him, watching the monitor, waiting. Oliver shows her his videos. His director's cuts. The one with Nonny first. Miranda watches intensely, as awed as he by the footage, taken decades and miles away. When it's over, she simply says, "More." Dutifully, Oliver plays her another and she has the same response. "More."

So he plays another and another until she's seen everything. She stands the whole time, captivated by Oliver's strange blend of sight, sound and text.

When the monitor finally returns to blue, Miranda looks at him. The buzz from all of the electricity in the room—the multiple monitors, hard drives, CD burner—seems for a moment to crescendo, like crickets after dark. It speaks for them, replacing their thoughts and their words with a single innocuous hum. These machines, with their own collective history so young and their own progress so tremendous, seem to be advocating for an optimism that would seem foolish to a nonmachine. Their forefathers were simple pulleys and levers not more than two hundred years ago. Look at them now! They can digitize life, separate people's heads from their bodies and reconstruct reality. Lovers in Lisbon and Calcutta can exchange messages and locate a cobbler's shop on a street in Tokyo. Technology keeps improving. It can reveal the deformities inside a person's heart. Death means nothing to a machine.

As the machines in Oliver's office keep on talking, buzzing their endless arrangements of ones and zeroes, creating connections, deciphering codes, making meaning, Oliver and Miranda stare at each other.

"Unbelievable," she finally says, her mouth bending into a strange, brilliant smile. "Everything I said to you, you already know. Why didn't you tell me?" She forms a fist with her hand and slugs him in the shoulder, still smiling. "Why didn't you show me? Oliver, *this* is your real work."

Oliver shrugs as the video screen throws an azure glow onto her face. She seems, for a moment, like an oracle, speaking to him from some other world. She has turned what he'd thought was obvious and unremarkable about his life into a revelation.

She places her hand on his shoulder. He is shivering.

"Here's the thing," he says, trying to modulate his voice. "Nobody wants to talk about it. My mom, my sister, they both just seem to want to forget. Or pretend to forget. Case closed. No revisiting allowed. I want to visit, Miranda. I'm terrified of forgetting. And I just thought that if there was a minuscule chance that Jared didn't want to be forgotten, that he was wondering about what might have been, I had to try. I had to."

She nods. "I get that."

Oliver chuckles bitterly. "He doesn't. He'd really like for me to forget him. Really."

Miranda slides her hand down from his shoulder to his wrist. "Sometimes we find people in front of the grocery store that are just strangers living next to us on the planet," she says, wrapping her other hand around his other wrist so that she's holding the weight of both of his arms. "And sometimes, in front of the grocery store, we do find our family."

❖

Betsy glances at the clock. It is already 10:30, but she lingers in the window, reluctant to believe her brief artistic interlude is over.

They had arrived home from their Monday evening dance class just in time. She covertly perfected her makeup in the hallway and wondered if this is what it might be like to ready oneself for an affair. Imagining, as you apply your lipstick and rouge, another's eyes upon you. There wasn't time to change clothes so she turned on the lights in the living room, still wearing her pale blue dance costume, and, catching her breath, she sat on the edge of the sofa. On the other side of the house, in their den with its wood paneling and big-screen TV, Martin had retired.

Crossing her legs at the ankle, she fixed her gaze on the front drive. She placed her palms in her lap and tried to imagine that it was any other night. That she was not being watched, photographed. What might she do, sitting here? She scanned the couch for her sewing bag. Not finding it, and afraid to leave the room lest she miss her appointment, she sat still. Betsy kept her eyes on the yard, allowing her mind to drift to the evening's West Coast Swing lesson. She could still hear the last song in her head. A slower, more soulful dance, to which Martin had had a hard time finding the beat. But Betsy loved it. Still sitting on the sofa, she let her feet rehearse the sugar push, the sultry horn blowing somewhere in the back of her mind. She stood to practice the basket whip and the two-hand-tuck turn, losing herself in the footwork, with her arms held out to an imaginary partner.

Now she is still standing in the middle of the room as though placed there and told not to move. She's sure that her brief encounter with some stranger's camera is over and she was caught dancing by herself. There was not anything true about how she must have appeared, like some lonely heart, not a woman whose husband is just in the other room, his own dance shoes kicked off next to his recliner. Nothing revealed except that she cannot sit still very well.

"Argh," she says, stomping her foot in frustration. But she continues to stand there, looking out at the dark night expectantly, still awakened to the possibility of being watched. She wonders if M.K. might still be out there.

"Honey?" Mr. Scrap says. He has brought her the last of their dinner wine. She looks at him, startled a little, then smiles as she holds out her glass for him to fill.

"Didn't mean to scare you," he says, trying to make eye contact. "You look stopped in your tracks. Did you hear something out front?"

Her forehead furrows a little. "Mmm," she says, a vague affirmative gesture. But for the inertia of her lips, she might move them to offer an explanation, an excuse for her distraction. A chipmunk, maybe, on the lid of their trash can again. Two birds tussling for a perch. The neighbors' dog splaying his front legs on the fence, hoping for a clearer view of the night. These are the kinds of sounds she might have heard, the disturbances that might make her stare out the window so intently. The innocent sounds of the world after dark.

But she doesn't clarify and he doesn't ask again. She knows he would chastise her if she told him what she'd done. He would turn out the light immediately and tell her that some pervert had invaded her privacy. She'd hoped he would go away and leave her to turn out the lights this evening, but he looks out the front window, nervous and accusatory.

"There's nobody out there," Betsy says, quickly, afraid of his judgment.

"Yes, there is," he says, pointing to the curb. A beat-up, unfamiliar car is parked right in front of their house.

He's up the stairs in a heartbeat, focusing on keeping his hands steady, wondering if he will be able to load the thing in time. It's wrapped in a pillowcase on the floor of his closet, beneath the row of dark brown hangers that sway with their gabardine loads. It tumbles out on the carpet in front of him. He's on his knees, fumbling with the barrel, trying to remember the instructions he'd received from the portly gray-haired man behind the counter at the discount store. A day after he'd gone for the vacuum bags and cream, he'd found himself in the same store again, standing over the glass case, his fingertips adding their own unique prints to the smudging.

He'd spent another sleepless night certain of noises in his yard, malicious intent swimming somewhere just out of sight. He was tired and frantic. "I'd like to see about something for self-defense," he'd said to the clerk, who looked at him skeptically from behind big, square glasses.

In response, the clerk had slowly pulled the keys from his pocket. He opened the case and placed two choices on the counter.

"Both for self-defense. Just depends on how many holes you wanna make," he said, looking away from Mr. Scrap, as though his real customers were elsewhere—the big-bearded guy looking at tackle or the young skinhead unzipping a tent. Men who didn't need instruction in loading a firearm.

Now, in the dim light of the closet, Mr. Scrap remembers the ease with which that clerk slid the bullets into place. One, two, three, four, five. With as much assurance as Mr. Scrap operates his dictation device at the office. Record, pause, reverse, play. He could do it in his sleep. Or blindfolded. Or in this goddamned dark closet.

He should have kept the thing loaded. To hell with caution. There were no young children around—knowing Oliver and Mary, there probably never would be. Nobody in his house would mistake this for a toy or fire it without understanding what damage it could cause.

Just keep the thing loaded, damn it, he thinks, as another tiny bullet slips through his fingers, falling into the dense fibers of the carpet. He fumbles after it, wiping his sweating palms across the shag.

Finally, when he's placed all five bullets—always fully loaded, the clerk had told him, never leave a chamber empty—Mr. Scrap begins toward the stairs.

But a car door slams from his own front yard. Downstairs, Betsy has heard it also. She's looking now, her footsteps edging closer to the window—he can sense this—completely unaware that she should not reveal herself. Completely unaware that she is in danger. There is a restraining order filed this morning at the courthouse with both of their names on it. Andy Rolondo's threat in the parking garage. The black car behind him on the way home from the big-box store. The smell of cigarette smoke so clearly coming from his own backyard. There was enough evidence to persuade the judge.

But Mr. Scrap knows that a man like Andy Rolondo would not be dissuaded by a document. He operates in a different world. Too often, Mr. Scrap has seen in his own practice how useless a restraining order can be: like pasting up the rules on a toddler's wall. Somebody has to be willing to dole out the consequences.

Mr. Scrap abandons the stairs and instead goes out onto the deck. He has a full view of the yard and street. A man has just stepped around the front of the car—a dark car. The same car? He looks for Andy Rolondo's face—his close-cropped hair, mustache and goatee, wraparound sunglasses. Hard to tell.

Mr. Scrap places his hand around the gun tightly. His index finger flutters over the trigger as a cigarette is flicked into his yard.

"There is a restraining order against you," Mr. Scrap yells, in a voice that narrowly escapes sounding panicked.

The man looks up in the direction of the deck. He puts his hands up, in surrender.

"Geez, isn't that a little paranoid," he says, his own voice strong, familiar with open-air confrontation.

Mr. Scrap is hidden, but the man is vaguely illuminated by the streetlight. It is not Andy Rolondo. It is some kid, a nondescript hoodlum.

Very smart. Of course. A man with money can hire anybody to do anything.

The screen door opens below him, its squeak like the call of a forlorn child. "Martin?" Betsy shouts from the front door. "What's going on?"

"Everything is under control, Betsy. Just go inside and close the door." Mr. Scrap's index finger has become more settled on the trigger.

The kid still has his hands in the air, though it is a halfhearted gesture. He is not afraid.

"Are you all right? Why does this boy have his hands in the air? Martin?"

Damn it. "I'll explain later. Please, just go inside." Why is she questioning him? Why isn't she afraid?

The kid steps forward now, looking up in the direction of Mr. Scrap's voice. "Why are you doing this? You seriously got a restraining order so I couldn't see her? That's outrageous, man."

"Stop talking," Mr. Scrap says in his courtroom voice. "Please." His arms should be tired from holding the gun this long, his biceps unaccustomed to the position. The adrenaline has made him strong. "Why do you want to see my wife? What business do you have here?"

Betsy has not gone back inside. This he can tell. She can certainly decipher the fear in his voice. His authority is compromised by her witness. If she would only do what he's asked her to do.

"It's okay, Martin," she says, scornfully, as though she is more capable of handling this situation than he is.

"I only had a couple of questions, man. Do you have a gun pointed at me, or what? What's going down here? Give me the score."

"There's no gun," Betsy says, her voice calm, soothing, as though she were trying to lure a stray animal.

What does she know about danger? About real trouble? "Right, Martin?" she says again. "There's no gun."

The kid lowers his voice. He speaks directly to Betsy. "Are you okay, lady? Has he hurt you?"

"There is a gun." Mr. Scrap's voice echoes from above them. "And it's pointed right at you, mister. So turn around and get back in your car. Get off my property, you goddamned loser, or it will end right here."

"Martin!" Betsy calls, stepping off of the porch, toward the visitor, terror in her voice. She looks up through the treetops, her hands on her hips. She searches for her husband's eyes, but he does not look away from his target.

The kid's got one hand behind him in his back pocket, and he's moving toward Betsy. But Mr. Scrap is able to keep him in his aim.

"Stop," he warns, but the kid keeps walking across the stone pavers that cut through the grass.

Why isn't anyone listening to him?

"My God, is that really a gun?" Her voice is accusatory. She doesn't think he knows what he's doing.

The kid won't put his fucking hands in the air. And he won't retreat. His face is becoming clearer in the light from the porch. There is something brutal about it, something threatening. As though he's already bleeding.

Mr. Scrap reacts, then, pulling back hard on the trigger and closing his eyes with just as much force. *Take that*, he thinks, as the explosion ripples through him. *Listen to this.* And then, because the noise of the blast and Betsy's scream scare him, he pulls again, without ever opening his eyes, without ever seeing Betsy run toward the boy, to his rescue. But when Mr. Scrap does open his eyes, Betsy is crouched on the grass below. The boy's head is in her lap; that bloody spot on his face is now cradled in her arms.

❖

The exterior of the house is washed in a red, pulsing glow. It could be an overzealous holiday light show or a disco. But it's not. Three ambulances, five police cars and a fire truck all responded to the 911 call. Their vehicles line the street, their drivers standing in huddles of authority across the lush stretch of grass in front of number 315. Three paramedics move the victim from the place on the ground where he's lain since they got there.

"Ma'am," the paramedic asks one more time, "is this your son?"

Her dress has a small spot of blood that is still damp and clings to her body.

"Will he be okay?" she responds. "Why is his leg doing that?" She points to his foot, which is twitching inside his canvas high-top. The boy had been holding a photograph of Paul, a photograph of her late husband that she's never seen before. It is in the grass now, staring up at her. She doesn't understand.

"They'll be able to tell you more at the ER. Is there someone who can drive you?"

She does not answer his question.

Instead, out of the huddles of unfamiliar faces, Oliver emerges. The sight of him causes her fragile composure to crack.

"Mom? What's happened?" he asks as he pulls her to him. "Are you okay?"

"Oliver," she says, unable to say anything else. "Oliver."

Then Oliver, too, sees the photograph on the ground. The picture of himself sitting by the side of the pool. Amidst a rush of dismay and denial, the recklessness of his own endeavor becomes clear. "What's happened? Mom? Who got hurt?"

He turns to Miranda, who is standing nearby, her camera hanging unused around her neck.

"That's one of my photos, Miranda. One of the ones I gave Jared."

Miranda places a hand on his elbow, then moves toward the photograph, bending to pick it up. She is stopped, however, by a policeman who tells her it's part of a crime scene.

"Crime scene?" She is incredulous.

"There has been a shooting, ma'am," he says, motioning for

her to step back. Miranda does so, falling into place next to Oliver, who is still holding his mother, her face now buried in his chest.

"Where's Martin, Mom?" Oliver asks, looking around for Mr. Nice Guy.

She doesn't lift her head but points in the direction of the front porch. There he sits, his head in his hands, flanked by two uniformed men.

One set of flashing lights recedes down the driveway as the ambulance with Jared inside pulls out into the street and launches its siren.

"Is Jared all right? Mom, is he going to be all right?" Oliver raises his voice over the blare.

"Who?" Betsy asks, finally pulling her head away from his chest.

"The kid. In that ambulance. That's him, Mom. That's *him*." Oliver stiffens.

"I didn't know what to do." She looks down the street and watches the ambulance until it has turned north, toward the hospital. "He had blood coming out of his mouth." She goes on, touching her lips. "And from his ear, too. Blood came out of his ear." She begins to cry again.

"I've got to go. To see how he is, Mom. Can I take your car? I'll be back. I'll come back in a while." His mother nods and wraps her arms around her own body. She's shivering.

Miranda volunteers to stay.

"Yeah," Oliver says, putting his arm on hers, "would you?" He kisses them both briefly before running up the driveway to the garage.

Miranda gently puts her hand on Oliver's mother's back.

"Mrs. Scrap," Miranda says, "you should sit down." Miranda

knows that she is not a Finley anymore. Oliver told her that his mom took Mr. Scrap's name, while Oliver and Mary kept Finley. Another confusion in Oliver's young life: invitations addressed to Oliver Scrap; friends ringing the doorbell of the house next door, forgetting, momentarily, about the move; big blue gift boxes arriving for Baby Finley before news of his departure had spread.

Mrs. Scrap is wearing the same pale blue dress she'd worn earlier this evening. Miranda had seen it through the window when the street was quiet and the night felt almost over. She had seen it through her lens as it swayed in a silent rhythm. They were photographs that Miranda instantly loved. The kind of pictures that some might call melancholy, but Miranda would call hopeful.

She had not seen any resemblance to Oliver and she had certainly not imagined that just a few hours later she would be holding the solitary dancing figure here in the driveway, the pastel dress spotted with blood.

Still shaking, Mrs. Scrap looks only momentarily at the camera slung across Miranda's body before she says, "I didn't know he had a girlfriend."

Miranda smiles and sets her glasses more firmly upon her nose. She wraps her arm completely around Mrs. Scrap, in an effort to stop the shivering. "Well," she says, "that could be awkward. But here I am. Girlfriend meets mother."

For a moment, Mrs. Scrap resists her grasp. But then, as an officer approaches to interview her about the night's events, she allows herself to lean into Miranda. When it becomes clear that Mr. Scrap will have to accompany the officers downtown, Miranda walks Mrs. Scrap into the house and through the living room that is already familiar to her. She offers to make tea or coffee, but Mrs. Scrap wants only a bath.

Miranda sits outside the bathroom door, listening to the dull rush of water. She wonders about what she cannot see. Is Mrs. Scrap crying? Is the tub overflowing? Is she soaking her dress in the sink? Finally, the water stops and there is no sound but the occasional drip and ripple of water.

"Mrs. Scrap? Everything okay?" Miranda asks from her cross-legged position on the floor.

"Betsy, please. I'm fine. I think." Her voice is calm but weary.

"Do you need anything?"

After a long pause, Mrs. Scrap says, "Are you the one?"

Miranda understands what it is she's asking. She doesn't want to have this conversation; she loves the photographs and knows that they will become something else if they talk about it. She sighs. The photographs have already changed; this woman is no longer a stranger and can never again be a stranger. Then Miranda says, "I take photographs, if that's what you mean."

"How did you find me?"

"Just the same as everyone. Like I said in the letter. Completely random."

There is no sound from the other side of the door. Miranda listens carefully, closing her eyes to imagine life on the other side.

"Betsy?" she says, finally.

Mrs. Scrap is crying now. "It wasn't for the boy, then?" she asks, her voice a thin wail.

Miranda shakes her head. "No," she says, her forehead leaning against the door. "It wasn't for him at all. Not at all."

"He had a photograph," she says, crying in earnest now. "Of Paul. And I thought that you . . ."

"I didn't," she says. "I didn't know who you were. At all."

"You're really just some girl, taking pictures of strangers?" she asks. A drop from the faucet lands in the bath with a hollow plop.

Miranda covers her mouth. She feels terribly alone sitting here on the floor, imagining the water and drips and the tears on the other side of the door that she can only hear. Her entire body is aware of the magnitude of this night. The moment the bullet traveled through skin and blood and bone changed everything forever and all of them now are bound by the night and its consequences. Her own ambition, her own certainty about closing the gap between people, seems small and foolish and utterly quaint.

"I'm just here," Miranda says, quietly answering Mrs. Scrap's question through her own tears. "I'm here if you need anything."

❖

On the way to the hospital, Oliver turns over in his mind what could have happened. Certainly his mother doesn't have a gun in the house. Did Jared bring a gun? Was he looking for revenge? Or did he stage a suicide there in the front yard? Did his mother and Mr. Nice Guy intervene?

In the emergency room, where he expects to find a flurry of activity and chaos, there is only the overfull waiting room and a surly triage nurse sitting behind Plexiglas.

"My brother was brought in an ambulance, just a few minutes ago with a gunshot wound. Where is he?"

She looks at him with glassy, tired eyes. "A nurse will be out to update you as soon as he's stabilized. And the officers will want to speak with you, too. Just have a seat."

But there is not one. Every chair is full. Oliver looks around at the bandaged wounds, pajamaed children and swollen eyes. Could this possibly be the place one comes for emergency, lifesaving care? It looks, instead, like a group of people who've given up on feeling better. They stare at the mute TV, which plays the headline news with subtitles. Images of a war still being waged, a people far away, who've lost their electricity and their government.

Oliver paces, unaware that he is triggering the automatic doors to open and close, open and close, until a security guard asks him not to linger in the entrance. He settles himself on the floor next to a young girl with a bandaged toe.

"I've been here since eleven o'clock this morning. My boyfriend ran over my toe with his scooter," she says to him, not looking away from the TV.

Oliver nods. "Ouch, must've hurt."

"Still does," she says.

He sits among them, envious, as they all are, of whomever's name is eventually called.

Finally, it is Oliver who stands and follows a nurse in green scrubs to just behind the triage doors.

"You're related to Jared Trizel?" she asks, looking at her clipboard.

Oliver nods. "His brother," he says.

"Okay," she says, still looking at the clipboard, as though her words are written there. "Well, he's going to be admitted to Neuro ICU. That's upstairs in the new part of the hospital. Fifth floor. It'll be a while before we get the paperwork processed to transfer him. The police may want to limit access there as well. You should go get a coffee or something."

"Is he okay?"

She looks up from her clipboard, right at Oliver's face. "He's been shot in the head. Never a good thing." She shrugs. "They'll be able to tell you more on the floor."

Oliver's hands begin to shake. "Thank you," he says, turning away from her and walking out the automatic doors, leaving the rest of the people behind, waiting. Suddenly, it doesn't look so bad not to know the trouble you're in.

He walks in circles around the entire hospital building. On his cell phone he dials Mary's number over and over again. She does not pick up. He leaves two voice mails. Then he calls home.

Miranda answers his mother's phone.

"Miranda?" he says, beginning to cry. The tears cloud his eyes and blur the streetlights.

"Oliver? How is he? Are you at the hospital?"

"They're admitting him. To Neurology. His head, Miranda. He was shot in the head."

She takes a deep breath. "Do you want me to come down?"

Oliver heaves, trying to stop the tears.

"Take a deep breath," she says.

"*I* did this, Miranda. Whatever I told him, must have, I don't know . . . he's my brother. I know you don't think . . ."

"Oliver, try to calm down. There's a whole part of this evening that we know nothing about. Okay? You had a conversation with Jared. That does not make you responsible for this."

"Shit, shit, shit. I'm going upstairs now. I've got to see him. Is my mother there?"

"She just fell asleep. Your stepfather's with the police. To answer more questions. I thought I should stay with her, even though, I mean, I'm just this strange girl in her house."

"Thanks," he manages to say. "Thanks for that."

"You are welcome. Oliver," she says, in a confessional tone, and then she's silent. "I'm sorry," she says.

Oliver nods. "I know."

She sighs, a disbelieving, sorrowful little noise.

There is something more Oliver wants to say. If he knew another language, he would tell her that the sound of her voice in his ear is surely more than he deserves. But, suddenly, all the words he knows seem ridiculous and impossibly insufficient.

The fifth floor is quite the opposite of the emergency room. Oliver does not see a single person walking through the wide corridors. He goes through a set of doors marked NEUROLOGY and then buzzes at a set of doors marked ICU. A woman's voice asks him who he is there to see and after he tells her, the doors swing open.

Inside, the smells of antiseptic and some other chemical he cannot identify overwhelm him. The nurse is standing by her station, waiting to assess him.

"Your brother is Jared Trizel?" She doesn't wait for an answer. "He's been seriously injured. The police are going over his chart. You'll have to wait to see him until we get everything in order. I'm not sure if they'll decide to do surgery or not. Doctors do rounds at six A.M. If you want to talk to them, you should be here then. Any questions?"

"Can I stay? Is there a place I can stay with him?"

She nods. "I'll clear it with the officer. There's a chair in his room. I'll let you know when we're ready." She turns and walks briskly down the hall into a glassed-in room.

❖

Mary is standing in the aisle, pouring refills. She did not expect to see this man again, but here he is, in 12B. She studies him. All men look the same in their sleep. Any distinguishable traits slip away as they snore, slack jawed, through the night. He could be anyone, she tells herself. He's hardly special.

She is on a westbound red-eye from New York. Doug boarded the plane, fiddling with his cell phone. He did a double take when he saw Mary, his eyes brightening. She welcomed him aboard just as she did every other passenger, offering him a pillow and blanket. He accepted gratefully and then, somehow, recalled her name. Mary couldn't help being impressed, although when they had danced together not more than a week ago, he had seemed ready to commit much more than her name to his memory.

As she poured his juice, they finally had the where-are-you-from and where-are-you-going conversation. He lives in a suburb of Atlanta, which is a frequent layover for Mary. But he's on his way back to Denver, where his mother is very ill.

"I'm sorry to hear that." Mary handed him a napkin.

"I wish I could've brought my girls, but it's just not practical. Spending all day in a hospital, with a four- and six-year-old." He shrugged. "I'm already exhausted."

Mary smiled at him. He did look weary. "What about your wife?" She couldn't help herself.

He raised his eyebrows, as if to begin a long story, and then motioned with his hand at her cart. "There might be a revolt if I keep you here any longer. Maybe we could talk later?"

Their conversation, she realized, had been heard by many greedy ears and eager eyes. She served the rest of her passengers and then walked slowly past his seat. He was already asleep.

She wants desperately for him to be as genuine as he seems. How, she wonders as she collects empty cans, can anybody ever know?

The business of stalking she could learn from Oliver—she could borrow his sunglasses and the video camera and become obsessed. They could sneak around together like they did when they were kids, speaking in British accents and trying to uncover everything. But she already knows how that ends.

She straps herself into the jump seat and tries to meditate. With her eyes closed, she visualizes an aircraft lifting into the air, pulling away from the tarmac, pulling away from the highways and back roads, pulling away from the green and brown and blue of earth, and lifting all of them up into this thin atmosphere, to a place where all that matters is if you're buckled in and sitting up straight. She breathes deeply. There are blankets if you're cold and soda if you're thirsty. The bathrooms, though small, can cradle you through any remorse that this pulling away creates.

Suspended in air by the wonders of physics and mechanics, you can watch a movie, eat peanuts, make a new friend, sleep.

At any moment, of course, the plane might fall back to the

green and brown and blue earth, where it would splinter into a million pieces, becoming the story of the day.

If this airplane crashes, there's no chance Doug will be a father who dies without much notice. His kids wouldn't be expected to just go on, as they might if his heart gave out on the kitchen floor one summer evening. There would be support groups and batches of sympathy cards from complete strangers.

If her father had fallen out of the sky somewhere far away, lost consciousness in the clouds and tumbled into the sea, then Mary and Oliver might have made a pilgrimage there with their mother, let the waves lap their feet and the salt water sting their eyes. They might have thrown roses into the waves and then, finally, come home to carry on. Home would not have become a house their mother was desperate to flee.

In the photo Doug had shown her of his girls—the one that's certainly still in his wallet right now—the older one was wearing a sparkly tiara. That spunk would be an asset if this airplane were to crash. At the makeshift information center in the hotel, Oliver would stand near those same girls and their mother, their shared circumstance making them instant companions. What a dose of irony, Mary thinks, if Oliver became their stepfather. If he took Doug's girls to the movies and to the pool and bought them bubble gum and ice cream, becoming their Mr. Nice Guy.

But probably, Mary notes, even as a sudden turbulence disrupts her reverie, this plane will not fall. Doug's children will not lose their father tonight. Oliver will not become the figure of his own loathing. They will all remain strangers to one another, by the sheer absence of tragedy.

❖

Miranda's camera has been abandoned on the kitchen counter. If it were allowed to capture the room around it, there would be photographs of a pair of wine glasses standing gallantly beside the sink, Mr. Scrap's necktie folded into a tidy blue bundle on the table, a pair of reading glasses abandoned beside the toaster. There is nothing to betray the events of the evening. It appears to be a kitchen like any other, midlife.

Miranda sits on the floor beside Mrs. Scrap's bed, remembering all that Oliver has told her about his mother and his father. About that summer and everything that was lost.

The phone rings. Miranda answers, thinking it will be Oliver again. It is not.

"Who are you?" Mr. Scrap asks, his voice stretched thin with fatigue and panic.

"I'm Miranda. Oliver's—"

"Of course. Where's Betsy?"

"Sleeping. Is everything all right? I mean, are you all right?" she asks.

"He came right at her. He could have killed her."

Miranda nods. "You shot him?" she says quietly, walking out of the bedroom and into the hallway, where she can talk without waking Mrs. Scrap.

"I had to," he snaps. "He was coming at her. I asked him to stop. He wouldn't stop."

"You think he was trying to hurt her?" She places a hand on the wall for balance.

Mr. Scrap sighs. "It is the only explanation for him to have been there, in our yard, trespassing on our property."

He's afraid, she thinks. He was afraid of Jared. Preemptive strikes and hasty decisions all over the world.

He continues. "He wasn't dead when they took him away. Right? He was moving. He was alive." His voice is awash with contempt and guilt and sorrow.

She nods. "Right." He has her sympathy for a moment, as she imagines him absentmindedly gnawing at his cuticles—a habit Oliver had told her about—his teeth slowly dismantling his own culpable skin.

She does not believe that Jared came here to kill anyone, and she can hear in Mr. Scrap's voice that he will not be spared this doubt, either. "Oliver is at the hospital now," she says.

"Oliver? Why is Oliver at the hospital?"

"Checking on him. Jared, is his name."

"You know this guy?"

"A little."

"Oh, my God." His voice breaks. "Why? I mean, *how*? Isn't he a good-for-nothing?"

Miranda bristles at this phrase. "I'm not sure what you mean. He bags groceries at Alfalfa's. He's an aspiring musician. Drums, I think. I'd call him a nice guy. Not a good-for-nothing. No."

"Well." His voice thickens. "Nice guys do stupid things when they're down on their luck."

Miranda looks at her hand against the wall, her fingers stretched wide. Each of us is capable of so much harm. "You're probably a nice man, usually. And tonight you shot someone."

"I defended my property," he says, raising his voice.

"There are euphemisms for lots of things."

"Please tell Betsy that I called." He hangs up.

Miranda takes a deep breath. Why had Jared come here tonight? She creeps back into the bedroom and takes her place on the floor.

"Was that my husband?" Mrs. Scrap asks.

"You're awake."

"What did he say? Is he coming home?"

Miranda furrows her brow. "He didn't say."

Pushing the sheet off, Mrs. Scrap sits up, pulls her knees into her chest, and lets her head hang over. Miranda can see that Mrs. Scrap's hair has dried askew but her robe is still tied tightly around her. She begins to weep.

Tentatively, Miranda approaches the bedside. She sits on the edge, placing a hand on Mrs. Scrap's back.

"Oh, God, oh, God, oh, God," Mrs. Scrap wails, over and over, finally leaning into Miranda. Curled tightly into a ball, Mrs. Scrap's entire body could fit on Miranda's lap. She holds her close, realizing that right now, they are two strangers alone together in the world. Here in this dark bedroom, they will have to survive this. Miranda is terrified of saying or doing the wrong thing. She has no idea how to proceed, so she strokes Mrs. Scrap's hair away from her face the way Miranda's own mother used to when she was upset.

Soon, Mrs. Scrap quiets down and begins to shiver. "I'm so cold," she says, wiping at her face with the sleeves of her robe. She turns away from Miranda and lies down again.

Miranda pulls the blanket up from the foot of the bed and covers her.

"What does any of this mean? I don't understand. He deplores guns. Why would he have one?"

Miranda keeps her hand on Mrs. Scrap's shoulder, trying to warm her. "Sometimes people don't feel safe," Miranda says quietly.

"We've never been burglarized. We've never had a single problem."

"What I meant is that he must not have felt like he could tell you."

Mrs. Scrap groans. "Do you think I'm awful? Has Oliver told you terrible things about me?"

Miranda shakes her head. "Not at all. Please don't think that. I didn't mean it that way at all."

Mrs. Scrap turns toward Miranda. Her face and eyes are red and puffy. "Tonight was supposed to be about being honest, right? Seeing each other for what we really are? But you never expected this, did you?"

Miranda smiles grimly. "It's been an awful night. I'm so sorry."

Mrs. Scrap's eyes are full of tears again. She blinks and they dampen her cheeks. "Please don't leave," she says, pulling the sheet tighter around herself.

"I won't," Miranda says, placing her head beside Mrs. Scrap's. "We're, like, forty-six-millionth cousins, remember?"

Mrs. Scrap smiles faintly before closing her eyes again.

10

The red-eye from New York does not crash, but lands in Denver at dawn as planned. As the drowsy passengers file past her, Mary wishes each of them a good day. Doug's hair is rumpled. "Here's my card," he says, extending his hand to Mary. "Please call me if you ever need help catching your breath." He smiles at the pilot who has poked his head out of the cockpit.

"Thanks," Mary says, confused, though his card quickly reveals that he sells breathing equipment for sleep apnea sufferers. She watches him walk up the Jetway. He turns and waves. She resists the urge to run after him.

On the concourse Mary retrieves two urgent voicemails from Oliver. In the first his voice is thin and tight, full of adrenaline. "Something's happened. You've got to come home. Now. Really, it's an emergency. Call me." In the second his voice is weary and quiet, as though he's talking from a tunnel. "Hi, Mary. So, I'm not sure if you'll get this tonight. But I'm at the hospital and I'm staying here. I'll be here all night. You should call me. Call me when you land."

Standing by the exit gate of her flight home, she calls him.

"Oliver? What is it? What's happened?"

His voice catches as he tries to speak. "Mary," he says, nearly whispering. "Hold on." There is rustling on the line and then he returns, his voice a little louder. "I had to go out into the hall. Okay. Where are you?"

"In Denver. On my way home. What is it?"

"It's impossible. I don't even know where to begin."

"Why are you at the hospital? What's happened?"

"I found him, Mare. I found our brother."

There is a long pause. For a moment, Mary thinks that Oliver has lost his mind. She imagines him standing outside the hospital's newborn nursery, pointing at a little tiny boy with a dark red birthmark, saying, "That's him. That's my brother."

"Oliver . . ." She wonders how to even talk to him. "What do you mean? Tell me what's going on."

"I've been watching him. I found him a couple weeks ago at Alfalfa's. But I didn't tell you. Or Mom."

She's almost relieved. At least her brother's not harassing neonatal nurses. "Yeah?" she says. "And?"

"So, I talked to him. I told him what I thought, about who he was, and I guess he went to see Mom. He went to see Mom, and Martin thought he was some kind of I-don't-know-what, and he shot him. Mary, he fucking shot him in the head."

Mary closes her eyes. She can tell from his breath pattern that Oliver is crying. "Holy shit, Oliver. Martin? Shot someone. Does he even own a gun?"

"Apparently," Oliver says, clearing his throat. "I just finished talking to the police."

"Police? Shit. I'll call Mom right now. I'm on my way home. Out of Denver. What can I do, Oliver? What do you need?"

"Besides the obvious?" Oliver snaps.

There is a long silence.

"Okay, you got me. The obvious being . . . ?"

"You and Mom to come down here. To see him. To be with me."

"Is he awake? Will he know us?"

"How would he?"

Oliver returns the gaze of an elderly woman in the room next to Jared's. Her lights are dimmed; she should be sleeping.

"How would he know you, Mary?"

"Then, I'm not sure that I . . . Is he going to be all right?"

"The doctors haven't rounded. I don't know anything yet."

Without thinking, Oliver smiles at the woman. She continues to stare. Her eyes are big and brown and relentlessly open.

"This is totally unbelievable. I mean, why in the world . . ."

Explanations don't matter to Oliver right now. The old woman's eyes, still staring back at him, don't seem to be registering anything—not Oliver or his smile or even the nurse who is now standing beside her, checking her lines and replenishing an IV.

"It's our brother, Mary. For fuck's sake. He's here. In Neuro ICU."

"I'm gonna miss my flight, Oliver. I'll call you again from the tarmac if I can."

"Later," Oliver says, hoping that he will hear from her again, that she will appear at the hospital, still in her airline-issued navy blue skirt and jacket, white blouse and fake wedding band, and take over.

He puts his phone away and walks slowly back down the corridor. The police officer leans against the nurse's station, writing on a clipboard. Jared is in the room adjacent to the picture window that looks east, where the sun is just beginning to burn above the horizon. The lights of the Wilds glisten in the murky dawn. Each is a house, a room, a life. Each life a beginning, a middle, an end. How many end here, in this place?

This was his father's hospital. His home away from home. The view must have been familiar to him.

A nurse sits at a small desk between Jared's room and the open-eyed old woman's room, looking over charts and printouts. She is his mother's age, with a long auburn ponytail and glasses. She seems to be oblivious of Oliver's presence.

Through the glass, Oliver watches the monitors glow and pulse mysteriously. Jared's face is obstructed. The tube going down his throat is taped across his cheeks so that only his nose and eyes are exposed. Everything is swollen and his flesh looks yellow.

Oliver puts his hands in his pockets. "Shit," he says, afraid of the morning, afraid of the certainties of daylight.

"Hard floor to be on," the nurse says, without looking up from her paperwork. "Hardest for families."

"Yeah?" Oliver says, surprised by her voice. "Yeah, I bet." He rubs his eyes. "You can't tell anything by all those machines, can you? I mean, about how he is, actually?"

The nurse rolls over toward Oliver on her wheeled chair. She pushes her glasses on top of her forehead and stands, leading him into Jared's room for a detailed tour of the equipment. She goes through each monitor, explaining its function very pedantically, then looks at Oliver and says, "But if we had you hooked up to all those monitors right now, there'd still be a whole piece of information missing. You could be giving me all the right numbers, but if you're not able to communicate with me—tell me, *Hey, Linda, I'm thirsty*—then we've got a problem. So the most important thing, the thing we pray for, is that he regains his consciousness. That's the piece that only he can tell us. Not the machines. And the sooner the better."

She smiles at him, finally, but it's a smile full of effort. "He's gravely injured. He wouldn't be here if he weren't. But people do walk out of here."

"Thank you," Oliver says, his eyes watching the numbers now, sensitive to every tick and change. "Thank you, Linda."

"Welcome," she says, returning to her rolling chair and repositioning her glasses over her eyes.

Oliver sits in the vinyl recliner near Jared's bed. The regular beeps of the monitors and the compressions of the ventilator are a perverse company. He stares at Jared's scrawny, naked chest moving up and down as the tube that travels down his throat pushes oxygen into his lungs. Does Jared know this is happening?

When a technician comes through and suctions the gunk from the back of Jared's throat, the violent, hollow sound turns Oliver's stomach. The shine of the floor, the frigid air blowing through the vents, are all suddenly unbearable, and he closes his eyes to stave them off.

He's falling into sleep, as though it were a slowly opening hole in the vinyl visitor's chair. There, he can see Jared seated next to him on his mother's couch, rather than prone unconscious in a hospital bed. They each have their heads leaning back, but it is in laughter, not sleep. And their giggles are the uncontrollable, non-sensical ones of childhood. Jared is a tough kid, his face made to seem intimidating by the stretch of jagged wine-colored skin. But his laugh is easy and soon they are joined by Mary, her serious, inquisitive voice eager to be a part of their silliness. She would have been welcome, in fact have been as essential to them as they were to each other. Mary would have given them each code names and historically accurate bios for their aliases, quizzing them on the table of elements and all the capitals of Europe. They probably would have all gone to medical school—all followed in their father's footsteps—and all established themselves as actual doctors. They would be the experts on the widening, giving desperate families an ambivalent nod of recognition, as illegible as the handwriting on the patient charts they carry.

The hole becomes darker; Oliver falls farther into a blackness that forces this vision away. He can no longer direct his thoughts. There are noises from the machines around Jared's bed, but these are indecipherable sounds. His fingers tingle. He cannot feel his feet. He's hanging, suspended somehow, in a pool of darkness. There is something he should do. Something he should say to stop the dislocation of his body. What is it? He's been told, he's sure. He could ask. Suddenly the words recede as well. He cannot conjure a sound. Not a whimper, not a grunt.

He's stuck in this black box, a surreal circus of invisible trapezes that cradle his limbs, disembodying him like a weightless acrobat. He is thirsty—parched, really—and desperate for something wet that might awaken his mouth. But without words, how will he get water? Will anyone ever think to drip some down his throat? How will he ever speak through such thirst?

"Oliver." He begins to recognize the voice. A hand is on his face, pushing his hair off of his forehead. "Wake up," the voice says, soft and gentle.

He finally understands.

He opens his eyes.

There's a glass of water in the other hand. "Here. You were dreaming. Talking in your sleep."

It's too easy. Oliver is ashamed of his good fortune.

He takes the water from Miranda. "Thanks," he says, his voice hoarse.

She leans over him, bending down until her head is against his chest. He feels his own heart beating against the curve of her cheek.

"Oh, Oliver," she whispers, raising her head so that it's level with his face, which is wet and crumpled and ashamed. Then she places her lips on his.

A kiss is not always a significant act. Think of how often a parent kisses a child, or a husband his wife, or a Frenchman his friend. It can be as thoughtless and inconsequential as a handshake or a nod hello.

He thinks of other kisses, but he cannot remember anything ever feeling like this. He understands that she is giving him a fragment, a fraction, of what she is. A widening of her life has just been transported in one brief pucker to his own.

This is the touch that signifies everything. She may as well have taken a scalpel of her own and opened his chest, pulled back his ribs and placed her lips onto his thick, red heart, or sawed right through his skull and grazed her mouth across his slick, ocher brain. With this little puff of her life, he is bound to her.

He knows it's not right and it's not fair, but he succumbs to the comfort of this touch and pulls Miranda onto his lap. Surrounded by Jared's sprawling, life-suspending equipment, Oliver kisses each curve of Miranda's face and neck and shoulders, giving her his entire life, acutely aware of the injustice of his every breath.

11

Missy Rolondo pushes the double jogging stroller up the last and final hill of her morning route. It's a beautiful morning, the hint of a new season evident in the angle of the sun. Her own shadow stretches slightly longer across the black pavement. As usual, Andrew is wearing the red cape his father brought him from Miami, and Missy can see him cuddled beneath it, holding a corner against his face. It is fraying at the hem, but this does not matter to the four-year-old. Her two-year-old, Max, is nearly asleep, his eyelids barely open, his thumb dangling from the corner of his mouth.

As she crests the hill, she sees that the massive glass-and-aluminum front door of their house is ajar. She slows her pace. She is certain she did not leave it unlocked. Especially when she's home alone, she is careful to lock everything.

Damn it, she thinks. Nearly the entire house is glass, but the sun reflecting off the windows makes it impossible for her to check inside. She doesn't know karate or tae kwon do, and her routine of pushing the double jogging stroller around the neighborhood hasn't made her strong, only tired. She managed to pack sippy cups and a package of pretzels in the stroller basket, but her cell phone is on the kitchen counter. What will she do if a stranger walks out through the open door to confront her, or abduct her, or maul her and make her sons bear witness to her weakness?

How, then, would she ever again reassure their little flushed faces after a nightmare?

Andy is tough. Just look at how he stood up to Mr. Scrap. As embarrassed and distraught as she'd been, she'd also been flattered and impressed that he fought for her. His refusal to back down or walk away is yet another way in which Andy has treated her differently than other men have. He won't allow her to fade away, even when she'd like to. Surely, this is worth something.

Often at night, when she hears a sinister creak from somewhere deep in the house, she sees the end. Frozen and quiet beneath the sheet, waiting to be done in, her mind's eye discovers two men with enormous biceps and thick facial hair suddenly standing on either side of her bed, staring at her still body, wondering aloud if she is awake or asleep. Here is the moment she worries about most: whether to roll off the bed and run to the boys' room, rouse them and carry them both down the stairs and out of the house, into the dark sloping street, and scream for help; or to feign sleep and let the criminals pursue their theft without interruption, hoping that their ambitions extend only to electronics and jewelry. If she could let them work around her, allow them to slip out the way they came in, unaware of her state of consciousness, perhaps she and her sons would survive without harm?

Inevitably, Missy cannot believe that she is capable of deciding between the two options, and it is no consolation that her marriage bed is too often just a single girl's vulnerable hideaway. Fear and uncertainty have become her most faithful companions.

As she stands at the crest of the hill, thinking of all of this, the front door still ajar, Missy decides she can no longer be who she has been. She can no longer be timid and afraid.

The assurance that whatever horrible things happen between them or to them in the dark will be shared—this is what she married for. Sex can be had anywhere, and they've proven that, she and Andy, but sleeping beside someone is why people marry. So that whatever terrible illness afflicts one of the boys at two A.M. would not confront her alone, nor would whatever news a frantic phone call might deliver in the middle of the night. She was after the solidarity of two people who nestle beneath the same sheet each night, effortlessly warming each other, their breaths mingling and softening all the hard edges of the room, making it full.

This is the reality of separating from Andy, the true pain of her impending divorce: the nefarious stranger that finds his way into the house will certainly face her alone. She must become someone new either way, someone different from the cowering wife always awaiting her husband's return.

She must become the woman who assuages her own doubts. Who can decide in an instant to take the children from their beds and run down the stairs in the middle of the night, away from whatever danger exists.

She must confront the door standing open in the morning light.

❖

The doctors have rounded. They are circling the patient like a flock of hungry crows, each trying to assess the damage. Oliver and Miranda are not allowed into Jared's room because the doctors have ordered a procedure. One of the residents is in there now, behind the drape, drilling a small hole in Jared's cranium so that she can insert a rod which will measure the pressure his brain is exerting on his skull.

"If his brain continues to swell, they will have to do surgery," an unfamiliar nurse explains to them on her way into the room with a tray of syringes and gloves.

Miranda turns away. "What is this place?" she says under her breath. Wiping at her eyes, she looks up at Oliver. "I mean, where the fuck are we? It's like a nightmare. A rod in his brain, for God's sake. The smell . . ." She covers her nose and mouth with her hand.

Oliver drapes his arm around her. Staring at the white curtain drawn in front of Jared's bed, he imagines a gloved finger poking at Jared's brain.

The doctor comes out, wearing a practiced look of ambiguity on her face as she passes. Miranda lets a little noise escape from her mouth, a stifled complaint against the universe.

But Oliver is smiling when they walk back into the room. For though the machines and tubes are all still pumping, forcing Jared's chest up and down, there is one startling change.

His eyes are open.

Oliver stands above his head, which now has a weird metal pole protruding from it. "Hey, man," he says quietly, suddenly embarrassed by his presence. "Miranda's here, too." He pulls at Miranda's arm and she steps toward the bed.

She gently places her hand on Jared's bare arm, stroking the tattoo of barbed wire. "Oh, my," she says. "Hi, there. You're going to be fine. Don't you worry about a thing, okay?"

The sound of Miranda's voice seems to interest him. His swollen eyes move ever so slightly toward her. He closes them, as if to acknowledge her.

"Are you thirsty?" she asks, still rubbing his arm.

He opens his eyes again, but this time he seems to be daydreaming, unfocused on anything in the room, replicating that terrible unseeing stare of the woman next door.

Miranda folds her hand around his. His feet twitch. The day nurse walks in. She looks at the probe, at the monitor that is connected to it. Then she looks at Miranda. "See if he'll squeeze your hand." The nurse stands on the other side of Jared and pats him roughly on the arm. "Jared, squeeze this pretty girl's hand, please. Come on, now," she yells like a bossy camp counselor. "Rise and shine."

"Did he lose his hearing or something? Why are you yelling at him?" Miranda asks quietly.

The nurse shrugs. "I don't know about his hearing. Brain injuries affect all neurological functions. But he's doped up right now, so you've got to speak quite loudly for him to hear you."

Miranda nods. After a long pause, she swallows hard and nods again. "Jared," she yells. "Squeeze my hand. Can you? Squeeze my hand or I'm going to take your photo."

Oliver is ashamed to be a part of this foolishness. As if it's not bad enough to be told you're somebody other than who you thought you were by some mournful nerd, then shot by the man who is technically your stepfather, then hooked up to all this shit, with a metal rod in your brain? And now everyone's going to start cajoling you into basic tasks like you're some kind of retard? By yelling at you? He walks out of the room.

Miranda keeps yelling. No shame. No guilt.

Soon enough, though, she joins Oliver in the hallway, her cheeks covered with the salty residue of tears.

She doesn't say anything for a while. She just shakes her head.

"It's okay," Oliver lies. "We're patient. We're not going anywhere, right?"

Miranda leans against him. "Holy cow," she finally says. "Is he really your brother, Oliver?"

Oliver shrugs and slides his hands deep into his pockets. He fiddles with his mother's car keys. Miranda's head rests against his chest. "Yeah. He is." She looks up at him, her blue eyes wide and knowing.

"Remember when I said that loss and abandonment didn't scare me?"

"Mmm," Oliver nods.

"Okay," she says. "You should mark that off any list of qualities that you admire about me. I was completely full of shit."

"Oh, yeah," he says, patting down his pants for an imaginary pad of paper. "The list." He wraps his arms around her and squeezes. "I already sent my list to Human Resources for final approvals. It will have to be in an addendum that you file with Gladys."

"Gladys?" Miranda murmurs, her own arms wrapped around Oliver.

Without a sound he shrugs. His mouth breathes hot on the top of her head. His arms tremble with the strain of holding her so tight.

"Funny," she says, though neither of them is smiling. "Soul singer or cubicle dweller. The only two options for that name."

"Yeah," he says, closing his eyes. "Funny."

The nurse is scraping the bottom of Jared's bare feet with a pencil. She begins yelling at him again. "Honey," she says, "look over here. Look at me. Can you watch me move?" She walks from one side of the room to the other.

Oliver and Miranda stare at his naked feet, yellowed, bloated, and motionless. They look inhuman, the wrinkled skin beneath his arches like an artificial casing for the tender underside of his feet.

The nurse repeats the pencil test. Miranda unwinds herself from Oliver. She covers her mouth and walks away.

After one more glance at Jared's wide eyes, Oliver follows her.

"Oliver," she says in a hushed voice while Jared's wide-eyed neighbor stares at them. "I don't mean this in any way other than what's proper." She pauses. "We've got to try to find his other family. I mean, who raised him. It's not good. If there are some other people out there, they need to know. He needs them to know."

Oliver nods, rubbing his eyes. He's been up for nearly twenty-four hours now. "You are absolutely right. Other family," he says, smiling, his instinctual response to the eyes that are looking but not watching them.

Miranda turns to the wide-eyed woman and waves. No response.

"Good God," she says. "She's beautiful."

Oliver frowns. The woman's back is curved into a slump, her hair is greasy and pulled back, her face shadowed by deep wrinkles.

"She's like an angel," Miranda says, waving again, her other hand fiddling with the seam in her blouse, the place where her camera should be.

Oliver squints. He would like to see this woman the way Miranda does. As in a photograph. But it's all too real. The sight of Miranda, standing there with streaked hair, red eyes, a man's shirt hanging open over her overalls, waving at a would-be angel, is the only beauty he can see in the whole place.

❖

Betsy won't get out of bed. She is transported, in her mind, by the drawn curtains and the daylight seeping in beneath, back to 1982. She remembers with clarity things that probably should, by now, have gone foggy and left her. For instance, when she walked into the kitchen that fateful evening, the first thing she noticed was his ludicrous sandals. Two thick pieces of suede buckled on the side with tattered white athletic socks underneath, stretched tight across his toes. The hospital was always cold, especially the pathology lab. This was what he wore to the hospital because it was comfortable, because he was on his feet nearly the entire time.

And why not? It was not that she objected to his wearing the sandals in the house. But combined with his houndstooth pants, the sandals looked like the ridiculous uniform of a senile old man. Inevitably, if they had to meet somewhere after work, he'd forget to change his shoes.

This nonchalance always unsettled Betsy. Mainly because she still so desperately wanted to impress him. Sure, he loved her. But not a day went by that she didn't make an effort to look the way she thought he liked her to look, with her hair loose around her face, small demure earrings, knee-length skirts that she fashioned from antique handkerchiefs and tablecloths.

Paul, however, never seemed to worry about impressing anyone. Not his wife or his coworkers, his neighbors or his friends. Only the children seemed to elicit his desire to oblige. For them, he'd wear a necklace made from raw pasta and string. For them, he'd speak the Queen's English. For them, he'd allow their felt-tip pens to travel up the smooth insides of his arms, scribbling little winged creatures and three-legged dogs and lopsided houses all the way up to his shirtsleeves. Later, the drawings would rub off on the sheets where he extended his arms to Betsy in the middle of the night. A black echo of the children they'd made, who slept on the other side of the wall in a desperate, serious, blanket-clutching slumber.

And then he wanted another. A child that they hadn't made, this time. An orphan, he said, the slight smile of self-satisfaction hidden behind his beard. They'd be saving a life, giving back to the world by sharing their home. He suddenly sounded like a politician pitching a tax hike.

"A baby?" she said, sitting on her hands.

He nodded enthusiastically. "A little fella."

"Already, it's a fella?"

He nodded. "As part of a study, they're using the ultrasound technology at the hospital on expectant mothers."

"So, you mean, you've already, there's already a mother?"

Again, he nodded. "She came into the ER, this girl. She's thirty weeks. Baby's due in August. It's a great opportunity." There, once more, was the politician's voice.

With her hands still beneath her, absorbing the creases and folds of her skirt, she leaned her head against him. It was a silent plea to slow down. I will let you save *me*. You can give *me* back to the world, more loved, more treasured. Her head against his shoulder meant this.

For one blissful moment, she was sure he understood. He cradled her face in the bend of his elbow and kissed her ear. The tickle of his beard and the heat of his breath arrested her. She closed her eyes, thankful. This was all, she thought. All I ever had to do was throw my head against him. Now, finally and forever, he will carry me.

"You're a wonderful mother," he whispered, his hot breath still mingling with her ear. "You'll be this baby's greatest blessing."

How could she argue with this? With him?

Heavens.

She gave in to buying diapers and formula once again. The women in her sewing group made blankets and bibs in varying shades of blue. Betsy resisted sewing anything for the baby herself. This was her silent protest. Her stoical dissent.

When she first saw those sandals on her husband's feet as he caused this chaos on their kitchen floor, she was vexed at their reminder of the reciprocal love she felt she'd been denied. For the last time, as she stood there in the kitchen, before she knew he was dead, she indulged this tender sorrow. Why, she wondered, had she acquiesced to nearly all of his desires while he still insisted on wearing those god-awful sandals that she had asked him a million times to leave at work?

It was this nettle she longed for after he was gone. Everyday, mundane sorrow becomes seductive when the unwieldy and exotic pain of tragedy has pinned you to the bed.

Here she is again. Pinned to the bed, thickened by the weight of her own insides. Her own heart, kidneys and liver harden in solidarity as they remember the unrelenting sirens and the flimsy despair of someone else's failing body.

Heavens. Miranda left early this morning, placing a glass of juice on the bedside table and promising to return. Betsy should do something. Call someone. Check on the boy.

Just the sound of that word in the quiet of her own head gives her shivers. Boy. Baby boy. Baby bee.

That is who Oliver said was in her front yard, bleeding, with Paul's photograph in his hand. The baby. The birthmark.

Never did she think a word could be so literal. The mark of his birth. A mark that Oliver had taken to be as accurate as a name tag. He had searched, she knew, all of these years, for a mark that would approximate his memory of the baby's mark. Such evidence would reveal the mistake for which he'd never forgiven her. This link to his identity, this mark of his misery, would become a mark of possibility.

To the children, she'd shrugged off the blemish. "Just a birthmark. Like a mole. Hand me his pacifier."

But, truthfully, that mark had terrified her when he was an infant just as much as it did last night, when he was lying across her lap, bleeding. Foreboding and angry, it looked like the map of a country ravaged by despair. Too much like the way she imagined Paul's own artery looked after it burst in his chest. Too much like her own chest felt that summer: thatched, torn, crimson.

She had always doubted that she could love a baby she did not bear. But she was terribly certain she could never love a baby who looked like that. That baby would need reassurances and protection she herself could not provide.

After all, she was not Paul. She was not altruistic, charitable or even very kind.

In those hot, interminable weeks of her most acute grief, she could not change diapers and prepare formula and sing any comforting words to anyone. The sour smell of the baby's spit-up and the flimsy crest of dark hair that rose from his scalp made her stomach turn. These were details she might have found charming if Paul had been looking over her shoulder, admiringly, his hands illuminating signposts on a road to loving this marked child.

Instead, she only wanted her husband back. And if he was cowardly enough to die on the linoleum floor wearing those ridiculous sandals as summer's most beautiful dusk turned the kitchen pink, then certainly she could be cowardly enough to give up on a baby boy who was not her own. Surely that was fair. She wanted something to be fair. Take my husband, I'll give away this baby. Tit for tat.

"Betsy? You awake?"

"Mmm," she says, with all the energy she can muster. She does not open her eyes.

Martin comes into the dim room and tentatively sits on the

corner of their bed. She can hear his breathing, the air whistling gently past the thick black hairs in his nose. He rests his elbow on his knees, fixes his eyes on the carpet.

"I thought you might . . . you might want something to eat." She opens her eyes. He pulls on a jagged cuticle.

"Are you home?" she asks, looking at his wrinkled, untucked shirt.

"Mary called." As if this explains everything.

"She's here?"

He nods. "She talked to Oliver."

Betsy closes her eyes again. *That's him, Mom.*

"Where's Oliver?"

Here, he turns his body toward her. "I can't say anything, Betsy. I can't find anything to say. They arraigned me this morning. I posted bail."

She shrugs, feeling the sheets drag across her shoulders. "I didn't know that you even had one . . ."

He nods quickly, anticipating her thought. "I know, I know. I should have told you."

Betsy closes her eyes again. The woman she passed the boy along to was a foster mother accustomed to all sorts of children. She'd give him a good home, Martin had said, until there was another adoptive family found. It was an immediate solution so that Betsy could have some relief and deal with her own children. Nurse her own wounds.

It was as easy as dropping off a casserole or returning a borrowed book. He didn't question her or challenge her or judge her.

He simply made a few calls and packed them in the car. This was the temerity of his love.

When she opens her eyes again he is weeping. Silent, flat tears stripe his face. She would like to turn away from this sight and curl onto her side and tuck her hands beneath her chin and wait. Like a gosling, as yet unhatched, she could wait and wait in the cramped and total darkness until a wiser creature than she broke off her shell, started her over again.

Who is she to dispatch mercy?

But she reaches out her hand and places it on the sheet beside him, as close as she can get to him without sitting up. She strokes the sheet as if it were a part of him. He seems to understand this. He grabs her hand in his and lowers himself to the floor so that he is kneeling. Placing her hand over his mouth, he holds it there so that she can feel the heat and depth of his pain. His teeth graze her knuckles, his lips quiver against her palm. Still, he makes no noise, but his chest heaves.

"It was an accident," she says. "A terrible accident."

12

Mary drives the forty-five-mile stretch of highway that connects the airport to her home without noticing any of it. While she was spanning the width of the country in an airplane, thirty-three thousand feet above any tree or shrub or roadside vista, her life as she's known it may well have fallen apart. Or come together. For all her apparent dismissal of Oliver's search, she secretly hoped, way down in the deepest part of her, that one day he would resurrect the world he hoped to find. If her life were a surrealistic Spanish movie, and sometimes she feels as though it might be, then it wouldn't be too unlikely for Oliver to ring her doorbell and have her father and the baby, now of course a strapping young man, propped up in the Ranchero. They'd go for a joyride, starting over together, even if one of them was dead.

That baby was, for Mary, a soft delight who made her arms feel strong. Anything she sang seemed in tune and her heart expanded with hope and resilience against the darkness of that late summer.

And then he was gone.

Mary blinks, trying to conquer the tears gathering in her eyes. She tells herself to take a deep breath, stay calm. With one hand, she searches in her purse for a tissue. She pulls out several, and with them comes the business card she had forgotten. Holding it between two fingers, Mary hears his voice in her head. *If you need help catching your breath.* Isn't that what he said? Doesn't she now need some help breathing?

In the car by herself, unsure of what it is she will encounter when she arrives home, Mary has a surge of reckless desire. She grabs her phone and calls him.

He picks up right away. "This is Doug."

Mary is crying, now, unable to stop. In the split second between hearing his voice and conjuring her own, she realizes how desperate she is.

"Hi," she says, barely audible. Then she laughs at her own audacity. "I need some help breathing."

"Don't panic. Just take nice even breaths. Who is calling, please?"

His voice is reassuring, even though he's confused.

"It's Mary. From the plane. I'm sorry to bother you—"

"Mary? Are you okay?"

"I don't know."

"Tell me what's happened. Are you safe?"

Mary gives him her abbreviated yet circuitous backstory and then tells him about Oliver's phone call.

"I'm not sure I have a machine for that," he says, his voice warm and full of concern. "But there is one thing I could suggest."

"What's that?"

"Don't hang up. I am a professional with the most sophisticated equipment available and as long as you're on the phone with me, I can make sure you're breathing. Let's check. Here we go."

Mary listens to the silence between them.

"Very good. You're going to be okay," he says, finally.

"You think? I'm not great with uncertainty. I prefer clarity."

"I'm on my way to a hospital as well. My experience is that there is very little clarity there. Ever."

Remembering his mother, Mary is suddenly embarrassed. "I'm sorry. You're dealing with a sick family member and I shouldn't have—"

"Mary. Please don't make it a mistake that you called."

"You've been very nice and—"

"You're much braver than you think. You will figure it out and you will keep breathing and I hope you'll call me again. Because I will be sitting in a hospital room, reminding my mother who I am and why I am there. I will be wracking my brain to think of things we can talk about, things that might remind her of the life she's lived."

"Oh."

"But probably I'll just be telling her about you."

"Me?"

"Talking to her now is a lot like talking to myself. So I might as well enjoy the conversation. Will you keep breathing?"

Mary lets the sound of her breath travel through the phone. "See?"

"Very good. Much improved."

They say good-bye and her thoughts return to the wounded boy. Even if he is who Oliver wants him to be, it doesn't make him their brother.

So much of her affection for Oliver grows from the accumulation of common memories. Would Mary have the same patience and sympathy for him if she couldn't close her eyes and picture his chubby five-year-old face as he stands in her doorway, asking for another snuggle? What if she couldn't summon forth the way he would lean his head onto her shoulder while she read to him in the shade of the porch? If they didn't have a shorthand between them that allowed for speedy communication? *Walter Pinkett*, the first boy Mary kissed, would always mean a huge interpersonal mistake; *rotten egg* was an invocation for competition, as in, "Rotten egg that parking space," or "Rotten egg the first piece of toast"; and *jolly good* was something Oliver always said to indicate he would capitulate to Mary's will.

Does intention count for anything? Does it matter that her father intended for them to have a little brother? The idea of finding something that's been lost has redemptive power, but life cannot recover every misplaced link. The kid that transferred out of her ninth-grade biology class might otherwise have become her lab partner, her eventual best friend, her soul mate, even. Where is he? Should she go looking for him? Find him and tell him that he's got to leave his wife and family and be with her because of what should have been?

No, Mary reasons against an unreasonable hope as she crests the last hill toward home. This so-called sibling that Oliver has found is just like a million other flukes in life. A passenger, late for his ticketed flight, stands in the window and watches the aircraft he missed taxi to the runway, take off, and then turn its nose to the ground and crash. What should he do, that man? Should he lie down and die?

❖

Funny how quickly a place becomes familiar, Oliver thinks as he and Miranda mindlessly maneuver the hospital corridors to the Neuro ICU. They are back from a dutiful but fruitless search for information on Jared's other family, having gotten only as far as a locked apartment door and a landlord who refused to help, saying the police had sealed the place off. The nurse who now buzzes them onto the unit has her microwaved lunch in one hand. Oliver wonders how in the world someone could become accustomed to eating amidst the noxious odors of bodily failures and their antidotes. He and Miranda look at each other, their eyes communicating their repulsion. How could you fork in a frozen ravioli while colostomy bags, liquid diets, partially removed skulls and vacant eyes surround you? Then he remembers the tuna sandwiches, leftover meatloaf and pasta salad his father used to fold up in waxed paper or scoop into Tupperware containers to take with him to work.

The sound of waxed paper being folded is still poignant to Oliver. It signaled that his father was about to leave them for work at the morgue, where he sliced through sections of preserved brain as though it were an offering on a cheeseboard. Scales like the ones behind the meat counter in the grocery store weighed livers and spleens and kidneys and hearts, and in between these tasks, whenever it was convenient, his father would remove the waxed paper and enjoy his sandwich there among smells Oliver cannot imagine.

Surely there must have been a break room with posters about workplace rules and regulations, maybe even a photograph of Oliver and Mary, a place where he could unwrap his tuna sandwich, slip out of his shoes and read the paper, emulating a regular office worker who does not have two more bodies to disembowel before quitting time.

Does this nurse with her bowl of ravioli in the ICU not have a break room where she'd rather be?

Sure enough, she disappears behind the nurses' station, only the smell of her ravioli lingering. Without a word, Oliver and Miranda confront the familiar hallway stretching out in front of them. The shiny floor, so friendly to wheelchairs and gurneys, is anathema to Oliver's sneakers, which noisily announce his every step.

There are two figures at the end of the hallway, standing in front of the window adjacent to Jared's room. As his noisy footsteps get closer, the figures simultaneously turn and look.

"Oliver," his mother says, a huge sigh exiting her mouth. "There you are."

She stands with her arms crossed in front of her body. Her eyes rest on Miranda only briefly and then she looks away, pretending they are not as acquainted as they are. Oliver had forgotten that he'd asked them to come. He wishes now that he hadn't.

Mary reaches out to him and he drops Miranda's hand in order to hug her.

"We didn't know if we were in the right place or not," Mary says in his ear. "Who's she?"

"Uh, yeah. This is the place. I was just, we went out for a little bit. I didn't know you were coming." Oliver glances through the glass into Jared's room where a nurse stands by the bed writing notes. "Mom, you remember Miranda?" he asks, as though a year has passed since last night.

His mother extends her hand. "Miranda."

Mary steps forward. "Miranda? I'm Mary. Oliver's sister." She gives her brother a disbelieving glance. "Are you, like, a social worker or something?"

Miranda smiles. She looks down at her own attire. The man's dress shirt hangs loosely about her shoulders. "I'm completely unqualified for that," she says, leaning gently against Oliver.

Mary shakes her head. "I'm sorry. I didn't know. I mean. Geez. I've been flying all—"

"Mary." Oliver interrupts. "Have you been in? To see him?" He gestures toward the room.

His sister shifts and puts her arm around their mother. "You asked us to come. We're here." The tone of her voice is somehow both flippant and accusatory, and the smile she is forcing is clearly the one she reserves for her overly demanding passengers.

His mother is crying now. Her tears are smearing her eye makeup, and when he touches her arm she turns away, biting her lip and staring at the floor.

"Oliver," Mary continues, "this poor boy—even if he is who you think he is, which he's probably not—has had an entire life—"

"He's twenty-one."

"Okay. But what I mean is, we're not the ones who should be here, holding vigil. There have got to be other people. Family." She cringes as she says the word.

"And if there's not? If he doesn't have anyone? Then what, Mary?" He hadn't wanted to argue. "He was standing in the front yard. In Mom's front yard. God knows what he was thinking, but he was standing there, and then this happened. His brain is bleeding and the machines are breathing for him and you're saying it's not our problem?"

"It may not even *be* him," Mary says. "I think you can appreciate, Oliver, how unlikely it is that he's actually the same boy." She still wears her polite, professional smile.

Oliver cocks his head. "Is that what you want?" he asks. "You want it to be over. Boom. Wrong guy. Pack it up. Hit the runway."

"And that would make me what? Less human than you? Do you expect me to sit at every kid's bedside? He *could* be a complete stranger, Oliver."

Oliver shrugs.

Miranda breaks the silence. "I'm going for coffee. Anyone else?"

"I'm so tired," his mother says, her voice hushed and quivering. "I just . . ." She trails off, digging in her purse for a tissue. "I think I could use a coffee," she manages to say before she turns and takes Miranda's arm, and they walk away, down the wide corridor, like schoolgirls.

"Nice," Mary says under her breath. "Nice drama, Oliver. And since when do you have a girlfriend who dresses like a janitor?"

"Me? I didn't do this. What's Martin doing that he needs a fucking gun, Mary?"

"The guy was skulking around the house. Trespassing. Loitering. Whatever you call it."

"Since when do you defend shooting someone just because they're in the wrong place?"

"Well, why was he in the wrong place, Oliver? Why would he be in their yard, peering in their windows? Why, Oliver?"

The nurse suddenly pokes her head out the door, looking past the two of them toward the nurses' station. She announces, calmly but loudly, "Crash cart."

Simultaneously, she flips a switch by the door that illuminates a blue light above Jared's room.

Another nurse, trailed by a doctor, runs into Jared's room, pushing the requested cart.

"Shit," Mary says. "We don't need to see this."

Oliver cannot move. He, too, does not want to see this or believe this or acknowledge this. But his sneakers seem to be attached to the shiny floor like suction cups, his eyes stuck on the paddles that cause Jared's chest to erupt like a seismic event.

This cannot be happening, is all he can think. Like stubborn lyrics, the words flood his brain and will not be supplanted. *This cannot be happening.*

Surprisingly, Mary stands beside him. She does not walk away, either. A hint of their reflection shines wearily in the glass. They watch as the paddles are used and reused; three times, altogether.

Time seems to slow and stretch, until after the third time, the doctor places the paddles back on the cart, pulls off his gloves and walks out of the room, as though he's just finished a friendly game of squash.

He stands disarmingly close to Oliver and Mary. "Okay, so this is what's happening," he says, running a hand over his bald head.

Oliver is buoyed by this phrase. It is present tense.

"We're having trouble controlling his pressure," the doctor continues. "The brain bleed is significant, we know that from the CAT scan, causing major damage to the left temporal lobe. We cannot even address those issues, however, until we can be sure he would survive surgery. At this point, he would not. As a result, the brain injury continues to worsen. This a bleak situation, I realize. It's lose-lose. For him and for you guys. And I'm sorry I can't give you a better prognosis. Questions?"

Oliver blinks. *This cannot be happening. This cannot be happening.* A puncture seems to open somewhere beneath Oliver's navel. Air and noise rush through him, widening this hole and making him weak.

"Um," Mary says. Her hand squeezes Oliver's.

"Let her know where we stand," the doctor says, his eyes moving to their mother, who, without their noticing, has returned and is looking now through the glass at Jared. Miranda is beside her. The nurses are raising his bed a bit, checking his lines. "Hang tough," he says, turning quickly and walking away.

The words spoken by this doctor—just as they are by others like him throughout this hospital and in every other, all over the country and the world, in well-lit rooms and dim ones, in big cities and pastoral countrysides, in delivery rooms and nursing homes—change everything. They have seen the widening, it seems, are tracking it and measuring it, and are still powerless against it. Death has begun its march and it will not be reversed.

What good are you? Oliver wants to shout. What good are you if at the exact moment that we need you most, you acknowledge defeat and walk away?

"What just happened?" Mary says, looking at Oliver. "Did he just tell us he's going to die? Is that what he said?"

Oliver drops her hand. He nods, speechless.

Mary puts her bag down on the floor in a gesture that indicates she'll be staying a while. She stares now, resolutely, at what she'd been so loath to acknowledge before.

It's harder, Oliver supposes, to walk away from a dying man than a living one. In some strange, cosmic injustice, it is easier to be there for someone in the finite, predictable preamble to death than it is in the uncertain clutter of life.

Unless you're a doctor.

"They would have taught *you* that, too," Oliver says to Mary.

"What?"

"How to walk away like that. Deliver that news and walk away. Just another piece of your day."

She nods.

"This cannot be happening," he says.

"I'm so sorry, Oliver. I had no idea . . ."

Of what, she's not certain because she does not finish her sentence. But Oliver is certain that what she had no idea about is this: that the death and the loss she's been hiding from somewhere far above the earth's surface, in a cabin filled with recycled air, would someday return. They are about to live through another death together. This is what Oliver, too, realizes he hadn't foreseen.

He'd somehow believed that by allowing his father's death to shape his entire life he could protect himself from all subsequent shock and dread. Surround himself with it and suffocate its power. He might as well have been riding shotgun to Mary's "Coffee, tea or juice?" routine. Each of them has been participating in a complicated delusional charade meant to deny the inevitable, as if they could hijack the pervasiveness of endings.

He and Mary stand shoulder to shoulder, just as they have so many other times, and look through the glass at Jared's yellowed chest mechanically puffing up and down. Mary's jaw begins to clatter and she clenches it shut. Unbidden, a memory comes of her dripping wet at the side of the pool in the fading afternoon sun, chastised by the lifeguard for lingering in the water past the final whistle, goose bumps covering her arms and legs.

"You want me to tell Mom?" she asks.

"She should just go home," Oliver answers, deflated, but certain of this. His mother should not be here. Neither should his sister. "You were right, Mary. He's a stranger. Just a guy."

"Maybe." She leans into him, her shoulder pressing against his in solidarity.

"No, really, Mary. I'm certifiable. You know that. I mean, I'm certain that I was wrong. *Am* wrong. About everything. There's no way he could be . . ."

Before he can finish, he notices a girl. Or is it a woman? Her age is unclear. Wearing black boots and ripped stockings, a T-shirt hanging loosely across her diminutive frame, she fiddles with the ends of her long dark hair.

"Oliver." Miranda is suddenly beside him, her hand on his arm.

"I know," he says slowly.

Miranda steps forward. "Hi." She smiles. "Are you a friend of Jared's?"

The girl's eyes scan each of them quickly. "Who the fuck are you?" she says quietly.

Oliver rubs his eyes. This question has become more and more difficult to answer. "I'm Oliver Finley. We're visiting Jared. You, too?"

"Does he know you guys?" she asks, her voice incredulous.

"Sort of, yeah. Are you related?"

"To Jared?"

Oliver nods. "Yeah, to Jared."

She looks away, checking the room numbers.

"Is he in there?" She points, still holding on to the frizzy ends of her hair.

"Yeah, he is. What's your name?"

"Sadie. I just went by Jared's place and the landlord said he was here. He told me that some friends of his had stopped by, but Jared doesn't really have any friends. I don't understand what's happened. Is he in trouble?"

Oliver takes a deep breath. "Yeah."

"He told me he was fucking clean," she says, rolling her eyes.

"Not that kind of trouble," Oliver says. "He's hurt. Pretty badly. But it wasn't his fault."

Behind him, Miranda is crying again. Oliver can hear her sniffling. Sadie looks at her. She scoffs. "Like, what, he's going to die?"

There is an awful silence that is answer enough.

Somehow, Mary anticipates what might happen next and has her arm around Sadie, guiding her to a bench in the hallway. Sadie begins to shake. Her face breaks out in red splotches and she yanks at the ends of her hair. "No, no, no, no . . ." She stands up and pulls away from Mary. Her boots squeak in protest against the shiny floor as she runs toward Jared's room.

There are two nurses inside who look startled when Sadie enters. They each take one of her elbows and walk her to Jared's bedside, as though she is a reluctant child on the first day of school. Her head continues its shaking and she seems to wilt a little as she observes Jared. Each nurse adds a hand to Sadie's back for support.

Betsy, who has been leaning against the wall, nearly forgotten, clears her throat. "Oliver," she says, her eyes on the floor, her voice barely audible. "Did you come here to be a spectator?"

It is a rebuke; he is quite familiar with this tone of voice. "What?"

"Go on," she says.

Struck by the resolve in her voice, he moves his feet across the wide hall until he's standing in the doorway of Jared's room. The nurses no longer have both of their arms around Sadie, but one of them continues to rub her back gently while the other goes about her official duties.

Sadie looks up. "Who are you?" Her eyes are wide and desperate.

Oliver wishes that his answer could be some comfort to her, but he knows it will not. "So, Jared was adopted, right?" His voice falters as he speaks. "And I think he's the one we were supposed to adopt. My parents. I was seven. It was 1982. But we didn't. My dad died and everything got messed up."

Sadie furrows her brow. "Does Jared know?"

Oliver sighs. "I told him last night. Before this happened. I wanted—"

"He talks about his birth mother. About where she is and if she'll ever try to find him. The people he grew up with . . . they threw him out the first time he got into trouble. Before he was even fifteen. He finished high school on the street. He hoped his real mom was out there, but I don't think he ever counted on finding a—what do you call what you say you are?"

"An almost brother." He swallows hard. "Are you his girl-friend?"

More tears swell from the corners of her eyes. "We had this big fight. It was stupid, really. I live in Grant so I have to take the bus to visit. And with picking up extra shifts, I can only come about once a month. Last weekend I missed the bus because of this girl at work who was late and . . ." She folds over at the waist, resting her forehead on the bedrail by Jared's torso.

Oliver rounds the bed to stand beside her. The second nurse resumes her duties, leaving him to tend to Sadie. He places his hand on her shoulder; her back shudders as she cries. Jared's face gives no sign, no glimmer of life.

Sadie rocks her head back and forth on the railing, as Jared's chest rises and falls with perfect mechanical precision. "He was mad," she says. "But there was nothing I could do. Because of his parole, he couldn't come to me. We were stuck." She stands up and looks at Oliver. "It was just one weekend. I thought he was being stupid. But maybe he knew . . ."

Oliver shakes his head. "No." The skin around both her eyes is black with smeared makeup. "He just missed you." He hears himself assuring her that the world is simpler than it is. Whatever shards of regret he can pull away from her, he must.

She is warm, the heat from her skin burning through to his hand, which he keeps pressed on her back. "You should have some water," he says, pulling a cup from the dispenser. He fills it at the small stainless sink and hands it to her, wrapping her shaking fingers around it with his own.

"Thanks," she says.

He nods and watches her drink. Such a simple thing. Why can't Jared tell them that he needs a fucking sip of water?

But Sadie's face goes pale and she pulls the cup from her mouth, barely making it to the sink before she heaves. Oliver pulls back her hair, the way he remembers seeing his mother do for Mary.

When she's finished she stands up straight and wipes her mouth with a paper towel. "Shit," she says, looking at Miranda and Mary and Betsy, who've gathered in the doorway. "I barfed."

Oliver lets go of her hair and places his hand on her arm. "Maybe you should sit down."

She nods.

He walks her around the bed and guides her to the same vinyl chair in which he spent most of the previous night.

"I'll get a bedpan," Mary says from the doorway. She turns, looking for a nurse.

"Why are his eyes like that?" Sadie asks, looking past Oliver at both his mother and Miranda.

"I'm sorry, dear. It's just awful," Betsy says, wringing her hands. She has yet to walk into the room, to really look at the boy whose life her husband has undone.

13

Horrible things happen all the time. People commit unspeakable acts of violence against one another. Sometimes people are made vulnerable by their own government or another country's government, so that they are not even safe in their homes in the middle of the night. An airplane can fly high above the landscape, your city's lights just another target, and its pilot, if instructed, can press a button to send a barrage of explosives into your darkened bedroom, so that the last sounds of life that bounce against your eardrums are glass shattering and children screaming and the deep roar of a fire beginning that will rage into the dawn, destroying everything.

Also on the same day, far away from this fire, a woman may awaken to the muffled whimper of fear. She will pull her robe around her and follow this sound outside, around the back of her house to the rain barrel that she's dutifully installed to collect water for her garden. Hoisting herself up with both arms, she will find the source of the whimpering at the bottom of the deep barrel: a bedraggled mutt left there by kids who were either bored or mean or both. The dog's back feet and body are covered by water.

His front feet are stretched up toward her, scraping the side of the barrel in a panic. His tail, though covered in water, begins to wag. The water splashes about. She reaches her arms down toward him. "It's okay, puppy," she says, her nightgown inching up against her thighs, revealing her pale flesh to the low morning sun. In a split second she falls, head first, into the foot-and-a-half of water, her feet sticking out of the barrel. Unable to hold her nose and mouth above the surface, she drowns, while the dog continues to wag his tail and lick her ears.

A man may hide inside the house where he once lived, the house for which he'd worked two jobs, convincing the woman he loved that he had it all together. They'd married in the yard, beneath a hot summer sun. He'd brought both his children home from the hospital and placed them in the front bay window in order to protect them from jaundice. This man may walk in one morning using a key he's not supposed to have anymore and hide in a closet so that when the woman he still loves returns, he will surprise her. When things don't go as he thinks they should, he will be ready, with a baseball bat and a hunting knife.

It's things of this kind that Missy Rolondo is thinking of as she pushes the stroller up into her driveway, toward the open front door. She parks the stroller at the far end, telling the boys she'll be right back. Purposefully, she lengthens her stride, trying to feel stronger, more in control.

Standing in front of the open door, she listens. There is no noise coming from inside the house except the dishwasher, which she set before their walk. With quivering hands and a racing heart, she puts one foot across the threshold.

"Hello?" she calls out timidly. She turns and takes another look at the driveway, where the stroller casts a long shadow. "Hello," she says again, louder this time. With both feet inside the house, she has committed to this course of action. She begins to wonder if she herself didn't leave the door open, somehow, despite having brought the boys out through the garage. She takes a deep breath. Maybe everything is just as it should be.

But there is an odor she cannot identify. Quietly, she walks toward the kitchen. Andrew has left his blocks piled high on top of the coffee table in the living room. His socks are strewn across the back of the couch. Oddly, the TV is on. But the sound is off. Was he watching it this morning while she fed Max? Possibly. But certainly not CNN.

Turning back quickly, her sneakers squeaking on the hardwood floor, Missy Rolondo does not make it to the front door before she is grabbed from behind. She screams but her mouth is immediately covered. Her feet come up off the floor as she tries to free herself.

"Shhh," he says in her ear. "It's just me."

Placing her back on her feet, Andy keeps his hands on her arms.

"For fuck's sake!" she says. She turns and punches him in the chest. "What the hell are you trying to do? I nearly died."

He takes her fist in his hand, pulling her close to him. "I'm sorry," he says into her hairline. "I didn't mean to scare you. I thought you'd be home. I just, I had a present for you guys and I couldn't wait. Come here." Andy wraps his arms around Missy. Though there is a part of her that despises him for this drama, the bigger part of her is so relieved to see him, to have his deep voice fill the house, to have his arms around her and the scruff of his unshaven face against her face, that she forgives him.

Everything. All of it.

Missy finds herself clapping, cheering like a spectator on the side-lines of some primordial contest, when he jogs out to the driveway to retrieve the boys from the stroller, carrying one over each shoulder, Andrew's red cape streaming behind him like a conqueror's flag.

This, she thinks, is our happy ending. If only the world would end today, this would be the right place for it to stop.

She follows her family inside and watches as Andy reveals a shallow cardboard box in the kitchen. There, curled up on a bed of shredded newspaper, is a silver puppy.

The boys squeal. Andy lifts the puppy out of its nest and lets each boy give it a snuggle. Missy sees a patch of damp papers, which accounts for the smell she'd noticed earlier.

"It's a Weimaraner," Andy says proudly. Then, looking at Missy, he adds, "They're great watchdogs and great family dogs. He's got a pedigree to die for."

Missy smiles as Max leans into the dog with a wide-open mouth, trying to administer a toddler's kiss.

"What do you say to Daddy?" Missy reminds them. But they don't hear her above their own giddy delight. The little boys' fingers pinch the puppy's extra skin with proprietary satisfaction.

Missy leans against the countertop.

"Are we all good, then?" Andy asks, his eyebrows raised in expectation. "I didn't want to do anything to upset you. We prob-ably should have spoken about it beforehand, but . . ."

Missy shakes her head. "No, it's fine. I mean, look at them. They love it." This dog will mark his territory, prowl the perimeter of the property, be with her when the phone rings or a fever spikes. She accepts him wholeheartedly. "Now I'm really outnumbered. The only girl in the house," she says, smiling.

He stays all morning, playing with the boys, tending to the puppy. Missy takes a swim and is reminded again when she emerges, wet and shivering, that the cooler days of autumn are not far away. That means school for Andrew; packing her baby off to kindergarten.

Forget about confronting burglars in the night, or prowlers in the morning. As Missy sits on the warm concrete, wrapped up in her towel, admiring the view of town below, she realizes that it will take all of her courage just to put Andrew on the bus.

She doesn't have the strength to endure an ugly divorce. Nor does she really want one. Having Andy in the house right now, fixing grilled cheese sandwiches for the boys, playing Jimmy Buffett too loud on the stereo and juggling calls on his cell phone, makes her content. But it will also, she knows, exacerbate the quiet that's left behind when he's gone.

When, though, is anticipating its loss ever reason to deny contentment?

She stands up to stretch and squeezes the water out of her hair. Andy greets her at the door with a beer. He has Andrew's red cape fastened around his own neck; an honorary, temporary hero.

"Good swim, babe?" he asks, handing her the bottle.

"Yeah, pretty good." She takes the bottle into the kitchen and sets it on the counter. "How long will you stay?" She hates that she even asks the question.

"Am I allowed to stay?" he asks, taking a drink from his own bottle.

She nods. "Yep."

"No more lawyers? No more divorce bullshit?"

"No more," she says, matter-of-factly, remembering Mr. Scrap's sentimental face as she tearfully told him about her courtship with Andy.

"Was it the puppy?" Andy says, smiling. "Or the cape?" He pulls the cape out around his neck, like an amphibian's mating call.

She gives no answer, only smiles.

They stand side by side, watching the boys roll on the floor together, the puppy asleep again in his box. Will they last like this, as parents, as partners through the boys' adolescence and adulthood? Or will this afternoon in the kitchen be one of a string of small, bright moments before an inevitable demise of their relationship?

Missy breathes a deep sigh. Andy takes another swallow of beer. She decides that at this moment, it doesn't really matter.

❖

Mary returns with the bedpan. She places it on the floor beside Sadie, who has a bit more color in her face now. Together they watch Betsy, who has hesitantly entered the room and approached Jared's bedside. Her head cocked, as though she's ready to listen whenever he's ready to speak.

"Mom?" Mary says, noticing her mother struggle to find a place to put her hand. Finally, it rests on Jared's swollen wrist. "I can take you home, if you want."

"Oh, please don't go," Sadie says in an urgent voice. "I don't know how to—I mean, there's no way I can be here alone." She sits by the bedpan with her arms wrapped around herself, rocking gently from side to side. Betsy approaches and smooths Sadie's hair back from her forehead, and Oliver is transported, momentarily, to the night after his father's funeral, when a stranger in a VW bug had left the baby with them. Without a plan, Betsy had brought the boy inside and suggested that they bathe him. Setting him in the countertop tub that their father had found at a yard sale, the three of them stood under the bright lights of the bathroom and took turns pouring warm water over his little, squirming body. Just the sight of his small, oval belly and chubby, bent legs had provided some much-needed, if short-lived, levity.

Now, watching his mother's diligent hands tend to the person that baby grew up to love, Oliver suddenly notices that sometime since this morning, Jared has closed his eyes. He looks more peaceful, more normal; if it weren't for the rod coming out of his skull and the tubes in his nose and down his throat, he might just be asleep. There had been no benign way to explain the way his eyes looked this morning.

And yet. They had been open.

Oliver has already forgotten just how disconcerting Jared's not-conscious open eyes had been. He is succumbing to the skewed reality of the ICU, in which, as one unbearable scenario is replaced by yet another even more unbearable scenario, the bystanders yearn for that first one. He longs to see Jared's eyes again. If they were to open now, Oliver would readily behave like a fool, screaming absurd commands and studying them carefully for some sign of recognition. He would forget to know better.

"There," Betsy says, letting her fingers linger, for a moment, on Sadie's temple. "I'll stay. Just as long as you like." She moves her hand from Sadie's head to the unharmed side of Jared's face. "He's handsome, isn't he?" She turns her eyes past Oliver, back to Sadie.

"Yeah," Mary says, taking Sadie's hand in her own, "he is."

The machines whir on and then suddenly there is an unfamiliar buzzing. It is Mary's phone. She reaches deep into her jacket pocket and walks past them, following the hallway out to the cell phone lounge. Oliver thinks it must be Mr. Nice Guy calling. Mary had told Oliver that he'd been released on bail this morning, after an early-morning arraignment.

But it's not Mr. Nice Guy calling. It is Doug.

"Can you breathe?" The sound of his voice nearly makes it so that she cannot.

"Thank God. Yes. All on my own."

"I didn't tell you to call me in that circumstance also."

"No, you didn't."

"I wish I had. My mother and I had a great conversation. She's the reason I'm calling, actually."

"The kid my brother found is bleeding in his brain."

"Oh."

"Yeah. ICU sucks. Worse than any airport anywhere."

"True," he says, thoughtfully.

"I don't want to be here. I wish I weren't here." She closes her eyes and remembers dancing with him.

"You'll be okay."

She almost believes him. "It's easy to be certain from over there."

"Yeah, I know. That's the thing about perspective."

"I'm glad your mom is better."

"No. She's worse. Much worse."

"But your conversation—-"

"Was with my dad. She was talking to my dad."

"Oh."

"Across the years. Across life. And death. She told him she wished he'd left her forty years ago. Just ended it so they could have been happy."

"Ouch."

"I had no idea. They seemed normal to me. Not miserable."

"That doesn't sound like what I'd call a good conversation."

"Really? I think it's going to save my life."

❖

"I really need a cigarette," Sadie murmurs.

Miranda has left to feed Jello. Mary is still on the phone. Oliver watches his mother tend to Jared, applying lotion to his sloping feet and a cool cloth on his forehead, unaware that he and Sadie have stepped out.

"Let's go." He takes Sadie's arm and leads her out. On the way, she rummages through her bag and places a cigarette in her mouth. All through the hospital and its maze of corridors and elevators, Sadie's eyes are cast down at her feet, her lips gently working over the unlit cigarette.

When they are standing on the sidewalk outside, near where Oliver stood to call Miranda last night, Sadie lights up and finally raises her eyes.

"Fuck." She looks directly at him. Then she begins to pace. "This is totally fucked up. What happened?" She begins to cry again. "I mean, how in the world did this happen?"

Oliver shakes his head. "I don't even know, really. For some reason, he was at my mom's house."

"Her?" Sadie motions to the building they are standing in front of. Then she wipes at her eyes with the heel of one hand.

Oliver nods. "Yeah. Jared showed up at my mom's and her husband—I don't know why—but he must have thought that Jared was some kind of intruder."

"He did this?" Her eyes move quickly, darting from Oliver to the street to the people passing by them. "Your stepdad?"

Oliver nods again. "But I—"

"And your mom's up there?" She throws her stub into the gutter and reaches into her satchel for another, pulling out a scrawny velvet stuffed monkey in order to dig for the pack.

Oliver jumps at the sight of the toy. "Fuck," he says, under his breath. "Fuck . . ."

"What? What is it?" She finds the pack. "You can have one of mine."

Oliver shakes his head. "No." He reaches for the toy and she hands it to him.

"It's his," she says. "He gave it to me for when we're apart. It smells like him, even."

Oliver holds the monkey close to his face.

It reeks of cigarette smoke but also of an unbathed child—a week's worth of sweat and dirt and sugar that seven-year-olds accumulate between their fingers, behind their ears and even on their eyelids. A sticky, salty, mildly pleasant odor that reminds him of his sister. You can never smell it on yourself, but Oliver can remember sitting side by side with Mary on a chaise on the porch, their bare feet blackened by the day's pursuits. She smelled just like this worn velvet monkey in his own hands now, the very same item he and Mary had chosen with their father twenty-one years ago, standing in front of the display in the toy store. Mary had thought to place it in Jared's car seat for his journey away from them. He must have kept up with it, somehow, ever since, imposing his own little-boy smell that is still somewhere deep inside. Oliver holds the toy to his cheek; only in the face of this confirmation does he realize how much doubt he'd harbored about his discovery. Even now, how readily his grief expands to encompass the certainty of Jared's identity.

Oliver and Mary had been right there with him all along, present in this monkey. Strangely, while he holds this artifact—the very proof he's so longed for all this time—he does not find any justification of his endeavor, only evidence of its folly.

Across the parking lot, two birds are fighting over a stray cracker in the gutter. Their wings shudder and flap, reprimanding each other. He shrugs his own shoulders. "I'm sorry," he says. "I'm really sorry."

Sadie furrows her brow and grabs the monkey back from him. "He can't die. That's all. He just can't." Her fingers shake as she brings them to her mouth and lights another cigarette. Her eyes spill tears that fall off her face into the small hollows above her collarbones.

Here is their widening. They will go on and hope and yearn and believe in another chance.

"He brought me here once when I had food poisoning." Sadie uses her chin to motion to the ER entrance. "He sat there in the waiting room with that stupid blue bedpan—just like the one upstairs—catching my puke." She rolls her eyes. "I hate this place."

Sadie smokes one more cigarette and then together they retrace their steps back through the labyrinth of elevators and corridors that lead to the ICU.

❖

The machines beep and blink and the sun sets with steadfast conviction. So many people in the room is against the rules but the night nurses have made an exception. None of them wants to linger on the reasons for this unexpected kindness.

Betsy studies Jared with a tenacity Oliver doesn't remember seeing before. Sadie strokes him occasionally, whispers in his ear, but cannot bear for long the proximity to the gurgling in his chest. She retreats again and again to the spot she's found between Oliver and Mary.

Miranda delivers water bottles and trail mix from a vending machine she's found. Nobody eats; she stacks the packages neatly on the counter, where they remain, like souvenirs from a recent trip.

Two nurses perform their duties around them, cleaning out the ventilator and barking salutations to Jared's closed eyes, until, without warning, one of them punches on the ominous blue light and the other runs for a crash cart and a doctor.

"Out, please," the first nurse says to them. "We need space."

The five of them file into the hallway, helpless and dejected. Sadie clings to Mary's arm. *Where have you been for the past twelve hours*, Oliver wants to shout to the horde of doctors and nurses now swarming around Jared. *Eating ravioli?*

They pound and electrify Jared's body with abandon. His arms stiffen momentarily in what appears to be a regaining of consciousness, and then flop again, useless. Over and over. Until they stop. A doctor they've never seen before glances at the clock and tells a nurse to note the time. He pulls shut the white curtain hanging from the ceiling and throws his latex gloves in the trash bin by the door in one seamless motion.

"You the family?" he says without inflection.

They all nod.

"I'm sorry. We did everything medically possible to save him. His injuries were simply too significant."

Sadie crumples. Mary sits beside her, holding her. Miranda goes for ice.

Oliver and his mother enter Jared's room. It is quiet. No beeping or whirring. Jared doesn't look much different.

Betsy places one hand on Jared's forehead. With the other, she touches Oliver's shoulder. She says only, "I'm sorry."

"No," Oliver says, shaking his head emphatically. "Mom, I've been grasping at straws. Clinging to a delusion. It's my fault."

"I could have done so many things differently," she says, lowering her voice, as though Jared might be eavesdropping. "I could have kept that baby." Her eyes fill with tears.

Oliver holds his mother. "I did this, Mom." He clings to the only parent he has left. "I did this."

"No," she says, crying. "No, no, no."

The moon is a white curve in the dark sky. Their own breathing fills the silence. Then there is a gentle knock.

Miranda comes in quietly. Without a sound she kneels, placing her forehead on one of Jared's hands. Then she stands and joins Oliver and Betsy in an awkward embrace.

In the hallway, Mary is holding the blue bedpan for Sadie. The nurses move around them in conciliatory arcs.

The light of dawn has begun to creep in through the windows. Mary offers to accompany Sadie to see Jared. She shakes her head vehemently.

"I don't believe in that shit," she says. "He's gone. His body—"

"It's okay," Mary says, absorbing Sadie's head on her shoulder. "Let's go, then."

Betsy, Mary and Sadie begin the long journey out of the hospital.

Miranda holds Oliver's hand. "You coming?"

He shakes his head. "I want a minute."

Wrapping her arms close around her body, she nods. "Find me in the cafeteria."

Oliver reenters the room.

There is one of the nurses who must have known this was what the night had in store for them. Glancing at Oliver, she smiles briefly. "I'll be a minute," she says, expecting him to turn and go. But he does not. He is compelled to watch her pull the remaining lines out of Jared. She collects the tubing and needles that have nested inside of him with a perfunctory precision. Like a video played in reverse. "Someone will be here in a moment for him."

"Can I go?" Oliver asks her.

"Go with him?" the nurse asks in disbelief.

"Yeah, walk with him?"

"You do know where he's going?"

Oliver shrugs.

"I think this is the better place to say good-bye," she says bluntly. "The morgue is not where you want to be."

Until she said it, Oliver hadn't realized exactly what would happen next. He'd thought he might escort Jared's body through the corridors of the hospital to a waiting hearse that would take him where? To a mortuary. Or something like that.

Now that she's said it, Oliver feels like his legs might collapse. The morgue. "He's not . . . he's not going to have an autopsy, is he?"

The nurse shakes her head. "No, but that's where he goes until the cops release his body. Then you'll have to choose the funeral home you want to use. That kind of thing."

"Oh. Right." Oliver watches her place a bandage over the wound on Jared's chest where his main line had been. A bit of blood seeps through. This is her final task. She pulls up the sheet to cover him completely.

"That okay?" she asks as she lets the sheet drape over his face. "It's how we do it. But, you're family, so if you want to leave the sheet off until they come up for him, it's your call."

Oliver nods. "Yeah," he says, "fine."

She takes a bag of trash and leaves Oliver alone. The light coming in the window is too bright. The hospital room suddenly looks worn and dirty. The Formica counter around the sink is pink and its seams are separating at the corners. The white paint on the walls is grim.

Sitting in the vinyl chair, Oliver leans his head back, closing his eyes.

You're an idiot, he tells himself, *a total fucking moron*. Soon, he is sobbing, his body thrown forward, his head hanging over his feet, saliva stretching from his mouth onto the shiny, shiny floor. The blood pulses in his head and his throat whines in desperation.

There is nothing with which he can reasonably console himself. The photographs, the whole charade of a dossier, was not about giving Jared the father he'd missed out on. It was all about indulging his own ludicrous desire to hit rewind and pause and splice together some semblance of what was meant to be or what might have been. He thought he was owed.

"Hey, man," a voice says from the door, "just let me know when you're ready."

Oliver sits up and sees an older man in a white coat standing at the threshold. "Are you?" he asks.

The man nods. "But take your time, kid." The guy is tall with a long sloping belly and wide shoulders. He has a dark black mustache and thick black eyebrows.

"Oh, no. Come on in. I mean, I'm done," Oliver says, taking a tissue from the counter. "Go ahead."

The man walks in and tucks the corners of the sheet all around Jared, so that the form of the body becomes more distinguishable beneath the sheet. Then he takes the folded blanket tucked under his arm and spreads it out on top of the sheet. Turning to look at Oliver, he says, "Tough shit, ain't it?"

This acknowledgment strikes Oliver as unusually kind. He nods.

After releasing the brakes on the wheels of the bed, the

attendant begins to pull it out into the hallway. Oliver follows along without a word, his hand on the sheet near Jared's head.

The attendant doesn't say anything but allows Oliver to help him guide the gurney out of the room. They wait for a freight elevator that opens onto the back of the unit. Through a small window in a door near the elevator, Oliver sees the nurses' break room. A few of them sit around a table, drinking soda and laughing, untroubled by the sound of wheels rolling by.

In the elevator Oliver is confronted with the attendant's smell: drug store cologne and Lysol.

"Father?" the attendant asks, solemnly.

"Sorry?"

"Is it your father?"

Oliver looks at the gold crucifix around the man's neck. "No, he's my . . . he's a friend."

"Well, I know it don't feel like it now, but time does heal these wounds."

Oliver can't help smiling. To him, it seems like time caused these wounds.

"He's long gone now, you can be sure. I know the soul has wings. It flies right out the window the minute that heart stops beating. This, here," he says, patting the blanket on top of what must be Jared's leg, "this is just the shell. Like those broken shells you find all over the ground in springtime. The baby birds don't need that shell no more. Not when they're living in the sky."

Oliver's doubt must show on his face.

"I've worked here twenty-five years," the attendant says. "I know what I'm talking about."

"Twenty-five years," Oliver echoes him, before he comprehends what the words mean. Then, when he does, he cannot refrain from asking, "Did you happen to know Dr. Finley?"

The attendant smiles for the first time, showing a mouthful of overlapping teeth. "Sure. My first boss. Good guy." He wrinkles his forehead and looks at Oliver. "You related?" he asks.

"He was my dad," Oliver says, nodding.

"No kidding? I see the resemblance. I haven't thought about him for years. He must have died when you were little. Quite some time now, it's been."

"Yeah, twenty-one years this summer," he says, realizing that Jared must have just had or been about to have a birthday. "Maybe I could ask a favor of you?"

"Sure, you bet," he says as the elevator doors open to the basement, admitting a blast of cool air.

Oliver wipes his hands on his jeans and follows the gurney into the morgue.

14

Mr. Scrap takes the bucket out of the trunk of his car. He has his old black rod over his shoulder and a rusty tackle box wedged inside the bucket. The day is more beautiful than it should be. Sunlight streams through the grove of cottonwood trees that line the riverbank, throwing a golden light across the water.

This is a popular spot for casual fishing; the opposite banks adjoin the Wilds, and on this side there is a small parking lot just off the main highway.

Settling himself and his gear on an empty stretch of the high bank, Mr. Scrap studies the untroubled faces of a half-dozen other fishermen scattered along the river. Their movements are slow and deliberate, as though they are performing the Caucasian man's tai chi. Reel, load, tie, cast. Reel, load, tie, cast.

He, too, hopes to lose himself in the rhythms of the sport as he pulls his tackle box out of the bucket and opens it. The trays are filled with nothing but crumbs and dried-up salmon eggs. He slams down the lid of the box, exasperated.

Fishing without bait.

He bounces the rod a bit, then looks around in the dirt for a worm. Tossing aside a couple of rocks, he finds only a family of small gray beetles, the largest of which he plucks from the underside of a stone and loads onto the hook, certain he has no chance of catching a fish with a beetle.

As he casts his reel out into the middle of the river, he tries to clear his head. To just be, like the other guys out here, just watch the line, wait for a tug, listen to the gentle current of the water, the buzz of insects, the occasional call of a blue jay or a finch.

Instead, though, he feels as if he is still standing on the deck in the dark, his eyes watering from exertion, struggling to discern the truth of what happened below. He is stuck on the precipice of regret. If he could only step back, get his feet solidly beneath him, he could save himself. He could reverse it all.

But, he tells himself, it does no good to dwell on what might have been. It is not the way he advises his clients to conduct their lives and it is not the way he wants to conduct his own. What's done is done. He will have his day in court. Surely, a jury will see that he made the best decision he could with the information in front of him in that moment. If allowed, regret and remorse could consume what's left of life. Like this perfectly good day of fishing.

Except it is not a good day of fishing without any bait. And he has no bait because his mind is a mess. The thought of living out the rest of his days this way—continuously backpedaling to keep from slipping into a freefall of despair—makes him afraid. In the very act of trying to protect his life, he's actually dismantled it.

The two bullets that came out of that gun seem to be lodged in his own throat, restricting his air supply. If he could just catch his breath, take a long, deep inhale, he's certain it would temper his anxiety. Instead, he feels like he is slowly suffocating, his brain starved for oxygen, for tranquillity.

Damn that kid for being in his yard. It's private property, just the same as if he'd stepped into his living room uninvited. Nobody knows anything anymore. People roam about, ignorant and careless. He was warned, Mr. Scrap thinks, jerking the fishing pole. He was told to stop. What gives people the idea that their own will is superior to anything else?

Civilization is going down the toilet. His generation is the last to follow rules, defer to elders, curse in private. And the younger generations are not ashamed to display this deterioration; as far as he can tell, obscene and inane tattoos adorn nearly every person under forty.

They're tough, these kids, with their extreme piercings stretching ever wider holes into their skin. The guy'll be fine, Mr. Scrap reasons. He'll collect disability. Really, he's probably done him a favor. Given him a battle wound, an anecdote to embellish and retell on every street corner.

It's all about who has been closest to the edge. Isn't that why Oliver is trying to make a career out of death? Trying to attain some credibility by facing, shaping and exploiting it? His own father's death has given him license to be odd and contrary. It's a hall monitor's note for strolling through the corridor without blame, while all of the rest of them go on with the work of life.

Unwilling to give in to this mess, Mr. Scrap thinks he ought to be able to recast it. Akin to a marital indiscretion, a skipped tax payment, a real estate foreclosure, this is something Mr. Scrap can disavow. Surely, it will fade into a forgotten corner. He does not have to own it, to carry it with him. It is your choice, he often tells his clients, how to go on from here. Hang on to the bad choices and disappointments, let them define you, or leave them behind. It is up to you.

Mr. Scrap begins to reel in his line and as he does so, a flash of red darts through the trees on the opposite bank. He is startled—afraid, even. He looks upstream to see if the fisherman there noticed it. But he is chewing on a toothpick and has his eyes on baiting his hook. Again, the patch of red, like a harbinger of death. Is he having a stroke? Is this the end?

Then a figure Mr. Scrap recognizes immediately emerges from the trees on the other side of the river. Behind him, darting from one tree to the next, skipping and jumping, is a small boy with a red cape tied around his neck.

Mr. Scrap sees that Andy Rolondo has a little plastic fishing rod in one hand and a jar of bait in another. He walks in long, easy strides, swinging these accessories blithely. The boy follows behind him, occasionally wrapping his hands around low tree branches and swinging like a monkey. Turning to watch the boy meander toward him, Andy Rolondo puts a hand to his eyes to block the midday sun.

He looks harmless enough, in his shorts and sandals, his dark hair damp, as though he's just out of the pool. But this is the man, Mr. Scrap thinks, who has turned me into someone who shoots at kids in the front yard. He is the reason for all of this grief. And just look at him, standing there, blameless. Mr. Scrap scrambles to his feet, accidentally knocking the tackle box closed. The noise causes Andy Rolondo to look across the river. Mr. Scrap must seem vaguely familiar, so much so that Andy Rolondo takes his hand from shielding his eyes and lifts it in a gesture of greeting.

"Don't come near me," Mr. Scrap says, a slight whine entering his voice. A couple of other fishermen raise their eyes, then look back at the water, uninterested.

"Sorry?" Andy Rolondo calls across the rush of the stream. Just then the boy jumps, with the cape spreading behind him as it's meant to, and Andy Rolondo catches him midair. Strangely, even as he clenches his jaw with animosity and his chest heaves with rapid, shallow breaths, this sight moves Mr. Scrap. It is an iconic gesture of all that a father can be—allowing the boy to soar through the air, cape flapping, and then successfully cradling him when the flight is over.

Mr. Scrap fights back tears.

The newborn had been so small, his fists so tight. He'd stood over the boy while Betsy paced and tried to justify her decision. He couldn't counsel her honestly; his judgment was clouded by his own desire. He only wanted what would make her more available to him, what would raise her esteem of him. When the slight, red-faced infant screamed, Mr. Scrap hadn't heard anything plaintive. He hadn't stopped to imagine the possibilities. He hadn't thought that the baby would become a child, a little boy who might want to hold his hand to walk down a darkened hallway, or laugh generously at his ridiculous wordplay, or bound about the house in a favorite costume, begging for a trip to the river. Now that he sees this boy nestled in Andy Rolondo's arms—in Andy Rolondo's arms, for God's sake— Mr. Scrap's remorse widens into something black and immovable.

As he holds his son, the red cape now wrapped against the curve of his little back, Andy Rolondo seems to understand who it is standing opposite him, across the river. His face changes, darkens.

Mr. Scrap struggles to breathe. Raising a slow, ambivalent arm in a gesture that is more of a paddle than a wave, he takes a series of short shallow breaths. When he drops his arm, he realizes his chest is heaving and his face is wet with tears.

Andy Rolondo places his boy at his feet and walks toward a shady spot, where they settle themselves in to bait the hook.

Mr. Scrap picks up his tackle box and his pole and retreats to his car, leaving the day's catch to the others.

15

In Mary's dream everyone is on the airplane together. First, there's her mother, sitting by the window, legs crossed, looking out as the plane passes through a never-ending tunnel of white. She is drinking from a plastic cup of wine with a wistful, faraway smile on her lips. Beside her, with his hand stretched wide across her mother's knee, is Mr. Scrap. He is wearing a bizarre brown helmet and he does not have a glass of wine. Instead, he has a bowl full of tiny fish; she cannot tell if they are alive, or if they are simply realistic-looking lures. He's holding it casually in one hand, as though it were a bowl of nuts or pretzels, and he's watching Mary carefully, following her arms as she points to the emergency exits. Across the aisle from them is her father. He is dressed in a pilot's uniform and a stiff pilot's hat. His beard is as shaggy as ever and he's wearing the same sandals he died in. Surprised to see him there, looking so nonchalantly alive, she wants desperately to go to him and hug him, but the safety demonstration is not complete and she cannot end it prematurely.

As she mimes the use of an oxygen mask, she notices the doctor from the hospital has his phone to his ear. This is against the rules, but he doesn't follow rules and she is not so foolish as to think that she can change him. He waves at her, flashes a good-natured smile, and then raises his glass, not in a toast but in a request for more soda. As Mary walks down the aisle, checking everyone's seat belt, she sees that Jared is stretched across a row of empty seats, sleeping. His clothes are ragged and he smells horrible. She reaches into an overhead compartment and retrieves a pastel blue baby blanket that somehow covers him entirely. Behind Jared, Doug and his daughters are making chirping noises. Their tray tables are little chalkboards and they are each drawing with long slender pieces of chalk. Doug is composing music for Mary, measures and measures of white quarter notes and eighth notes flung all over his slate. She immediately understands it to be a lullaby. It is beautiful.

Over the wing in the exit row sit Oliver and Miranda. They are dressed all in black and they each hold little silver binoculars up to their eyes, aimed at the seat backs.

"Huge, right?" Oliver says to his companion, without taking his binoculars away.

"Absolutely," she says, smiling. "Gigantic."

Sadie sits behind them, smoking, waiting for one of them to give her a turn with the binoculars.

Mary walks on by, fastening and unfastening a sample seat belt. Then, with a shot of adrenaline, she remembers her father. He isn't just her father—he is the pilot. Which means, if he is sitting there across from Mr. Scrap and her mother, there is nobody in the cockpit.

They really will be crash-landing. They really will need their oxygen masks and seat cushions and emergency exits. She turns and runs to the front of the plane, but it seems to have stretched, and she just keeps jogging past row after empty row, never reaching the front.

Her cell phone rings, buzzing beside her ear like a distress call.

Quietly, so as not to wake her mother or Sadie, who are both sleeping after the long night in the hospital, Mary tells Doug about this dream.

"I never got to the front. It was like the aisle turned into this enormous treadmill. Ugh. It was awful." And then she remembers. Reality is rarely worse than the nightmare. But today it is.

"Anxiety dream," he says. "Everything's up in the air—no pun intended—"

"No, actually, it's not." She sighs.

"What do you mean?"

"Nothing's up in the air anymore."

"Oh, God. Mary. I'm sorry."

"Yeah. Me, too."

"How's your brother doing?"

"I don't really know. Probably not very well."

"Do you want me to come?"

Mary pauses. They've spoken several times during the last twenty-four hours. He's been a comfort and a distraction, both. But she hasn't wanted to think of what happens next. "No," she says. "Don't do that."

"Why not?"

Mary closes her eyes and can picture Doug sleeping, a

passenger on her flight. Just another body in a seat. How did he turn into this? Their connection to one another is tenuous and undefined, but also tenacious. His voice on the phone is both necessary and remarkable. Is this her doing? A fantasy she's given in to? A voice to whom she's assigned too much?

He could be anybody.

On any given flight there are countless pairs of eyes, sets of hands, dozens of delicate mouths. She imagines each passenger hooked up to monitors, half a skull missing. It is a nightmare even more vivid than last night's dream. But would she go to their side, any of them, sit next to their fading body and hold their hand? Though she knows the answer, she wonders why not. Could not each of them have some unknown link to her? A dear friend's mother or aunt, a future in-law or stepson, a neighbor or a long-lost cousin? A girl with the same pair of favorite shoes or a boy who might have been her brother? A man who might, one day, matter to her. Where do the connections ever cease?

We all have belly buttons. We all swallow. Also this: We all will end.

Mary's thoughts are jumbled, as though she's actually lost a brother. Her defenses are dismantled, her nerves scrubbed raw. She doesn't bother fighting back the tears. All she can manage to say is, "Keep moving, Doug."

She's been taught to form a human chain during an emergency evacuation through smoke, to urge passengers to hold hands in order to stay together. In this cult of human connection, passengers are to hold tight to the person in front of them.

16

As far as Betsy can tell, not much has changed about the funeral industry in twenty-one years. She and Sadie sit across a round wooden table from a middle-aged blond woman who reveals that she chose this line of work recently, after the death of her sister. Betsy can see that she hopes this gives her an authenticity and authority when she counsels them that they will not regret any money they spend here. "It is not the time to skimp," she says, with her head at an angle, her brow furrowed.

Sadie hunches over the table, watching with vacant eyes. Betsy remembers the way everything receded after Paul died. People and events were so far away, even if they were right next to her. The shock of being left behind surrounded her with a dense wall of thick air that hardly anything got through.

"Listen," Betsy says, surprised by her own confidence. She puts a hand on Sadie's back. "We know what we want. There is no need to give us a pitch. We already have a plot, we just need the box. For ashes."

The woman's smile thins out into a grimace. "Cremains."

"Yes," Betsy says. "That's right."

"Of course." The woman studies Sadie with a look of disdain. Betsy recognizes the assessment. It is one she's made time after time about people. Unkempt hair, sloppy clothes, dark eye makeup. But her empathy has squelched these judgments about Sadie. She's watched her sleeping on Mary's couch with her face scrubbed clean, her hands curved into unknowing arcs, the large blanket pulled over her doing nothing to keep her from looking small and vulnerable. Suddenly, Betsy is self-righteous in her affection for this girl. This woman thinks she knows something about Sadie and her trouble just because of the thick smell of cigarettes clinging to her clothes, the tattoo of a snake wrapped around her wrist.

After they've been shown the boxes for cremains, the woman asks what they want engraved on the marker.

"I gotta go outside," Sadie says, standing up.

Betsy is left alone with the blank form in front of her.

❖

Oliver has not slept in three days and hasn't shaved in a week. Miranda comes and goes, her equipment slung across her body, her face a closed door. Mrs. Wilcox has left two terse messages on his answering machine, unaware of his trouble. He's finished her video. It sits on his desk, ready.

Mary has called. Her voice is tired but sure on his answering machine. "Oliver. I know you're there. This is, has been, I can't even say. What this is. Shit, actually. If you need help figuring things out, don't call me." She laughs, then continues. "Mom and Sadie, they're okay, I think. Rotten egg you to mental health, okay?"

Each evening, he drives the Ranchero to Alfalfa's, sitting in the darkness, watching the store shut down: the checkers inside, counting their drawers; the baggers sweeping up, collecting carts, replacing stock.

Surely, this is not where Mary would advise him to look for mental health.

But he hasn't wanted to see anyone or go anywhere else. Not Mary or his mother or even Miranda. His whole body aches. He feels unfit for life.

Tonight, with his head on the steering wheel, the windows down, his feet crossed, he closes his eyes. He thinks of the nurses on the Neuro ICU, with all new patients, all new family members, their lives a series of heroic efforts among gruesome facts.

What would his father think of the trouble Oliver's found? A new set of columns has been written, flanking a new division that marks his days as either Before or After. Though drawn against his will, against his hope, this line is his own doing. The most significant action of his adulthood was born of his most tragic flaw.

He desperately wishes for a different outcome. A different After would have reminded each of them not of life's fragility, but of its resiliency; not how unjust it can be, but how merciful it can be. How the widening can, in fact, reveal the way to a reversal. How a brother can be lost and then restored.

What he has is *this* After. This is the set of circumstances he will have to navigate.

In the darkness of his closed eyes, Oliver remembers the small brown envelope he brought home from the hospital. Across the front, in dark slanted script, are the words, *Please Transcribe*. The envelope is encircled with a brittle green rubber band. He wasn't sure, even when he made the request of the orderly, if he'd ever have the nerve to listen.

But Oliver has a glimmer of desire.

This is what he's never really had the courage to do.

End it.

He goes home and stands in the doorway of his bedroom, watching Miranda sleep. She is also on this After side of the line, he reminds himself. It is a mercy of life. Her chest rises and falls with every breath, and in the space between each Oliver recognizes a new kind of widening.

When the sun appears, he creeps out of the house alone, except for Jello, who slips out the front door in between Oliver's feet. They drive up to the Wilds. Oliver parks the car on the side of the road and hikes, just as he had with his father, up the east side of the peak. He has the video camera in his backpack. The archaic tape recorder is already loaded.

He cannot help thinking of Patty Wilcox as he makes his ascent. Here is where that string of destiny started twenty-one years ago. Beginning with the girl's feet, as she tumbled and fell, woven through his father's heart, as it puckered and seized, and then through his mother's heart as hers, too, puckered and seized in its own way, and now laced through Mr. Scrap's culpable heart and tied into an angry, bleeding knot inside Jared's brain.

They all would surely have wished for a different bond. But this is what is. This is Oliver's past.

As he stands on the top of Bear Peak, he cringes thinking of how Patty Wilcox had thrown him the finger as he stared at her from the tree, his seven-year-old face blank with dismay. Her adolescent voice seems to call to him from somewhere down below. *Do you always spy on people? Do you?*

The answer? Yes. Here he is. Even now. Still spying, camera in hand.

He watches Jello carelessly lift his nose to the air, sniffing all around him. What, Oliver wonders, might he be picking up?

He paces the perimeter of the cliff, trailing Jello until they've worn a path. Then he sits and dangles his legs, the adrenaline racing through his torso as his shoes hang with nothing beneath them. He places a pinch of dirt on his tongue and pushes it against the roof of his mouth, fighting tears. Its grit scrapes and grinds into the crevices of his teeth. He stands and walks to the center of Bear Peak, bows his head and finally, with shame and rage, props the camera on his shoulder and pulls the old relic of a tape recorder out of his bag.

He doesn't remember the voice, what it will sound like.

When he pushes the play button and listens to his father solemnly stating the girl's name and home address, Oliver's palms begin to sweat as he realizes that, in fact, he does remember. His father hits every *t* with a hard, crisp ending that is immediately familiar. His deep soft voice could somehow carry down a hall, from the front yard to the back—through a closed door, even.

The body is that of a well-developed, well-nourished, adolescent white female who appears the stated age of thirteen years.

Body height is fifty-three inches, and body weight is sixty-nine pounds. Scalp hair is black. Decedent's body was found at the base of an approximately two-hundred-foot peak, clothed in a T-shirt, shorts and sandals.

At autopsy, rigor mortis is generalized to late; livor mortis is posterior and slightly blanching; the body is cool to touch. Artifacts of decomposition are absent, and evidence of medical and postmortem care is absent. There is obvious evidence of contusions and trauma to the back of the head, sustained from the impact of the fall.

While his father's voice continues speaking, Oliver lets himself imagine one last visit to that afternoon.

Through his shoulder, down his back, there is pain. Like a muscle spasm.

But it does not end.

This should worry him.

The tingling begins. At first it must be pleasant. A little creeping. Something to remind you you're alive and always changing.

A sip of coffee will taste good.

Something is not right.

Where are the kids? They're too quiet. Always trouble. Little whispers. Where? So beautiful.

The first squeeze is startling, disabling. The newspaper falls out of his hand. How did that happen?

Shit.

The kids. So little. Too small for this. Too many things they don't know.

But what? What have I kept for later?

Everything important.

Betsy.

The baby.

Help.

Don't let them see this. Don't let this be their life.

Keep breathing. You can come back from this.

The second squeeze turns the room into black, only small flecks of red and gold remain. Are they real?

The only real thing now is this crushing pain, the dizzying spin that does not end.

Oliver runs toward the edge and hurls both devices out to the abyss. His father's voice falls away from him. The video camera records this descent. This terrible, last descent of two machines plunging to their death. The sky and earth must be tumbling over in a succession of rapid somersaults.

Oliver stands on the edge of Bear Peak, watching all of it go. Jello barks twice and thrusts his wet nose against one of Oliver's clenched hands, beckoning his reassurance. Oliver opens one and lets Jello lick his salty palm.

The video camera and the tape recorder fumble against the rocks at the bottom and skip and jump to their end.

❖

Miranda cannot help herself. The darkness comes and she wants to be in it. Scooting quietly out of bed, away from Oliver, who is awake and staring at the ceiling, she pulls on her sneakers and escapes into the night.

The air is changing and with it the landscape. There are small signs of fall's approach. Wilting flowers, edges of yellow creeping into the green canopy, and apple tree branches bending under the weight of their fruit.

Most houses are dark; it is past midnight and Miranda takes comfort in the concrete beneath her feet, the never-ending stretch of sidewalk turning at corners and continuing ad infinitum.

Soon enough she is where she has been itching to return. Mr. Scrap's lawn is immaculate. There is no sign of any disturbance. The morning after, when Miranda stepped off the front porch, there had been, imprinted in the grass, a darkened rectangle made by the weight of the paramedic's bag, and next to it the grass had surrendered to Jared's body like a summer snow angel. The silhouette had been as innocuous as a shadow.

Now there is nothing. The blades have resumed their previous posture. She kneels and touches this grass with her fingertips. What happened here is tucked away and hidden by nature's own insistence that it carry on.

When Miranda stands again she realizes that she is not alone. Sitting cross-legged on the deck above his yard, Mr. Scrap is looking down at her. She is startled and places a hand on the camera around her neck as though it is a source of protection.

He does not say anything and neither does she. For a moment they are each like an animal who's been caught in the other's territory.

"Go on," he finally says, his voice surprisingly clear.

Miranda is certain of his meaning, but she does not oblige. She knows too much for this photograph to be compelling. The truth of his isolation that is apparent in this moment would be poignant only to a stranger. As though a ghost, she walks silently off the grass and into the night.

17

For Sadie's sake, there will be a service. Betsy has planned it as she would a dinner party. Beautiful flowers, an engraved program, a single guitarist to stand beside the grave. The details are perfect. She has kept herself busy with this task, ignoring the parts of her life she has sidestepped like a deep hole: the house she has not returned to, the husband whose voice speaks to her over the phone each night in anguished pleas.

Sadie has allowed Betsy to take her shopping and buy her a suitable black dress with a jagged hem that appeals to them both. Betsy feels obliged to attend to these considerations, spurred on by the guilt she cannot escape, but she is surprised by the affection that continues to grow inside her for this scruffy, forthright girl. Sitting in the passenger seat of Betsy's sedan, Sadie reveals little bits about her life that Betsy had always thought a daughter would share with her mother, but Betsy never had, nor had Mary. Sadie tells her about the concert where she met Jared and about his aspiration to form his own band someday. She says they sometimes spent all weekend in his apartment, eating macaroni from a box, listening to music and marveling at being naked for so many hours.

She also confesses her lurking doubts. With so many days between their visits, Sadie had frequently wondered if Jared were really clean and then hated herself for wondering. She worried he would never outrun the addiction that had chased him since adolescence. And she worried she would either be too patient or not patient enough.

Betsy listens hungrily. As though awakening from an anesthetic, she remembers when her own life was full of tremendous pain. Not just Paul's death, but before that, even—the wince of having to say good night, the ache of wanting to see him again the next day. Love, she supposed, was what she'd forgotten. The burning, aching urgency of love.

Certainly, she loves Martin. Even now. She admires his intellect, appreciates his helpful nature, acknowledges his devotion. But it is nothing like the way she once felt about Paul.

She wants to tell Sadie to hold on to this feeling, to remember it even when life's circumstances debate its relevancy. But she curbs this impulse. Platitudes do not pay the bills or get a person out of bed in the morning.

But when Sadie reveals that the nausea she had in the hospital has returned each morning since and that the stick she peed on turned blue, Betsy tells her it is a silver lining. Betsy tells Sadie what nobody told her about that small screaming infant in their grief-stricken house: that together they will make it work.

❖

As the sun rises, Miranda looks around the bedroom. She reaches for her camera on the nightstand the way someone terribly nearsighted reaches for eyeglasses upon waking. Her few belongings are packed in boxes. The message that a group of her photos will be shown in a gallery in Santa Monica next month came as a small bright spot in an otherwise very dark week. Oliver is not sure he should go with her.

"He was my brother," he says quietly, without lifting his head from the pillow. This conversation between them never begins or ends.

"Identity is shit," Miranda says, fingering the camera on her belly. "We're all imposters."

Oliver barely smiles. "That's nice. Another title for your show?"

"Better than *Is That Legal?*"

Oliver turns his head to look at her. "I imposed my entire life story onto him. He was trying to survive, that's all."

She's quiet for a moment. Then, placing a hand on the pillow so that it's grazing his cheek, she frowns. "We all reach out for what we want. An apple, a sports car, a lover. On the way, shit happens."

He reaches out his hand and lays it on her bare shoulder. "How'd that go? Anybody hurt?"

Miranda rolls her eyes. "Mock me," she says. "But I speak the truth."

Oliver closes his eyes. Miranda keeps her hand on the pillow, near his face.

Oliver lifts his head and props it up on one elbow. "I appreciate your efforts, Miranda." He puts his hand on top of hers. "But there's no assuaging this."

She nods. "Things happen in life that change you. Good and bad. And every story overlaps someone else's." Oliver looks down at their hands, stacked. Miranda follows his eyes. "And every connection is formed and broken without any idea about what lies beyond," she says, fixing her lens on their hands and snapping a photo.

These could be anyone's hands, Oliver thinks. They could be his parents' or the Wilcoxes' or any other couple's on earth. This innocent gesture is part of the standard repertoire of forming a union. *Give me your hand. Take my hand.*

The start of something.

The end of something.

This coupling happens over and over. Across species and continents. It begins and it ends.

18

Oliver and Miranda pick Mary up in the car truck. Miranda scoots to the middle of the bench seat to make room.

"Wow," Mary says as she pulls the door shut. "This looks like a bad sitcom."

"If only," Oliver says.

The Ranchero pulls away from the curb and heads through town.

"When I was a kid I used to wish for an album with all of the sitcom theme songs. *Love Boat, Three's Company, It's a Living.* Those were great songs." Mary and Oliver glance at Miranda with dubious faces. "Do you disagree?" she asks, smoothing her navy blue skirt across her lap.

In the absence of an answer, she begins to hum the tune from *Three's Company.*

She gets through a few bars before both of them erupt with laughter. It is contagious and irrepressible. The cab is filled with their abandon, each of them grateful for the momentary return of humor that has eluded them for over a week.

But soon it fades and they ride the rest of the way in silence.

It is a beautiful spot. An elegant stand of aspens marks either side of the entrance. There is a wide black iron gate that announces the destination. Oliver takes the gravel drive according to his mother's instructions. There are lots of trees that obscure and shade the orderly rows of stones.

His mother's car is parked off a ways and Oliver pulls up behind it. He can see her standing in the distance, her petite figure clothed in a black skirt suit with a purple blouse peeking through the jacket.

"Ready, ladies?" he asks as he pulls the keys from the ignition.

"Mr. Nice Guy called Mom this morning after she'd left."

Oliver throws the keys under the seat and leans forward to look at Mary. "And?"

"And he's going to plead. The prosecutor knows him. He'll get a lot better deal than at trial."

"I don't have a suitable reply."

"I just thought you'd want to know."

"Fuckin' life," he says, resting his forehead on the steering wheel.

"It's not a bad title for the sitcom," Miranda offers after a moment.

Without warning, their collective hilarity returns and the three of them laugh in the old car in the middle of the cemetery until tears streak their faces.

When they finally climb out of the car, there are a couple others parked behind the Ranchero. A few employees from Alfalfa's and a friend of Sadie's from high school gather around the old leaning ash tree that was just a sapling when they buried Oliver's father here.

Crossing the unkempt grass, their footprints leave deep imprints behind them, like stones being dropped from their pockets. Mary and Miranda go to Sadie, who is leaning against the ash tree, smoking, looking wholly unlike herself with her hair pulled back off her face and an expensive dress draping her slight frame.

Oliver stands over his father's marker and glances at the space near it that is covered with a black cloth, awaiting Jared's ashes. The Latin on his father's grave that his mother has arranged to be repeated on Jared's, finally makes some sense to him. *To the stars,* indeed.

His mother stands silently beside him, putting a hand on his elbow in greeting.

"You didn't have to do this, Mom. Give up this spot. For a complete stranger." His father's gravestone has a few brown pine needles left from a previous autumn. Betsy kneels and brushes them off. Her fingers linger on the stone before she stands again. "I have regrets, Oliver. I'm not perfect. You were both so young and I was scared. I don't think I'll regret this."

Oliver nods. "But, still. It's really an incredible gesture."

His mother stares into his eyes. "Looking behind you never ends, Oliver. It only means you have your back to the world. And I worry so much about you. That you've turned your back to the world."

It's the first time her concern has not been laced with rebuke. Or, maybe, he thinks, it's the first time in a long time that he's listened. "Yeah, I know, Mom." He wraps his arm around her shoulders. "I know."

The guitarist begins plucking a Bach piece and the dozen or so people gather tightly together. Oliver keeps his arm around his mother, who holds Sadie's jittery hand. Miranda and Mary stand beside them.

Only Betsy is not surprised when the guitarist stops strumming and begins speaking. He is musician and preacher, both. Right off the street corner.

First there is a prayer. Then a brief eulogy to youth and lost chances. There is no mention of addiction or abandonment or guns in the night. Jared may as well have been a valedictorian or a cancer victim. The blandness irritates Oliver, but he knows it doesn't really matter. It is nice that this man in his woolen necktie and corduroy jacket is here. That he quotes the Bible and blesses Jared's spirit, even though his subject was an atheist, is irrelevant. Jared is long gone.

Finally, Sadie steps hesitantly forward and lifts the box of cremains from the makeshift altar. She is crying; nearly everybody is. From behind one ear, she slides a single pristine cigarette. Holding it up briefly for everyone to see, she smiles a little before placing it under her thumb, an offering on top of the wooden box.

A gentle wind lifts the edge of her hem and the loose hairs around her neck. Sadie turns her head toward this breeze, as though she is listening for its instructions. Standing very still with the box in her hands, she waits.

Oliver slips his hand through Miranda's. He remembers riding to the cemetery for his father's interment in the back of a black limousine. It was hot and his pants were itchy around the waist. His mother sat between Mary and him, her hands grasping the ball of tissues she'd acquired at the church. Oliver had thought only of how he wished his dad were there right then to see the car with its TV screen and refrigerator and facing leather seats. He had been unable to forecast how much he would miss his father for the rest of his life. He'd only known how much he wanted him in that moment, to see them all in the fanciest of cars.

Oliver wonders if this is a little bit of how Sadie is feeling—wishing Jared could see this gathering. The solemn-eyed preacher, Jared's would-be family, the tall ash tree. Or is she forecasting, thinking of the coming days and nights when the pain of his absence will expand before it recedes? Either way, she eventually places a kiss on the box before installing it in the ground.

A car door breaks the reverent quiet and all eyes turn to see who's arrived.

Initially, Oliver thinks it is Mr. Nice Guy and he shudders with disdain.

Mary says, "No, way," and steps away from the circle, toward the approaching figure. The visitor walks through the grass deliberately, undeterred by the audience. Mary meets him halfway and they stand facing each other before she leans into him.

"What are you doing?" Mary asks when she's breathed her fill of his scent. "This is crazy."

He holds her face between his hands and presses his forehead to hers. "No. It's the only thing that isn't."

He takes her hand and they return together to the circle. With all eyes still on them, Mary shrugs. By way of explanation, she says only, "Doug."

There is a final blessing and a final guitar piece. The crowd drifts into embraces and quiet conversation.

Sadie doesn't move from her place in front of the hole.

Miranda kneels beside her. She presses her hands into the grass and keeps her eyes on them. "Everything in my head sounds stupid right now."

"Me, too."

"Maybe we could make flash cards for grief. So, you know, we wouldn't have to say all those stupid-sounding words in our head."

"Fuck. My pictures would all be stupid, too."

"Mine would just be repetitive. And stupid."

"That's why people wail. In other countries, right?"

Miranda nods. "I have some amazing photos of him. I'll print them for you."

"Okay."

Miranda lifts her hands out of the grass and looks at the imprints they made there. Sadie puts her own hand inside one of the imprints and says, "That's not a bad flash card."

❖

Oliver and Miranda are alone again in the Ranchero, the last of the vehicles that have become a small unofficial recession, winding away from the cemetery and back into town. Mary has strapped herself into Doug's rental car, and Sadie into Betsy's sedan.

"My first funeral." Miranda pulls her legs under her like she's riding sidesaddle.

"Maybe you didn't notice. Our sitcom has been canceled. But it sounds like a good book," Oliver says, looking at her.

Miranda smiles. "You're funny. But, really, it was."

"Yeah? Nobody in your family ever—?"

She shakes her head. "Good genes, I guess. Or bad. Grandparents gone before I was born."

He nods.

"Are you coming with me tomorrow? To the land of sitcoms?"

Oliver turns west, splitting off from the cars in front of them.

Miranda frowns, confused.

"Wilcox video," he says in answer to her unspoken question. He's had it in the glove box for days—the last of its kind. "It would be nice if we'd met in that Swedish bathhouse, right? Spent days and nights just—what—soaking? No dying, no funerals. Just us."

Miranda cocks her head. They drive slowly, passing house after house that she's stood before, taking pictures of strangers.

Oliver knows that whenever he thinks of meeting her, he will also think of Jared and the horrible end to a foolish quest. It's another thing he's sorry about—that he can't compose a pristine, uncomplicated memory of their courtship.

"I hear there's Legionnaires' in bathhouses. What's your point?"

Oliver reaches his hand across the seat to her. "How is it that the very best thing in my life came along at exactly the worst time in my life?"

"Some people call that religion."

Oliver smiles. "And you?"

"I vote for calling it remarkable."

"Done." Parking the Ranchero along the curb in front of Mrs. Wilcox's house, he slides close to Miranda and kisses her.

After he's slipped the DVD through Mrs. Wilcox's mail slot, he pauses on her porch for a moment. The sun's globe lingers just over the horizon, streaking the clouds pink and orange. The steep western face of Bear Peak is hot with the end of the day. A hawk circles its crest, banking into the light, angling its feathers toward the last of the day's heat.

Oliver climbs back into the car beside Miranda and watches in his rearview mirror as the bird soars effortlessly on the currents until, finally, it is swallowed by the distance.

Acknowledgments

I'm indebted to the photographer Shizuka Yokomizo, whose work was an early inspiration.

My remarkable agent, Molly Friedrich, and the astute Lucy Carson have both provided wide and deep guidance.

For her unflappable confidence and wisdom, I am grateful to Molly Stern.

Liz Van Hoose's boundless passion, specificity and dedication to this book took my breath away.

For my family—lost and found—thank you is not enough.